9-1-1

A Peter Andrassy crime thriller

D.J. Maughan

Hulyeseg Inc

This book is dedicated to the brave men and women who gave their lives responding to the attacks on the World Trade Center on September 11, 2001. Your bravery and sacrifice will never be forgotten.

Preface

On September 11, 2001, I drove to the airport to fly to San Francisco when I heard a report of a plane striking the north tower of the World Trade Center in New York City. The voice on the radio reported that all planes in the United States had been grounded and that airports were closed. My wife and I returned home and watched in horror as the towers crumbled.

At the time, I was a university student working in the reservations office for Delta Airlines. For the next week, I took phone calls from people whose travel plans had been altered by the attacks. One call I'll never forget. It was a woman who had lost her mother in the plane that hit the South Tower. She was making plans to return home for her mother's service. It was a tough call, and the authenticity of the attacks never felt more real.

A week later, Delta Airlines closed the reservations office I worked in. I lost my job, along with all my colleagues. It was a difficult time but, thankfully, two weeks later I found new employment that gave me experience in my chosen major.

I hesitated to write and publish this book. I know there will be those who say writing about 9/11 is in poor taste. That I'm profiting from a devastating event. I respect their opinion but disagree. I've read multiple books about Pearl Harbor, the Holocaust, and other horrific tragedies. I wasn't alive during those events, but the descriptions I read in the books made them more real for me. I had a greater depth of understanding as a result. That's my hope for this book. I wish for all who read it to have a deeper love and reverence for those who gave their lives that day.

D.J. Maughan

Part I

Chapter 1

Scott

September 2001

It's the phone call I've dreaded for years—the call I always expected but believed would never come. My assistant said only my name, and I knew...

"What is it, Roxanne?"

A pause on the other end of the phone.

"Scott?"

"Yes."

Hesitation. "Someone's here."

I step away from the squat rack and press the phone into my ear while plugging the other with my index finger. Music blares all around me in the gym. "Who?"

"A client."

"Man?"

"Yes."

"Is he near you? Can he hear me?"

"Yes and no."

I stare at my reflection in the gym's mirror. The muscles in my forearm compress and stretch against the skin. "What's his name?"

She hesitates. "Shane Larkin. He's...furious. He wants to see you." I hear a man's voice in the background. "He's demanding to see you. He won't leave until he does."

I turn back to the squat rack and notice a slight bend in the bar. I've got three plates on either side. Anytime I squat over three hundred pounds, the bar curves. The more weight, the more pronounced. I'm halfway through my five sets of five reps. I hate not finishing.

"Tell him I'm on my way. I'll be there in twenty minutes."

Eighteen minutes later, I enter my office building and ride the elevator to my floor. I step out, walk down the hall, and brace myself as I turn the door handle to my company, Sound Security Title. My assistant, Roxanne, sits at her desk. Her legs are crossed, and she's wearing a short skirt that highlights her shapely calves. She looks up from the computer, relief in her eyes, and nods to the man sitting on the couch. I turn and look at him. He's at least ten years older than me. He looks at me above the *Time* magazine he holds and scowls as I take a step toward him.

"Mr. Larkin?" I ask, extending my hand and forcing a smile.

He glances at it, then back up into my eyes. His eyes smolder.

My smile fades as I stand awkwardly before him. Finally, I drop my hand and gesture with my other hand, palm up. "Will you join me in my office?"

He returns the magazine to the end table and stands. He's a small man. No taller than five feet eight, one hundred and fifty pounds.

I'm just short of six feet, but I tower over him. I wait, indicating he should go before me. He doesn't. Instead, he stares up at me, his face menacing.

I take the cue and lead him down the hall and into my office. I ask him to take a seat next to the desk and close the door. I sit opposite him behind the desk.

"What can I do for you?"

He leans forward in his seat and jabs a finger into the cherry wood desk. "I want my money."

I frown. "What money?"

"The money you stole from me."

Shock registers on my face. "Excuse me?"

He shakes his head, his dark eyes menacing. "Don't play dumb with me."

I raise my hands. "Sir, I have no idea what you're talking about."

He sneers. "I contacted my mortgage company. They never received the payoff you promised to deliver. A month ago, I started receiving notices. Past-due statements. I've never been behind on a mortgage. It had to be a mistake. I let it slide. But when I received another, I called them. They said the loan was still open. It was never paid and closed."

I frown. "That's impossible."

"Is it?"

I nod. "We wired the payment. We always do immediately after closing. I can prove it."

His expression changes, and a moment of doubt creeps into his eyes. There's a gentleness in his expression for the first time since I entered the office. "How?"

"I have proof of the wire." I stand from the desk and hold up a finger. I exit the office and walk down the hall to Roxanne. I know exactly where the receipt is, but I ask her in a booming voice for his benefit. "Roxanne, can you find Mr. Larkin's file for me?"

Her eyes have been trained on me since I came around the corner. There's a question there, but she doesn't ask. "Sure."

"Thank you."

She moves around the desk, and I watch as she passes me on her way to the server room. I follow, smelling a hint of her perfume. She opens the filing cabinet and, without looking at me, whispers, "What's going on?"

"It's nothing," I whisper back. "It'll be fine."

She shuffles through files and stops on the one with Larkin written on the top. She hands it to me, and our eyes lock. There's worry in her eyes, but I give her an assuring smile. I walk down the hall and reenter my office. Mr. Larkin watches me as I place the file on the desk, leaning over it. I flip pages to the wire verification and point to the confirmation number.

"See? It's right here. Here's the confirmation number. And here's the dollar amount." Next to the confirmation number is the amount of $427,324. "The exact amount for the payoff of your loan."

Larkin leans forward, scrutinizing the document.

I point lower on the page. "And here you see the amount leaving our escrow account and entering the mortgage company's account."

His head lowers as he looks further down the page. Finally, he looks up.

"I paid the amount. They haven't accounted for it correctly. I've had this happen a time or two. I'll reach out to them with the confirmation number. It's just an accounting error. Give me a week, and it'll all be cleared up."

He shakes his head. "Why would it take a week? Call them now."

I point to the clock on the wall. "It's too late. It's already four thirty."

"So?"

"Mortgage companies close at four. Nobody will answer."

He stands and crosses his arms. "I'll be back Monday."

I shake my head. "Today's Friday. I can't call until Monday. I won't have proof from them yet."

"Tuesday then."

I sigh. "Okay."

He doesn't shake my hand as he exits the office.

When the exterior door is shut, I turn back to Roxanne and give her an encouraging smile. My face masks the anxiety I feel.

Chapter 2

Peter

Peter Andrassy stands on the outskirts of the group of ten Hungarian National Police officers crowded around their captain. All are dressed in uniforms and armor, anticipating a firefight. Peter is the only member of the group who wears civilian clothing. He isn't technically a member of the National Police. That is, he's not a sworn police officer. He works as a consultant. A former New York City detective, he returned to his home country of Hungary after retiring from the New York Police Department. Now, besides his work as a private investigator, he consults the National Police on complex criminal matters. That's why he's here.

While Captain Zsida gives final instructions to the group of officers, Peter surveys the neighborhood. Who would ever guess a human trafficking ring would be operating in this place? The group is congregated on a secluded street in Egerszalók. A small village on the outskirts of a larger city in Eastern Hungary. Like many places in Hungary, Egerszalók is known for its thermal baths and rich tradition of delicious wine. Nestled in a small valley between two hills, it's the type of town you might see pictured on a postcard.

Peter hears a clicking noise and turns to the young officer beside him. Her gun clipped to her belt rocks back and forth, bumping against her radio. She sees him looking and stops fidgeting. Peter hears his name and turns back to Captain Zsida.

"Officer Bako will hang back with you. You're not to enter the house until I come out to get you."

"Understood."

Captain Zsida looks from Peter to the young officer. She nods. Satisfied, the captain motions, and the other nine officers step behind him. They head toward the trafficking house up the street. When the group rounds the corner and passes out of sight, Bako glances at Peter and then moves forward.

"Bako?" Peter questions.

She looks back at him. "Zsida said we aren't to enter the house. He didn't say we had to stay here." Without waiting for a response, she moves forward, and Peter hurries to catch up.

As they walk, keeping distance from the primary group of officers, he wonders about her. She's young, at least twenty-five years his junior. Average height with a lean build, dark-brown hair, and bright blue eyes. Although he doesn't know every officer at the headquarters, he's seen most and can't remember seeing her before.

Bako turns and notices he's watching her. "What?"

"Nothing. I was just curious about you."

She gives him a look but doesn't ask.

"I haven't seen you before. How long have you been with the National Police?"

"Two weeks," she says, then stops, squaring her shoulders at him. "But I'm not new to police work, if that's what you're thinking."

It wasn't. But Peter says nothing while she searches his face. After a moment, she turns and starts walking again. "Where were you before?"

"Kecskemét."

Peter nods. "Did you grow up there? Is that home?"

"Sort of."

They've reached the house now where officers circle the lot.

After a beat, Bako steals a glance at him. "So, what's with you?"

"Hard to say."

She gives him a quizzical look.

"It would help if you were more specific."

Her gaze goes back to the house. "I mean, you aren't part of the National Police. Why are you here?"

Peter watches as Zsida motions to two officers. "I worked as a detective for the NYPD in America for twenty years. I came back to Hungary a year and a half ago. I've been helping the National Police ever since."

"You're Hungarian?"

"Yep. Born and raised in Pécs."

She nods. "Is that it?"

"What do you mean?"

"I mean, I've only been here for two weeks, but I've already heard your name a few times. Seems like you're a big deal."

Peter shrugs as she eyes him, waiting to see if he'll say more. After a moment, they turn back to the house as Captain Zsida and another officer ascend the front steps and position themselves on either side of the door.

"I don't need you babysitting me, you know? I've been in more dangerous situations than this."

Peter frowns. She's misread the situation. He's the civilian. Not her.

Zsida and the other officer breach the front door and stream into the house. Two officers follow, and more enter from the back. Gunfire sounds from within, and a chorus of male voices yell back and forth. A woman screams, and the final two officers enter the large structure.

Seconds later, a window opens at the top of the house, and a man emerges dressed in only boxer shorts and a gold chain. He scrambles onto the balcony and flips over the side. He slides down the column extending from the ground to the balcony, and within seconds, he exits the front gate while Peter and Bako watch from across the street. His feet are bare, and although in obvious pain, he runs along the pebbled road. None of the officers inside the house see him escape. Bako tears after him in hot pursuit. Peter, not wanting her to be alone, runs after her. The man looks back and sees them pursuing. He darts across the street, steps on a rock, and hesitates.

"Stop," Bako yells, raising her gun.

The man looks at her, then dashes down a side street. Bako continues after him, gaining on him. She's about two hundred meters in front of Peter when she and the man vanish behind a house. Peter slows his pace as he comes around the corner. Neither person is visible, and a German shepherd chained in the yard next door is losing its mind. It foams at the mouth and pulls against its restraint. Peter strains to hear above the growling and barking. There's no sound from Bako or the fugitive.

Peter withdraws his gun, readies the weapon, and moves forward. When he reaches the edge of the house, he peeks around the corner. The fugitive is behind Bako, holding her neck with the crook of his elbow in a choke position. With his other hand, he holds her own gun to her temple. His eyes meet Peter's. Peter trains his gun on the man's forehead.

"I want out of this. Just let me go," the man says.

Peter shakes his head. "I can't do that."

The man squeezes Bako's neck harder, and she cries out. "I'm going to kill her."

"That's only making an unpleasant situation worse."

The man frowns. "I didn't do anything. I was only following orders."

Peter nods. "I believe you. It's your boss we want. Now is the time to prove that. Let her go, and let's talk."

The man glances at Bako, then back at Peter. "How do I know I can trust you?"

"What choice do you have?" Peter motions to the man's feet with his gun. "You won't get far without shoes. Your feet are already bleeding. More men are coming behind me. You have nowhere to go. If you kill her, I'll have to shoot you. You don't want to die here. Put down the gun."

Peter hears boots on the street behind him. They're coming fast.

"You're out of time. My colleagues are here. Put the gun down. They'll shoot first and ask questions later. You don't want that. Drop the gun."

The dog next door had calmed considerably, but now, hearing the approaching men, it resumes fighting against its restraint.

Peter comes out from behind the corner. "I'm trying to help you. I mean it. Drop the gun."

That does it. The man lets the gun fall from his hand. Bako grips the man's arm and forces him to the ground. She puts a knee on his back and handcuffs on his wrists. Peter holsters his weapon as Captain Zsida comes around the corner.

"What happened?" the captain asks.

Bako looks at Peter, but before she can answer, Peter steps toward the captain.

"Sir, this man snuck out of the house, and Bako and I pursued. I wasn't able to keep up, but Bako was. She chased him down and subdued him before I arrived. She did a fantastic job. She's a fine officer."

Captain Zsida looks from Peter to Officer Bako. "Is that right, officer?"

She looks past the captain and notices Peter wink.

"I'm just glad we were here, sir."

Twenty minutes later, after searching the house and finding multiple trafficked women, Peter exits. When he reaches the street, Officer Bako approaches. "Peter?"

"Officer."

She looks around, making sure nobody is listening. "Why'd you do that?"

"Do what?"

"You know what. Why'd you give me the credit? He took my gun from me. I was negligent. Why didn't you tell the captain?"

Peter rubs his salt-and-pepper beard. "I meant what I said. I think you're a fine officer who wants to make a difference. You made a mistake I know you'll never make again."

Out of the corner of his eye, Peter sees a man approaching.

"Peter?"

He turns and sees Detective Farkas, leader of the Human Trafficking Task Force of the National Police. "Don't you have somewhere you need to be?"

Peter looks down at his Breitling Chromate watch and can't believe the time.

"Exactly," Farkas says, "get in the car. Your wedding is in three hours. Zsuzsa will never forgive you if you don't make it on time."

Chapter 3

Zsuzsa

I brush back a strand of blond hair as I analyze my reflection in the mirror. Today is a day I've dreamed about since I was a little girl. True, I thought it would come earlier. I imagined myself younger. But many things in my life haven't gone as planned.

I turn to the side and follow the curve of my white gown from heels to shoulder. It really is a gorgeous dress, and at this moment, I no longer regret the diet I've forced myself to follow these last four weeks. I can't recall a time when my body looked better. I lean closer to the mirror and inspect my face. Makeup can only cover so much. Faint lines surround my eyes and mouth. I'm an old bride. Next month I'll be thirty-six.

For the last six years, I've doubted this day would ever come. That there was a man out there for me. Then Peter walked into my restaurant. Nine months ago, he sat down at a barstool and ordered a Dreher and beef stroganoff, and my world changed. I didn't know it at the time. How could I? He could have been just another attractive older gentleman flirting with me on a random weeknight.

The attraction was immediate between us. It was undeniable. He was much more than any other man. He was different.

Within a week, he was back asking me out. I never dated patrons of the bar. They would try, but I never gave in. This time, I found myself saying *yes* before I could even think it through. That night, he admitted why he had come into the restaurant. He was a private investigator following my boss. The restaurant owner. Over the next several weeks, things escalated quickly. My life was in danger multiple times. But each time, Peter was there. He transformed before my eyes. He morphed from an attractive man to someone I didn't think I could live without. He was someone I could trust. Someone I could rely on. I was in love, and I didn't even know it.

Then he was arrested and forced to return to New York City. I thought it was over. I was shocked when, less than a month later, he returned. Hardly a day has gone by since his return that I haven't been with him. He's my everything, and I can't imagine my life without him.

A knock at the door wakes me from my thoughts.

"Come in."

The door opens, and I watch in the mirror as Kata, my friend and maid of honor, enters. She smiles and comes toward me. "Oh, Zsuzsa," she says and takes my hand as we stand side by side looking at each other in the mirror, "you look so lovely."

"It's quite a dress."

"It's magnificent on you. I love how you've done your hair."

I reach up and brush at a strand. "Is it too curly?"

We turn toward each other, and she puts a hand on my shoulder. "Not at all," she says, shaking her head.

I smile. "I think I'm ready. Let's get this show on the road."

She grins, but I see a hesitation in her eyes.

"What?"

"It's Peter."

My stomach falls. Did something happen?

"He's late."

"How late?"

She shrugs and winces. "He should be here in less than an hour."

Chapter 4

Peter

Detective Farkas pulls the car to a grove of trees in the hills above Budapest and orders Peter out. Peter exits as swiftly as his bones will allow and sees his friend and best man, Lantos Tamás, standing along the side of the dirt path smoking a cigarette

"It's about time. Zsuzsa almost had to marry *me*," Tom says, then pauses and blows a puff of smoke into the air. "On second thought, get back in the car and get lost."

Peter gives him a look and hustles down the path as Tom puts out his cigarette.

"Your monkey suit is in the small shack just around the corner."

Peter walks down the path one hundred meters until he reaches the opening in the cluster of trees. Anxiously awaiting his arrival, every member of the congregation turns to look at him. He avoids their eyes and ducks into the shack. A tuxedo hangs on the rack inside the door. He grabs it, steps behind the privacy screen, and undresses. A few seconds later, the door opens.

"No rush. She already left," Tom says.

Peter stops unbuttoning his shirt. "Are you serious?"

"No. But she should have. What's wrong with you, anyway?"

Peter sighs as he continues to undress.

"You've got to stop this, you know."

"Tom...don't start."

"Someone has to. By the way, what's my title in this wedding thing?"

"Huh?"

"My title? I think it's best man, isn't it? It should be best looking, but that's not the point. Best man," he pauses for effect, "that means I'm here to help and support you. It means I get to offer advice, and since you're the one who gave me the job, you have to listen."

Peter rolls his eyes, but Tom can't see it because he's behind the privacy screen.

"What? I can't hear you."

Peter still says nothing.

"Are you going to listen to me?"

Peter doesn't answer.

"Well?"

"What, Tom?"

"Are you going to listen?"

"Fine."

Tom nods and crosses his arms. "I love you, Peter. I love you like the brother I never had. It's because I love you, I can say this to you." He pauses. "You don't deserve her. She's so much above you, it's not even funny. And I'm not just talking about looks. You and I both know she saved you. Before you met her, you were broken. Do you remember?"

Peter stops after pulling on his jacket. He knows Tom's right. After leaving New York City following the murder of his wife, Peter came back to Hungary in desperation. Searching for a reason to live. Zsuzsa had given him that. Without her, he knows he wouldn't be alive. She gave him purpose and joy.

"I remember," Peter says.

Tom steps up to the privacy screen. "Peter, you need her more than she needs you. Never forget that. You've been married before, but she hasn't. You've already shown up late to her wedding. Get it together. Be the husband she needs. Stop thinking about yourself. Think about her."

Peter turns and looks at Tom over the screen. An understanding passes between them.

"Now, I'm going to go back out there and do my job. I'm going to make sure she sticks around and marries you. Hurry and finish dressing. I'll meet you at the front next to the arbor."

Five minutes later, Peter stands at the head of the chapel. Tom and Peter's former brother-in-law, Gary, from America, are to his left. The music changes, and everyone in the congregation rises. Zsuzsa appears at the back of the aisle of chairs. Her uncle stands beside her. They begin to walk toward him, and Peter feels a rush of excitement mixed with anxiety. Looking at this gorgeous woman, he feels inadequate. She deserves better than him. Tom's right, he has to be better.

When they reach the front, Zsuzsa's uncle places her hand on Peter's and steps back. Zsuzsa looks up into Peter's eyes. He expects to see anger, but instead, he sees curiosity.

"How did it go?" she whispers.

They turn and look at the wedding officiator, and Peter is again reminded how lucky he is to be standing beside this woman.

"It was accurate. That's where they were operating."

"I want to know everything…but later."

An hour passes as the sun sets over the tip of the hills just beyond them. Peter sits beside Gary, his former wife's brother. They watch as Zsuzsa's friends and family dance around her.

"When are you going back to New York?" Peter asks.

"Tomorrow. We need to get Rachel back for school. It starts next week."

Peter's niece leaves the dance floor and stands in front of her father and uncle.

"Uncle Peter?"

"Yes, my favorite niece?"

"I'm your *only* niece."

"And your point is?"

Gary laughs.

"What is it, my *only* niece?"

"Can you do something for me?" Rachel says.

Peter smiles. "Maybe. Depends on what you need."

She grins back at him. "Can you translate for me?"

"I'll make you a deal. I'll translate if you can say her name correctly."

Rachel sighs and gives him a look.

"Those are my terms."

"Fine…," she says, rolling her eyes. She says the name poorly.

Peter shakes his head. "No, listen to me. Zsu-zsa. It's like the middle part of the English word measure. Z and S together in Hungarian is like the letter J in French. Ju-Ja."

Rachel tries again, and this time, it sounds perfect. He nods and motions for her to lead the way, then follows her as she approaches a group of women dancing on the grass dance floor. Zsuzsa is in the middle, flanked by Kata and a few other friends. She sees Peter watching her and stops. He motions for her to come over.

"My niece, Rachel, has something she wants to say to you."

Zsuzsa gives him a quizzical look, then looks at Rachel.

"Zsuzsa," Rachel says, then turns to Peter, "tell her I hope when I get married, I look as lovely as she does."

Peter translates and Zsuzsa smiles.

"That's so sweet. Thank her for me."

Peter grins. "Tell her yourself."

Zsuzsa laughs. "I can't."

"Yes, you can. It'll be good practice. Come on, you know how to say thank you in English."

Zsuzsa looks at Rachel. "Thank you very much, Rachel."

Rachel beams, and the two embrace.

Zsuzsa turns to go back to her friends, but Peter grabs her hand and nods to the band. The leader smiles and stops playing, motioning to the others. Everyone watches as Peter leads Zsuzsa to the middle of the grass field. When the music plays, he takes her in his arms, and they dance as everyone watches.

After a few seconds, Zsuzsa pulls back from his shoulder to look up at him. "Peter?"

"Yes?"

"What did you mean, *practice*?"

"Huh?"

"You said I needed to practice my English. Why?"

He smiles. "You told me, when you were a little girl, you had a poster on your wall. What was the poster of?"

"New York City."

Peter nods and goes back to dancing. She lets him lead her but keeps her eyes on him.

"That's it?"

He grins. "What?"

She shakes her head. "Tell me."

He stops and looks her in the eye. "Did you pack your bag?"

"Yes."

"Good. Tomorrow, I'm taking you to America. It's about time you see my other home."

Chapter 5

Scott

I sit at my desk on the 105th floor of the World Trade Center's south tower and stare at the file before me. I arrived early, skipping my normal workout. I spent hours yesterday doctoring the documents in the file. I got here much earlier than I would have liked to print them and have them ready for when Mr. Larkin arrives. I only hope he'll be convinced.

The front door to the office suite opens, and anxiety shoots through me. The light flips on, and I can hear Roxanne's keys jingle. I take a deep breath and stand at my desk.

"Scott?" she calls from the small reception area?

I exit my office and walk down the hall. She's standing by her desk, purse draped over her forearm. Her sunglasses are lodged in her straight, dark hair. She's wearing a short skirt with tall, open-toed, black heels. The outfit accentuates her firm body.

"I thought that was you."

"Yeah, I had some work I needed to get done for a closing later today. I decided to get an early start. How was your weekend?"

She smiles and bends over, placing her purse on her desk. She moves her mouse, and her monitor comes to life. She took yesterday, Monday, off. "Pretty quiet. I didn't do much. Had some drinks with a couple of girlfriends. You?"

"I worked more than I would have liked."

She's bent over the desk, keying in her passcode. She looks up and frowns. "I'm sorry. Maybe the week will get better," she says, and winks.

Did she forget about Larkin's visit on Friday? How could she not remember?

"Maybe. By the way, could you do me a favor?" I pass her an envelope. "Can you make a quick run to the bank? I forgot to get this deposited yesterday, and I've been worrying about it."

She takes it, looks me in the eye, then looks beyond me to the clock on the wall. "The bank won't be open until nine." She sits down in her chair. "I'll wait until then."

I was afraid she'd say that. "Actually, would you mind going now? You can be there right as they open. It'd mean a lot to me."

She frowns, and I can see questions in her eyes. "Okay. I guess I could run to the mailbox first. That'll save me a trip later." She stands and picks up her purse. As she passes me, I reach out and put my hand on her arm.

"Thanks, Roxanne."

She looks up at me, irritation on her face.

"I've missed you," I whisper. "I can't wait until tomorrow."

She gives me a long look, and I can see she wants to ask, but she doesn't. Instead, she smiles and sways past me to the door. She leaves, and only the faint scent of her perfume remains. I take a deep breath, then head back to my office, looking out the window. To my left are the Hudson River and New Jersey in the distance. I can't see anything directly north, only the other tower. I stand transfixed as I stare at the water far below.

I don't know how long I've been looking out when I hear the exterior door to the office suite open behind me. I turn and see Mr. Larkin. The small older man hasn't seen me and closes the door. He looks around the office. "Hello?" he calls out. I walk to the threshold of my office and wave. He looks over and sees me.

"Hello, Mr. Larkin. I'm ready for you in here."

Larkin nods and comes forward. I extend my hand to him, and this time, he takes it.

"How was your weekend?" I ask, ushering him into the space.

"Fine," he says. He's more pleasant than Friday, but the iceberg that sunk the *Titanic* still had more warmth.

"Have a seat." I round the desk and sit in my chair across from him.

He folds his arms and looks at me.

I lean forward across the desk and open the file. "I was able to reach your mortgage company yesterday. They confirmed receipt." I point to a paper on the top of the file. The sheet has loads of information, and I've highlighted the dollar amount, bank account number, and property address in yellow.

Larkin comes forward in the chair, keeping his arms folded. He gives the document nothing more than a glance, then leans back. "You're a liar," he says. His voice is cold and flat.

I frown, feeling a churning in my gut. "What are you talking about?" I motion to the papers. "Here's your proof."

His eyes bore through me. "You're not just a liar. You're a thief and a fraud."

"What's your problem? This wire receipt clearly shows I transferred the money."

He smirks and shakes his head. "You're going to keep this up?"

"Keep what up?"

"I got a letter dropped at my front door last night." He reaches into his sports coat and withdraws an envelope. He slides it across the desk. I open the envelope and find a note printed in block letters: SCOTT LYON IS A LIAR. BELIEVE NOTHING HE TELLS YOU.

I look back up at him.

"Turn to the next page."

I do and see it's a bank statement. It's *my* bank statement! My heart drops as I examine it. It's the trust account for my title business and clearly shows the deposit of Mr. Larkin's escrow money. It also shows an immediate transfer out.

"If you look closely at the account number my money was transferred to, you can see it wasn't the account you have listed here." He leans forward and points to the wire transfer I showed him earlier.

I drop the pages to my lap.

"Now, where's my money?"

I stare at him, trying to come up with an explanation when a loud pop sounds from outside the building. Larkin jumps, and my eyes go to the window. We both stand and approach it. There's a hole in the other tower. A fireball expands out, and smoke pours from the floors just below us. Our eyes are riveted to the scene as thousands of papers fill the sky.

"A bomb?" I whisper. It's not unprecedented. There was a bombing in that very building eight years earlier in 1993.

Suddenly, figures surround the opening. One person jumps, then another. We watch in shocked horror.

"It's the heat," Larkin says. "They can't stand the heat. They'd rather jump than burn to death."

Several seconds pass as we watch people fling themselves from the building.

Larkin blinks and steps away from the window. "We've got to get out of here," he says, worry lines creasing his forehead.

"What? Why?"

"There could be more." His eyes go wide. "The structural integrity..." He steps back to the window, pointing. "Look at the size of that hole. The entire building could be compromised. If it is, it's only a matter of time..."

"A matter of time until what?"

"The whole building collapses."

I stare at him and remember our brief conversation when he came for the closing of his house sale. He had said something about architecture. Or was it engineering?

Larkin grabs my arm. "Come on. We've got to go. Down the stairs." He pulls me toward the exit. I shrug him off and stare at him. "Come on," he yells, "now! We can't take the elevator. It's unsafe. We don't have a lot of time. We've got to move." He tugs at my arm and turns away from me, starting down the hall when an idea forms in my head.

Reacting on instinct, I hurry toward him and wrap my arm under his chin. As I take him from behind, I give little thought to the consequences of my actions. I support my wrist with the other arm and squeeze as hard as I can. I'm much stronger than he is. He reaches up, scratching at my arm as I choke him. My grip is so tight, the only sound is the shuffle of his feet as he tries to get leverage against me. I grit my teeth and keep the pressure under his neck, my bicep bulging. He shakes, and his right arm reaches up for my face. He claws at my cheek, and I think he's drawn blood as his nails sink into the skin. I jerk back, applying even more pressure. Finally, his body goes slack, and he shakes. He's unconscious, maybe even dead.

I drag him toward our server room, open the door, and pull him inside. The room is small, no larger than eighty square feet. Barely enough floor space for me to fit his body. I bend his legs, and before I close the door, I turn back to look at him.

A voice erupts from the PA system, saying that a plane flew into the other tower. It assures us that our building, building two, is secure. It admonishes us to stay calm and remain at our desks. I look down at Larkin. I wonder if he's dead. I didn't check his pulse. I wish I had time, but if what he said is true, every second counts. I've got to get out of here. I shut the door and rush back to my office. I grab the papers he brought and jam them into his closing file. I check the window and see the sky is now full of black smoke. It's billowing from the other tower, and flames are visible. The fire's growing. A lurch of fear grips me, and for the first time, I'm afraid for my life.

I turn away from the window, scan the office, and check to see if I'm missing something. I notice the Yankees hat on the shelf behind my desk and grab it, jamming it on my head. This plane crash might just give me an opportunity. I reach inside my desk, knowing I've got some cash, and rush down the hall, bolting for the stairs.

Chapter 6

Peter

Peter wakes to see the other side of the bed empty. The hotel room is small. Barely large enough to allow someone to walk around the bed. Light filters through the curtain, providing him some visibility. He surveys the room, wondering about Zsuzsa. Then he hears it. The shower turns off beyond the bathroom door. Relieved but still exhausted, he drifts back to sleep.

Moments later, he startles awake. Zsuzsa sits beside him on the bed. She's wearing only a towel. Her long blond hair is pinned up in the back. "No more sleeping," she says. "You can sleep when we go back to Hungary."

Late last night, they had arrived at John F. Kennedy Airport and got a taxi to the hotel. It was dark, and although Zsuzsa had anxiously watched from the car window, she couldn't see much. Just two days ago, they were married in Budapest. After spending their wedding night in the city, they boarded a flight to New York City. She slept on the plane, but he didn't.

Peter smiles and turns away, closing his eyes. "Five more minutes."

"Fine. If you won't go with me, I'll go see New York on my own."

He opens his eyes and turns back to her. "Oh, yeah? Do you know the city? Do you know the language?"

She stands and turns away from him, dropping her towel. Exposing her naked backside. She's playing games with him, and it's working. "If you aren't interested, I'm sure other handsome American men will help a poor, lost foreign girl." She turns to look at him, sucking the tip of her finger.

She was trying to be playful, but it does more to him than make him chuckle. "Come back in this bed," he commands.

She shakes her head and takes her clothes with her to the bathroom. "Get up. You can't have me until I've seen the city."

Minutes later, they walk out of their hotel and into the bustling streets of New York City. Zsuzsa holds a coffee in one hand, Peter a tea. Their other hands are intertwined. Peter guides her in the direction he wants to go.

"Where are you taking me?" Zsuzsa asks.

Peter smirks. "Weren't you telling me just a few minutes ago that you'd see the city without me? I assumed you were in charge."

She rolls her eyes and lets him escort her. It's her first time out of Hungary, and everything is different: cars, street signs, buildings. Even the people look different. It's a Tuesday morning, and the sidewalks are jammed with pedestrians. Many carry briefcases or have mobile phones pressed to their ears, speaking English. There's an energy found nowhere in Hungary, not even in Budapest. It's a vibrant late-summer morning, and although the sun is up, it's nowhere visible. The buildings are too tall. Zsuzsa feels like she's in a movie.

They turn right, leaving the busy street, and the signs change. Some still have English, but most are Chinese. The signs are bright and hang over the shops, many with open markets. Colorful canopies distinguish one vendor from the next.

Zsuzsa stops in front of a tank full of lobsters. "What are those?"

"Um," he chuckles, "I actually don't know the Hungarian word for them. *Tengeri rák, lehet*?"

She nods. "Are they good?"

"Very. Want to try?"

She turns away from the tank. "Now?"

He chuckles. "No. I'll take you to a restaurant that serves them. Would you like that?"

She nods enthusiastically.

He looks down at his watch. "Come on, there's something I want to show you."

They walk several more blocks and exit Chinatown. They reach the Manhattan Bridge arch and Zsuzsa says, "What does that remind you of in Budapest?"

Peter frowns, examining the arch as they walk past. "I don't know. The Chain Bridge?"

"Maybe a little," Zsuzsa says. "I was thinking more Heroes' Square."

Peter frowns and looks back. "Really?"

"Kind of. At least the columns."

Peter shrugs, not sure, and they walk along the pedestrian path of the Manhattan Bridge. After five minutes, he stops and points through the chain-link fence. "That's Lower Manhattan. You probably recognize a couple of the buildings."

"Those two," she says. "World Trade Center?"

"Yep. I've always liked this view—" Peter stops, his eyes glued to the north tower. A fireball bursts near the top of the building, and black smoke pours from all sides.

Chapter 7

Scott

I rush through the door to the stairwell of the 105th floor of the south tower. It's eerily quiet, and I wonder if I'm making a mistake. Should I go back? I shake my head. No, I've got to get out of here. Larkin was terrified. I run down two flights of stairs and hear people below me. I reach them after only a few seconds. It's three men and a woman. She's obese and creeping along, huffing and puffing. The men walk beside her, encouraging her. When she sees me trying to push past, she turns to the man closest to her.

"Just go without me. I'll take the elevator."

"No," he says, shaking his head and gripping her arm. "If something happens in this building, you'll be trapped. This is the only way."

One man looks at me, and I nod, dropping my head as I squeeze past. I continue down the stairs, occasionally passing people as I go, always ducking my head to avoid eye contact.

I consider what that guy told the fat lady. Larkin had said the same thing. *Avoid the elevators*. I wonder what they know. Why are they so sure we've got to leave? It was the other tower that was hit. Not this one. Surely everyone will be fine once the fire is out in the other building. That thought only increases my urgency. I've got to put as much distance between myself and the office before Larkin wakes. If he ever does.

When I reach the tenth floor, a crash sounds from up above, and the ground shakes. Dust falls all around me, and the white metal railing vibrates in my hand. Voices scream as I look up at the stairs above. Another bomb? Another plane? If that's true, the first one wasn't an accident. We're under attack. I pick up my pace as alarm sirens blare. When I reach the third floor, I hear voices below me. My only thought is getting out of the building as quickly as possible. That's why I'm so surprised to see people ascending the stairs. Two firefighters push past me with grim expressions. They're headed up to the explosion. I wonder what they'll find when they get there. Will they find Larkin? Did he die in the explosion? I don't let the thought fester as I fly down the remaining floors, squeezing past people on the descent. I even shove a slow old man who isn't moving fast enough and won't step aside.

When I reach the ground floor, I fling open the door and enter the lobby. I barely recognize it. It's chaos. People are everywhere, running toward the exits. I push past several, hiding my face. Seconds later, as I clear the exit, I stop and look up. Both towers are on fire. Smoke billows from both, and I can see flames. I run across the street and can't help myself. I stop and look again. White sheets of paper float down all around me like giant snowflakes. A woman standing beside me screams, and I look over just in time to see a body splat on the ground in front of us. People are jumping from my building.

I think about Larkin and lean back to get a better view of the tower. The black hole with smoke pouring out is roughly three-quarters of the way up. The center is probably level seventy-five. Even if Larkin's alive, he's above where the plane hit. He's likely unreachable for the firefighters. If they can't get to him, he'll die from smoke inhalation. And if the towers implode, like he said...

To my left, I hear rhythmic voices penetrating my ears above the screaming. A van sits beside the curb, the radio blasting. Two men are talking about the towers. They say it's a terrorist attack. It wasn't a bombing. Two commercial planes intentionally flew into the towers. They wonder if more are coming, and I realize that, even after exiting the building, I'm not safe. I've got to get out of here. I resume my plan and duck away from the crowd. I run up West Broadway. Cars are stopped all around me. Some people walk while others run. Some stand in the street, pointing and talking. I pass them, ignoring the urge to look back. When I reach Walker Street, people standing in the street looking back shout. I turn to see Tower Two, my tower, collapse in on itself.

A mushroom cloud extends from the site, and the ground shakes. I turn away, sprinting. I'm in far better shape than most and easily outrun those around me. People wail and scream, tears rolling down their cheeks. One woman trips and falls beside me. I jump over her and continue on. After two blocks, I look back over my shoulder and see the cloud expanding toward me. Dust and smoke fill the street. A reporter and cameraman stand on the road ahead. I duck behind a parked car. I don't want to be seen. I don't want anyone to know I'm alive.

I look back and see the smoke and dust have filtered down the side streets. The smoke cloud isn't as potent as it was in Lower Manhattan, but I can still see grime in the air. Several hundred feet below, people stumble from the cloud, covered with dust. Many hold their shirts over their mouths and noses to prevent breathing the particles. Police and FBI emerge on the street and begin helping people. Directing them uptown.

A siren blasts, and fire trucks pass, picking their way around the survivors. The trucks disappear into the dust when people shout and yell again. Tower One, the first tower hit, is collapsing. We can see it over the dust cloud. A new jolt of fear strikes, and I pick up my pace as people run all around me. Within seconds, I taste iron. My throat feels gritty. I slow my pace and cough hard. I get some relief and take off again.

I reach Canal Street and turn left. Just before I turn right on Varick, I see her. Roxanne is across the street, just outside the bank. She's standing with a group of people. Almost as if she senses my presence, she turns and looks in my direction. I duck behind a car. I curse and scurry around the street corner. Staying low behind the cars.

I stand and run, wondering if she recognized me. Dust covers my clothes. I'm wearing my Yankees hat. She couldn't know it was me. Could she? I can't remember ever wearing a hat around her. She was on the opposite side of the street. Chaos all around. I'm covered in dust. Surely, she didn't know it was me.

I get another couple of blocks up the street and slow my pace. Penn Station is visible now. My sanctuary. I wasn't planning on disappearing today, but fate stepped in. This chaos gave me exactly what I needed. I couldn't have planned it better. As long as I can reach it and not run into anyone else I know, I can do exactly what I hoped. I can disappear. And now it's even better. Nobody will know I'm alive.

Chapter 8

Peter

Peter and Zsuzsa watch from the bridge. A plane hits the other tower. At first, they think it's an accident. Now, they know it isn't. People line the bridge beside them. The mood is quiet. Somber. Nobody moves as the first tower crumbles. When the second follows, cries of shock and anger reverberate. Peter feels sick. He thinks he may vomit. How many people have lost their lives? Fathers, mothers, grandparents, sons, daughters. Who could have performed these atrocities? And why?

Hours pass as Peter and Zsuzsa stand on the bridge watching and waiting. Finally, they decide to return to their hotel. Dust and smoke cover the area around the hotel. People wander the streets in a daze. Police officers aid those in most need. They guide and tend to the wounded. As Peter walks past, he can't help but feel he needs to do something. Just two years ago, he was one of them. A cop. A member of the NYPD. Now, wandering the streets, he's just another civilian rattled by the day's events.

He wants to help. To stand side by side with his brothers and sisters on the force, but he can't. He has Zsuzsa. If not for her, he might try. But she's in an unfamiliar country with a language she barely knows. He looks at her and sees her fear. He could never leave her alone. She's his world now, and he has to keep her safe.

They arrive back at the hotel and go to their room. They turn on the TV and watch with the rest of the world as news reports inform them about the day's events. Peter translates. They learn of additional attacks. One at the Pentagon in DC and another in a field in Pennsylvania. Unsure where else to go, they wait in their hotel room. They barely leave the room for two days, having nowhere to go. Their plans are ruined and seem insignificant now. They talk about flying back to Hungary, taking a rain check on their honeymoon, but decide against it. Air travel was halted, and even when it resumes, they know it will be nearly impossible to get home without significant delays. Better to wait until some normalcy returns.

On the second day, knowing they can't go much longer in such cramped quarters, Peter places a call to Gary and his wife, Becky. They insist Peter and Zsuzsa come to stay with them. Peter agrees.

When they arrive at Gary and Becky's, Peter and Zsuzsa are shown to the guest bedroom.

Peter looks at Zsuzsa. "Sorry about this," he says as he places her suitcase on the bed.

She frowns. "About what?"

"This," he says, motioning to the surrounding room. "Some honeymoon, staying with my former wife's brother and family."

Zsuzsa shakes her head and mutters something.

"What?" Peter asks.

She looks up from her suitcase, having opened it. "I said you've got a warped sense of reality."

Peter frowns. "Uh...how's that?"

"Did you have anything to do with the terrorist attacks?"

"Of course not."

"Then why are you apologizing for them?"

He starts to respond but stops. They stare at each other until he finally shrugs. "I just wanted you to have a wonderful time. To see the city I came to love."

Her face softens, and she comes around the bed to him. She puts her hand on his cheek and looks into his eyes. "What we've witnessed is horrible. But that's no fault of yours. Maybe it hasn't been the honeymoon either of us imagined, but I wouldn't trade it for anything. I get to be here with you."

They stare at each other, and Peter leans forward and kisses her. She wraps her arms around his neck and kisses him back.

The door behind them opens, and they quickly release each other and turn to see Rachel, Peter's thirteen-year-old niece. She stands in the doorframe, her cheeks burning. "Sorry," Rachel says, looking down.

Peter puts an arm around Zsuzsa's shoulder. "It's okay. But maybe knock next time."

"Okay. Sorry," she says timidly, looking up at him.

"Is there something you need?" Peter asks.

"Mom said dinner's ready."

"Okay. We'll be right over."

Rachel hesitates, then turns away.

Peter looks back at Zsuzsa. "I guess that's another unexpected twist to our honeymoon. Nothing like getting interrupted by your niece," he says, chuckling.

"She's cute. She's an only child. She doesn't know any better."

Peter and Zsuzsa go to the dining room. Becky already has the table set for the five of them. Gary sits in the family room in his recliner watching the news while Rachel stands in the kitchen helping her mother.

"Where do you want us?" Peter calls to Becky.

She comes around the corner carrying a bowl of salad. "Over there," she says, gesturing toward the side of the table. She places the bowl in the middle and heads back to the kitchen while Peter and Zsuzsa take their places. Gary turns off the TV and joins them at the head of the table beside Peter.

"You went back to work today?" Peter asks.

Gary nods, and Peter turns and translates to Zsuzsa.

"You don't have to translate everything for me. Just talk to your family. I'll keep myself occupied with the food. You can tell me what they said later."

Peter looks back to Gary and sees he's watching them.

"That's got to be hard," Gary says.

"What?"

"Being here in a foreign country with all of this going on. I imagine she's scared."

"If she is, she doesn't show it." Peter looks at Zsuzsa, and she smiles.

Becky and Rachel come in, and Becky tells them all to "dig in."

"How was work?" Becky asks Gary.

Gary, Peter's brother-in-law and brother to Peter's deceased first wife, is an attorney for the US State Department. Today he went back to work feeling confident the attacks were over. School hasn't resumed for Rachel. Gary sighs while picking up the salad bowl.

"Gary," Becky scolds, "let the guests go first."

Gary looks at her, then turns back to Peter and gives him a sheepish smile.

Peter takes the bowl and holds it for Zsuzsa.

"What a mess this whole thing is," Gary says.

"Shocking," Peter says.

Gary nods. "These attacks took everyone by surprise. There was talk, there always is. But nobody saw this coming. We weren't prepared for our own planes to be turned into weapons against us."

Peter puts the salad on his plate and passes it back to Gary. He takes a portion and then passes it to Becky and Rachel.

"International travel is going to be a mess for a while. I think you should plan on staying for at least another week."

Peter nods.

"Speaking of, since you're going to be around. There's something maybe you could help me with."

Becky looks at Gary, and an unspoken message passes between them. This is planned. Peter frowns but waits.

"Have you met any of Becky's side of the family?"

Peter looks at Becky and shakes his head. "Maybe a couple people. Only in passing."

She nods. She's letting Gary do the talking.

"Well, she's got a cousin who's about ten years younger. She lives up on Long Island. Not far. Anyway, her husband worked in the towers."

Peter looks at Becky. "He didn't make it?"

Becky shakes her head.

"Oh, I'm sorry."

Becky looks down.

Gary scoffs. "Yeah, well, don't be too sorry. The guy was a real piece of work." He drops his voice and leans toward Peter. "I never liked him."

Becky clears her throat, and Peter looks at Rachel, moving the food around her plate but paying close attention to the conversation.

"What floor was he on? Which building?" Peter asks.

Gary shakes his head. "I'm not sure, a hundred and something. He hasn't been seen since the towers went down. He was in Tower Two."

It was the second tower to be hit, but the first to collapse. Peter chews on his lip and looks at Zsuzsa. She's watching them, but he can't tell how much of the conversation she's picking up.

"Anyway, it's bad enough that she lost her husband in the attack." He stops and looks at Becky. "Maybe it was a good thing."

She gives him a shake of the head.

"Becks, the guy was a jerk." Gary spears a piece of chicken and then looks at Peter. "Well, it turns out the guy was embezzling money. A lot of money. He was being investigated by the New York Insurance Commission and had multiple complaints against him. He owned a title-insurance company. He's accused of keeping clients' money and not paying off their mortgages."

"Okay?" Peter says.

Now Becky jumps in. "Cindy says she knew nothing about it, and now the insurance commission has frozen his assets. She can't get access to his bank accounts. He's dead, and she doesn't have any money for her and the kids."

Peter frowns. "How many kids?"

"Two. Both are quite young. A girl, five, and a boy, four."

"Wow."

Gary nods and bites his lip. "Anyway, she has no money and can't afford a lawyer. I'm the only one she knows, and she's asked me for help. I don't know what I'm getting myself into, but I'll try to help. Tomorrow I'm meeting with her and the insurance commission. I think a detective from the police will also be there."

"And you want me to go?" Peter says.

"Could you?" Becky says, her eyes pleading.

Peter looks at her and knows he can't turn down Becky. He looks away and watches Zsuzsa. She smiles back at him. He wonders how he's ever going to explain this to her.

"*Mi*?" (What?) Zsuzsa asks.

Peter turns back to Becky. "Just this one meeting. I'm on my honeymoon."

Chapter 9

Scott

I stood at Penn Station for two hours before finally getting a train out of the city. I took the first available option, Philadelphia. The train was packed, and hardly a word was said the entire journey. People sat or stood in stunned silence, looking at their shoes or staring out the window.

When I reached Philadelphia, I exited the train and found a near-by hotel. I had my wallet but knew I couldn't use any credit cards. I only had the cash I'd grabbed out of my desk, four hundred and forty-four dollars. I found a motel that charged by the hour and didn't ask for identification. Yes, I could have shown two different driver's licenses, but why leave a trail? The one ID is nonnegotiable. That man is dead. The other isn't alive until I get to my destination.

After opening the door to the room, the scent of disinfectant overwhelmed me. Something about the smell made the motel seem less, not more, clean. It was like a teenager who thinks they can douse themselves in cologne to cover their lack of bathing. The room was straight out of the 1970s. I think I remember seeing the furniture set in a Sears catalog. Even the orange shag carpet, with multiple stains, complemented the whole motif. When I pulled back the covers on the bed, I swear a cockroach scurried over the side. I'd been duped. I spent twenty-nine dollars to spend the night with my clothes on, in a wicker chair, with my feet on a table.

I slept less than two hours. At six the next morning, I gave up and went back to the station. I purchased a ticket on an Amtrak headed for Chicago. The fare for a coach ticket was one hundred and seventy-nine dollars, and the trip took nearly two days. As soon as I boarded, I found a secluded window seat, rested my head against the window, and dropped into a coma-like sleep. I was out for hours.

When I finally woke, my stomach felt like it might start eating itself. I realized I had only eaten a small bag of potato chips since the disaster. I counted my cash and saw I had less than two hundred dollars left. I knew I had to make that stretch as far as possible. I found the dining cart and ordered the least-expensive meal, a ham sandwich. It only made me hungrier. It made me long for Des Moines and the millions I had waiting there.

I ate one more time on the train before it reached Chicago. When I exited, I ached for a hotel room and bed. I longed for a decent night's sleep, but after my experience in Philly, I kept going. I bought a ticket on the Greyhound from Chicago to Des Moines and got what sleep I could. Finally, after three days, very little sleep, and two small meals, I reached my destination.

Three months ago, I began putting this plan into motion. I had never been to Des Moines. In fact, I didn't even know which state it was in. Selecting it as my temporary home was nothing but dumb luck. I wanted somewhere with no ties to me. Someplace in the middle of America where nobody would ever think to look. A place I could disappear. I sat in my office with a map of the country laid across my desk. I closed my eyes, raised my finger, and pointed. Truth be told, my index finger rested on Perry, Iowa, with a population of less than seven thousand. It was too small. I needed somewhere I could easily find an apartment and disappear. So, I planned a "business trip," told my wife I'd be going to Chicago for a couple days, and flew to Des Moines.

The first order of business was finding an apartment. I rented a car and drove downtown near the capitol when I spied a For Rent sign. The building was perfect, near downtown on Locust Street. It looked like any other apartment building in small-town America. I found a pay phone, dialed the landlord, and met him an hour later. I needed a fully furnished place, and this was. After only five minutes of making a show walking around, checking it out, we agreed to terms. I signed a six-month lease, handed him a wad of stolen cash, and he gave me the keys.

With a new Des Moines address, I headed to the Iowa State Bank off Highway 6. When I walked through the doors, I waited for the first available teller and introduced myself as Joshua Staples. Thirty minutes later, after meeting the bank manager, "Josh" had an apartment, a bank account, and a new identity. All he had left was to visit the nearby Hy-Vee grocery store, stock the apartment with nonperishable groceries, and get back on a plane for home. That was three months ago.

I walk up the stairs to the third floor, get out my keys, and unlock the door. The smell is stale. I close the door and look around. It's exactly how I left it. I open a cupboard and find Top Ramen. I'm not sure why I bought it. I don't remember the last time I had ramen, but I'm glad I did. Nothing has ever tasted better. I take a shower, climb into bed, and look up at the ceiling. Tomorrow, I'll go to the bank, get an ATM card, and start my new life as Joshua Staples, a millionaire bachelor. I'll give my cousin's name the life he never could.

Chapter 10

Peter

Peter sits in an Albany, New York, conference room. Gary sits beside him. When Gary asked him to go along to the meeting of Cindy Lyon and the New York Insurance Commission, Peter assumed it would be somewhere in Manhattan. He likely would have declined if he knew the meeting was here, over two hours away from Manhattan. Ordinarily, the meeting would take place in Manhattan, but because of Mrs. Lyon's location, and the proximity of the Insurance Commission headquarters to Ground Zero, here they sat.

"She should be here any minute," Gary tells Peter, noticing he's looking at his watch.

Peter looks up and nods. It isn't Mrs. Lyon Peter is worried about. Since their marriage, Peter had been with Zsuzsa every minute, and he worried about leaving her. He only agreed because Becky had promised to take care of her by inviting her to do some shopping. Now he wonders how the two women are faring with the communication barrier and Zsuzsa's unfamiliarity.

The door behind them opens, and a woman enters. She's striking. Of average height with long brown hair, lovely eyelashes, and a trim figure. Knowing she's the cousin of his sister-in-law, Becky, he can see some family resemblance. She holds a purse in one hand and turns toward the two men as they stand. She's wearing an off-white blouse and a tan skirt.

"Hi, Gary," she says, extending a hand. "Good to see you again. I can't tell you how much I appreciate this."

"You already said it enough on the phone," he says, motioning toward Peter. "Do you know my brother-in-law, Peter?"

Peter holds out a hand. "Mrs. Lyon."

She takes his and smiles. "Cindy, please. Nice to meet you, Peter. You look familiar. I think I might have seen you before."

He nods, and Gary motions for her to sit beside him. "Before they come in, I wanted to talk for a few minutes," he says.

She nods, placing her hands on the table. Worry lines etch her mouth.

"I'll be honest with you; this is not my area of expertise. I'm not a criminal lawyer. As I told you before, I think you need one."

She shakes her head. "Why? I did nothing wrong."

"Yes, but your husband did. Allegedly. They're going to argue that you benefited from his theft and that everything you own should be sold and the money given to his victims. We've got to convince them you had no part in it. That you're a victim of his too."

"I am a victim," she pleads.

Peter can see in her eyes that this is a conversation they've had before. He's not telling her anything she doesn't already know.

"I need to ask one more time. Did you know anything about Scott's business practices? About his fraudulent actions?"

She shakes her head emphatically. "Nothing. He never mentioned it. I knew nothing."

Gary nods and looks at Peter, then back at Cindy. "Then I think you need to tell them that. Be honest. We need them on your side."

Cindy nods.

Gary stands. "I'm going to ask them to come in now. If you need a break or aren't sure what to say, just look over at me. I'm here for you. We want to cooperate, but you should always be comfortable. Okay?"

She nods, and Gary opens the door and leaves.

Peter looks at Cindy. "I'm sorry about your husband."

She looks at him, and her face drops. A wave of sadness clouds her eyes. "Thank you. This is all so confusing. I don't know how to feel about him anymore. It's like he left for work that morning and became a dead villain. Like I never knew him."

Gary comes back into the room. He's followed by a woman and a man. The woman is in her mid-fifties. Her hair is light, cut to her shoulders, a serious look on her face. The man is short with a graying beard and receding hairline. He's a few years younger than the woman. Maybe late forties. Peter recognizes him.

Gary walks them over to Cindy. "Cindy, this is Debbie Egan. She's the investigator assigned to look into Scott's business dealings. She works for the New York Insurance Commission."

The two women shake hands, and Investigator Egan turns to Peter. He extends his hand. "My name is Peter Andrassy. I've been asked by Mrs. Lyon and Gary to be here."

"Peter," the man who hadn't been introduced yet says, stepping up to him and slapping his shoulder, "I thought you'd left the country?"

Peter turns away from Investigator Egan and smiles at the man. "How are you, Eric?" he says, extending his hand.

Eric Kramer takes it, grinning. "It's so good to see you," he says, beaming at Peter.

"It's good to be seen."

Both men chuckle.

"Well," Gary says. "I see you two don't need to be introduced."

Kramer laughs and releases Peter's hand, extending it to Cindy. "Mrs. Lyon, I'm Detective Eric Kramer of the NYPD."

Cindy shakes his hand. Egan and Kramer move around to the opposite side of the table, and Cindy, Gary, and Peter sit together.

"Thank you for coming today, Mrs. Lyon," Investigator Egan says. "We really appreciate it. Mr. Lombardi," she motions to Gary, "has told us you're willing to help us with our investigation. We're grateful."

"I'd like to help," Cindy says. "Whatever I can do to put this behind us."

Both investigators nod, and Investigator Egan looks at Gary and Peter, then back at Cindy. "We'd like to ask for your cooperation in answering some questions. I understand Mr. Lombardi is acting as counsel for you?"

"Yes."

"And you want Mr. Andrassy present as well?"

"Yes."

"Very well," Egan says and opens a file. She places a pair of reading glasses on the end of her nose, a pencil in hand. Kramer leans back in his chair.

"What did you know about your husband's business dealings?"

"What do you mean?"

"Your husband owned a firm by the name of Sound Security Title. Is that right?"

"Yes."

"What was your involvement in the business?"

Cindy shakes her head. "My involvement?"

"Yes."

"Nothing. I didn't work in it. Scott ran the company. We have two kids. I stayed home taking care of them."

"You're a homemaker?"

"Yes."

"And you didn't work in the business? Not even to help manage the finances? Anything like that?"

Cindy shakes her head.

Egan makes a note in her file. "Tell me what you knew about your husband's business."

Cindy folds one hand over the other, placing both on the table. "Well, as you said, it was called Sound Security Title. Scott started the business about five years ago. It was something to do with real estate. I don't really know what. I never worked in that industry. He would tell me things about it here and there, but I never understood it. I think he'd verify information with the buying and selling of houses, and they'd pay him for it. I know he worked with a lot of different real estate agents."

Egan nods. "What about money? How would he get paid?"

Cindy looks at Gary, then back at Egan. "Um... I guess people would pay him for checking out the property and for making sure everything was done right? He always had closings when people would sell their houses, but I don't really know what that meant."

"Okay. Did he ever mention something called an escrow account?"

She puts a finger to her lips. "No, I don't think so."

"Do you know what *escrow* means?"

Cindy shakes her head.

"It's a holding account. When two parties agree to sell and buy a home, money needs to be transferred. A third party, a title company, like your husband's, acts as the fiduciary of those funds. They ensure both parties are legitimate and serious about the transaction. They hold the money until the transaction is complete. When the sale is final, they're contractually obligated to deliver the money to the agreed-upon accounts. Does that make sense?"

She nods. "Yes."

"Most houses have notes or mortgages. Loan obligations the owner is required to pay. Are you familiar with those?"

"Loans?"

"Yes, exactly. Like your home has a mortgage, correct?"

"Yes."

"Well, when a house sells, a seller needs to pay off their mortgage on the home. That way, the new buyer has a clean title. Sometimes, that money could be substantial. Again, your husband's company was responsible for taking the loan-payoff funds and transferring them to the mortgage company to satisfy the debt. Your husband held those funds in trust until a designated time when he was supposed to transfer them over." She stops and looks at Cindy closely. "Did your husband ever mention any wrongdoing when it came to the escrow funds he was given? Any time he used them for personal reasons?"

Cindy shakes her head. "No. Is that what Scott did? Did he not pay the money?"

"Most of the time, he did. There are only a few times that we know of, when he didn't. All of those times are fairly recent."

"So, he stole the money?"

"We think so. Unfortunately, we can't ask him. That's why we're talking to you."

Cindy's face falls, and her voice grows husky. "How much did he steal?"

Egan looks at Kramer, who says, "Based on what we can tell, he stole over three million dollars from his clients. It might be more..."

Cindy's eyes fill with tears. Gary puts a hand on her shoulder. "Cindy? Are you okay?"

She shakes her head. "I'm fine."

Detective Kramer comes forward in his chair. "Where's the money, Cindy?"

Gary puts up a hand to stop Cindy from answering. He glares at Kramer. "She just told you she has no idea."

"I didn't ask you, Mr. Lombardi," Kramer says. He looks at Cindy. "Where is it?"

Cindy wipes a tear from her cheek. "I don't know."

"This is ridiculous," Gary says. "She clearly doesn't know what you're talking about. Why are you asking her for the money?"

Kramer looks at Gary, then says to Cindy, "Did you withdraw the money? Do you have it?"

"No," Cindy says.

Kramer looks at Egan, then back to Gary. "Several days ago, there were multiple large cash withdrawals from the escrow account of Sound Security Title. Totaling over three million dollars. It's our job to find that money. And if we can't, we'll be forced to make the clients whole by other means."

Gary frowns. Cindy looks at him. "What does that mean?"

Kramer looks at her. "We'll seize any assets belonging to Scott Lyon, including his house, cars, and anything else of value. Until that money is found, you own nothing."

Chapter 11

Scott

When I wake, I look at the clock on the wall. It says it's six thirty, but it seems too dark. I prop myself up on my elbow and look out the window. The sky has a purple hue with only the first touches of the day's sunlight. I stand from the bed and walk to the clock. I watch it, listening intently. It's silent. I examine it and see the smallest, barely visible hand isn't moving. I pull it from the wall and check the back. The battery looks old. It's covered with rust. I'm sure it's dead. I put the clock back and walk into the kitchen. I remember I bought instant coffee when I went to the store three months ago. Now I'm glad I did. I've never had it before. The reviews have been less than encouraging, but desperate measures... I open the freezer, remove the coffee, fill a saucepan with water, and place it on the stove. Once it's heated, I pour the contents into a cup, add the water, and stir. I take a gulp and almost gag. It's revolting.

I abandon the cup and try to ignore my pounding head. I walk to the bathroom and rub the sleep from my eyes. I don't know if it's the travel or the adrenaline rush of almost losing my life, but I feel like I'm walking in quicksand. I turn on the shower and force myself inside.

When I return to the kitchen, the coffee has cooled to room temperature. I look at my wallet on the kitchen counter. I've got a ten, a five, and two ones. I can't afford to buy any other coffee just yet, and I know I can't get through a day without it. I pick up the cup, take a deep breath, and force the bile down my throat. I grimace, fighting my gag reflex, and wash out the cup with my eyes shut. I bend over the sink and scoop a handful of water into my mouth before spitting it back out. I shake my head and go back to my wallet. I remove my ID from the plastic cover, which reveals the second ID I have hidden beneath. I purchased it several months ago, unsure when I'd need it. I search through the rest of the wallet, removing credit cards and anything else that links me to Scott Lyon. I consider throwing them in the trash, but stop and look around. Where can I hide them? I look at the heating vent. I examine it and go back into the kitchen and get a butter knife. I use it to unscrew the vent and place the ID and credit cards within. I replace the vent cover.

I return the knife, put the wallet in my back pocket, and run my tongue along my upper teeth. I can't stop tasting the bile I gagged down earlier. The aftertaste is even worse, if that's possible. I look back at the kitchen. Today has to be the day. I can't take another one of these. Poor isn't a life I've ever wanted. I've worked too hard and come too far to live this way. Today, if all goes right, I'll have enough money to buy any coffee I want. I'll get the very best.

I exit the apartment, ride the elevator to the ground level, and walk out the exterior doors. I blink against the bright sun. Although the rays cover the street, it's still cool. I take a deep breath. The contrast of the air here is stark from Manhattan. There, the oxygen always has a smell. It's tinged with an aroma from whatever area it last passed through. Sometimes it smells like bread from a pizza restaurant or exhaust from the cars. Whatever the smell, it's not fresh. This is. It's cool and clean, and I don't like it. It conjures memories. Those I'd just as soon leave buried. I remind myself this is only temporary.

I gaze up and down the street, getting my bearings, then walk down Locust Street in search of Iowa State Bank. Prior to today, I've spent no more than thirty-six hours in Iowa. I feel like a fish out of water. I know where only three things are located, and the bank is one of them. I won't be here long, but I don't mind the walk. It gives me a better sense of the city.

While walking, I windmill my arms. They feel cramped and under used. It's been days since I last worked out, and I can already feel my muscles growing soft. When I'm done at the bank, I'll go shopping, then find a gym. That'll help. That's probably what's causing my lethargy. Later in the day, maybe I'll find a used car. Something I can buy with cash. Using an ATM, I'll only be able to withdraw so much. It might be a couple of weeks before I can take out enough to leave. I wonder where I should go. Chicago maybe? No. I want something west. Somewhere warm. LA? I've always been interested in California. What about San Francisco?

After fifteen minutes, I reach the bank and enter. I step up to the open teller window, and a cute girl in her early twenties with light-brown hair and dark eyes smiles at me. She and the boy in the other window were talking about the terrorist attacks as I approached. They said President Bush went to visit the site of the towers.

"Welcome to Iowa State Bank. How can I help you?"

"Yes, hello. My name is Joshua Staples. I set up a bank account a while back but realized I never got an ATM card. Can you assist me with that?"

She smiles. "Oh, certainly Mr. Staples. Do you have your account number?"

I pull out my wallet and read her the digits on the note I've had hidden away. She types into the computer and then looks back at me. "Do you have your ID?"

I pull out my wallet but don't remove the identification from the clear plastic window and extend it to her. She examines it, then turns back to the computer. "Thank you. Let me just get that card for you. I'll need a couple of minutes."

She walks away, and I turn back to look out across the lobby. I can feel eyes on me. There's a woman in her mid-thirties sitting behind a desk. When she sees me notice her, she drops her eyes back to the computer. I keep my eyes on her, and eventually, she looks back up and smiles. She's attractive, a little on the thicker side. She has long blond hair and bright-pink lips that match her nails and dress. She could be very attractive if she spent less time in front of a mirror and more time in the gym. She sneaks another glance at me, then looks away.

The teller returns, and I turn back.

"Thank you for your patience, Mr. Staples." She hands me an envelope, and I can feel the outline of a plastic card. "You'll need that card and your pin. Do you know the pin?'

"I do. Thank you."

She smiles, revealing slightly crooked teeth. My attraction to her droops. She should have worn braces when she was younger. "Will there be anything else?"

I shake my head. "No, thank you." I turn away, but then stop and turn back. "Actually, can I use this card at other ATMs besides Iowa State Bank?"

"Yes. They can be used at most ATM locations. They don't have to be our bank; however, some ATMs will charge a fee. You'll see a star on the back of the card. Any location with that star won't charge a fee. Look for that."

I smile. "Thanks for the tip. I'll go try it."

She gives me a funny look, then glances back at her computer screen.

"What?"

She hesitates. "Well...are you expecting a deposit or something?"

I shake my head. "No. Why?"

"Your account doesn't have enough money to withdraw anything. It won't work."

My heart drops, and I stare at her. "What?"

"Well, I mean, you have twenty-two cents in the account. But you won't be able to withdraw that little. I just didn't want you to think the card wasn't working."

Panic shoots through me. I feel a searing heat emanating from my chest and place my palm at the center. There's over three million dollars in that account. There has to be some kind of mistake. She must have looked up someone else's account in error.

"Are you sure? That account should have a lot of money in it."

She shakes her head. "I'm sorry. You're the Joshua Staples on Locust Street, right?"

I nod. She gives me an empathetic smile. I reach over and try to move the computer screen toward me.

"Sir," she says, turning the screen away from me.

I realize what I've done and take a step back. I can't describe what I'm feeling. Is this shock? My head spins, and my knees wobble. I put my hand on the counter to steady myself.

"I could print out the last statement for you. Would that help?"

"Please," I whisper.

She hits several keys, and a printer sounds beside her. She hands me two sheets of paper to review. Immediately I see it. Multiple large withdrawals within two days. I slide the pages back to her with my finger on the withdrawals. I fight to control my voice.

"These withdrawals. I need to know where they went. Who made them?"

She shakes her head. "I don't have that information. Maybe the branch manager can help. I can go get him." She begins to turn, but I've already drawn too much attention to myself. I've got to get out of here. I need time to think.

"No," I exclaim. I make a quick scan of the room and see everyone is watching me. "I'm sorry. I just realized what had happened. I'm so sorry. I forgot about a few transactions. It's fine. Everything's in order. My mistake." I back away from the teller window, holding the statement. I wave and turn for the door.

Chapter 12

Zsuzsa

It's been a week since we left Hungary, and today is the first day I've been homesick. I went shopping with Becky. I was excited, and it was so nice of her to invite me, but after only a few minutes, I knew it was a mistake. She knows no Hungarian, and my English is so poor that we had to communicate with hand gestures. We spent the day in Midtown, visiting stores like Macy's and other enormous department stores.

I've never seen shopping centers like those. I couldn't get over the styles and variety of clothing. I felt like I was in a different world. Even the price tags meant nothing to me. How much is an American dollar? Peter told me, but I forgot. I tried to ask Becky, but gave up after only a few gestures. She looked at me like those sea creatures in the tank in Chinatown were crawling from my ears. I missed Peter. He's handled everything since we arrived. When I've been with him, I've felt safe. Comfortable. That's why I feel this way. It's the first day I've been away from my husband since we got married.

Becky sensed my uncertainty and tried to help. She'd pick out clothing and hold it up to me. I'd shake my head or nod, then she'd lead me to the changing rooms. I'd try on the clothing and model for her. She was trying to be supportive, but I felt like I was a little girl shopping with my mother. She's only ten years older than me, but she's in a position of authority, and I felt helpless. The longer we stayed, the worse it got. Realizing Becky had an agenda and wouldn't stop until I had three outfits, I picked them out quickly. I no longer cared what they looked like. I wanted to be done.

As we left the last store, Becky suggested we get lunch, but I indicated my stomach was upset. We came back to the house, and I retired to bed. Illness gave me a good excuse to stay hidden until Peter returned. Now I can hear a commotion below and realize he's finally back.

I stand from the bed, fuss with my hair, and straighten my clothes. I can hear him coming up the stairs. I want to run into his arms when he opens the door. But I restrain myself. I lay back on the bed, spreading my hair on the pillow. I lean forward, pulling my top tighter.

"*Szia*," he says when he opens the door. I see him notice the tightness of my shirt.

"*Szia*," I say back.

He comes forward, and his eyes drop to my chest, then back up.

"I missed you," I say.

He leans forward and kisses me. "I missed you too. Becky said you aren't feeling well?"

"I'm fine now." I pull him down to the bed.

Twenty minutes later, I untangle myself from his arms and stand. I was hungry before, but now I'm starving. I pull on the jeans and blouse Becky bought for me and stand in front of the mirror as he comes up behind me. Peter has put his clothes back on, but his shirt remains unbuttoned. I'm impressed by the firmness of his body as he presses against me. He's always taken such good care of himself. I look at him in the mirror when a knock sounds at our door.

"Yes?" he calls out.

There's a muffled reply. It's Rachel. I wish for more separation, but at least she's learned to knock. He says something back to her, but I can't make out the words. English is becoming less foreign sounding, at least. I still don't understand much, but I can distinguish words now.

He leans down and breathes into my ear. "Becky has dinner ready."

I look back at him in the mirror and frown. "Do we have to?"

"What do you mean?"

I turn around and put my arms around his neck. "Can't we have dinner, just the two of us tonight? You were gone, and I just want it to be us."

He watches me for a moment. "What should I say?"

Fire flashes in my eyes. "That your new wife wants to have dinner with just you on our honeymoon?"

He falls back a step, and I feel bad. Even I'm surprised by the sudden turn in my mood.

"Of course. I'm sorry."

I reach out and take his hand. "No, I'm sorry. I didn't mean that. I just...I want to spend time with you. *Only* you."

He nods. "You're right. Let me go tell them. Becky will under-stand."

Fifteen minutes later, we're on the street in front of Gary and Becky's house. He's leading me and seems to be in no hurry. I don't want to push him, but I also worry he's forgotten how hungry I am. I almost mention it but decide against it. After all, I'm the one who turned down dinner with Becky. I'm just going to have to wait and hope my stomach doesn't start chewing on my spine. I make conversation to distract myself.

"How did it go today?" I ask.

His eyes are distant, and he takes a second to realize I spoke. "Huh?"

"Today? How did it go?"

He looks away from me, back to the sidewalk. "Oh, it was inter-esting."

"Interesting how?"

"Well, you heard what Becky and Gary told me about them."

I smile. "I heard, but I didn't understand."

He grins. "True. But I told you later. Well, a few minutes after we got there, she came into the room. She was young, maybe early thirties. She insists she knew nothing about what her husband was doing."

"Do you believe her?"

He looks at me and frowns. "I think so."

"You're not sure?"

He shakes his head. "It's not that. I just don't know what to think. It just seems so unbelievable. Her husband steals all this money and then dies in the towers. It's a crazy story."

I don't know what to say, so I remain silent, watching him.

After a beat, he says, "The investigators think she's guilty. They think she knew what Scott was doing."

"Why do they think that?"

He shrugs. "They can't find the money. It was withdrawn in large increments from his escrow account, but they can't find where it went. It's like it vanished. I don't think they think she has it. I think they want someone to blame."

"How sad."

He shakes his head. "I know. I think she's a victim, just like the people he stole from. She's got two little kids. The investigators have frozen her money. She's in a tough spot."

"Is Gary going to help her?"

He nods. "He wants to."

"And he wants you to help?"

He nods again, but then shakes his head. "But I can't."

"Why?"

"I'm here on my honeymoon. We won't be here much longer, and we need to spend time together. There are still things I want you to see. The city is still crazy, but not as bad as before. We'll be able to go back soon."

I see something in his eyes. There's more he isn't saying. Then it dawns on me. "You're worried about me."

He holds my look but says nothing.

"Peter, I'll be fine."

He watches me, then gives me a slight shake of the head.

"I'm a big girl. I'll be okay. She needs you." But even as I say it, I don't believe it. I was out with Becky for only a few hours today, and it was torture. How can I go day after day waiting as Peter investigates and helps this woman? I'll go mad.

We've reached Chinatown, and the street looks familiar. We were on this road the morning of the attacks. Peter grips my hand and pulls me toward a restaurant with a large merman holding a trident in one hand and a red bucket in the other. We come through the front doors, and the place looks more like a cafeteria than a restaurant. I'm elated that we're going to finally eat, but I was hoping for something nicer. I give him a quizzical look, but he only smiles and waits while a man comes up to greet us. The place is busy with nearly all the tables occupied. Peter talks to the man, and they seem to negotiate. Finally, Peter hands him some cash, and the man shows us to a table. We sit below a large wall painting of an octopus. The host gives us plastic menus and walks away.

Peter looks at me and laughs.

"What?" I ask.

His green eyes sparkle as he watches me, rubbing at his salt-and-pepper beard. "Not what you were expecting tonight?"

I look around, then motion to my dress. "I was thinking it would be fancier. I feel overdressed."

He gazes at me, and his smile is gone. He looks serious. "I don't care if you're overdressed. You've never looked more beautiful."

The compliment catches me off guard, and I look down. "Thank you," I whisper.

Moments later, a woman approaches in a white shirt and black pants. She wears a black apron around her waist and a name tag. She speaks to me rather than Peter. I look up at her and know she's greeting us, but don't feel comfortable responding. I look over at Peter. He hasn't jumped in. He's leaving it to me. She sees my hesitation, then looks at him. Her cheeks fill with color, and a line appears on her forehead. She knows him. Peter recognizes her too, but his demeanor is calm. She says something to him, and he nods. They talk in hushed voices. At one point, her eyes fill with tears, and she brushes them away. Right before she leaves, he motions to me, and she looks over and smiles. How do they know each other? I feel a flash of jealousy. Did Peter date her? No, that can't be it. He was married when he lived here. What is it? Who is she?

She finally steps away, and I look at him expectantly.

"Well, that's weird," he says.

"What? Who is she?"

He leans forward, his voice barely more than a whisper. I have to lean forward to hear him. "I put her husband in prison. I investigated him." I wasn't expecting him to say that. "He was running a money-laundering scheme only a few blocks from here."

She returns to our table, and we lean back in our seats as she slides two glasses of water before us. Mine has no ice. I never understand Americans and their ice. She says something to him, and he turns back to me. "Do you trust me to order for you?"

I haven't even looked at the menu. Ordinarily, I'd be annoyed if a man ordered for me. But, with the menu all in English, I shrug. If I can't trust him, who can I trust? He points to several things on his menu, hands it to her, and then she takes mine and walks away.

"So?"

"So what?"

"So that's it? You put her husband in jail for money laundering?"

He takes a drink from his water. "Well, yeah. But what's so weird is that she was about the same age as Cindy is now when it happened. She also had two kids. She claimed to know nothing about what her husband was doing. Just like Cindy."

"And you believed her?"

He shakes his head. "I thought she was guilty, even though she repeatedly told me she wasn't. She claimed to be a victim, and I didn't believe her. Months later, it was proven that she knew nothing about her husband's laundering. In the meantime, she lost everything. She says she's been working two jobs since he went to prison. She barely sees her kids." He frowns and looks away. "She's had it rough."

I look away from him and find her. She's hustling around the room, helping several tables. She looks tired.

"Was this an accident?" he asks. He's not looking at me. He's watching her. He's thinking aloud. "Is it just coincidence?" His green eyes come back to me.

"What do you want me to say?"

"I don't know. Have you had times like this? Times when you see someone or something and think maybe it was meant to be? Like maybe God put them in your path?"

We've never talked about anything religious before. I don't even know if he believes in God. "Yes, there's been times when something happened that seemed almost too miraculous to be a coincidence. I don't know if it's God. I don't know if I believe in a God. Do you?"

He watches me, then looks down at his water. He picks it up and takes a sip. "God and I have had a funny relationship. I grew up believing in God. But after some things I saw as a cop, I had my doubts. I wondered how a God could allow some things to happen. When Karen was murdered and my daughter died, I was convinced there was no God. I didn't believe in anything anymore. My world was taken from me. When I went back to Hungary, I knew God wasn't real. But then my mind changed again." He pauses and stares at his water glass.

"Peter?"

His eyes focus back on me.

"What made you change your mind?"

"You."

I'm taken aback. "Me? I'm not religious."

He shakes his head. "It's not anything you said. It's just *you*. When I met you, I had nothing. I didn't even see a point in living. I didn't want to live. You changed my life, Zsuzsa. You gave me purpose. I wanted something, and that something was you." He shrugs. "Some people may say that's cheesy, and that's okay. From the outside, it might be. But I'm entirely convinced I was meant to walk into Szép Ilona's that day. God put you in my life."

What do you say to something like that? How can I even respond? So, I don't. I reach across the table, and he gives me his hand. We stare at each other.

"Peter?"

"Yes."

"You've got to help her."

"Who?"

"Cindy."

He shakes his head.

"Peter, she needs your help."

He still shakes his head.

"I'll come with you."

"What?"

"You know how much I like detective work. Let me help. Today was hard because I wasn't with you. I won't understand much, but at least I can be with you." I grin. "We're still on our honeymoon, after all."

He chuckles, and the server returns with something I can only guess is our food. She places a large platter in the middle of the table. It's full of all kinds of seafood. Lobster, shrimp, crab. It also has corn and potatoes. She looks at me and smiles, then holds up a bib and motions to me. I give Peter a look and he laughs. She ties the bib around my neck and hands me plastic gloves, then does the same to Peter. She says something and smiles, then walks away.

Peter laughs as I look at the platter. "You were so fascinated by the lobster the other day, I knew I had to bring you here."

I look back down at the table, starving but unsure of where to start.

"Don't worry, I'll help. *Jó étvágyat*!" he says.

I repeat it back, and he hands me a shrimp. I unpeel it and pop it in my mouth. The flavor is nothing I've ever tasted before. It's delicious.

He smiles at my reaction.

"What is this sauce?" I ask.

"It's Cajun. We don't have anything like it in Hungary."

"Cajun?"

"Yeah. Weird, huh? You wouldn't expect Cajun food in Chinatown."

For the better part of an hour, we go on eating. Peter instructs me and gives me tips while I enjoy a totally new cuisine experience. When we leave, he gives our server a very generous tip. I don't know how much it is, because I don't know American dollars, but I can safely say it's more than is customary.

As we walk hand in hand back to Gary and Becky's house, I see Peter is lost in his thoughts. I don't speak, knowing he needs his time. I'm sure he's thinking about that server, and I only hope he's not being too hard on himself. I snuggle in close to him, and he puts his arm around me while I make myself a promise. I don't know how, but I'm going to help him. Cindy won't be another victim on his conscience.

Chapter 13

Scott

As I leave the bank, my head spins. How? Who? Nobody had access to that account. Nobody even knew it existed. Nobody, except...Roxanne. I stop so abruptly a woman passing by nearly runs me over. I look around, staring at the building across the street. Roxanne? She couldn't have. Could she?

I mean, she knew the account existed. But she didn't know what it was. I never told her anything about it. Yes, she dropped off checks for me at the bank, but I never gave her access to the account. I always filled out the deposit slips. She never did anything more than take the checks and slips to the bank. How could she know?

No. I shake my head. Even if she knew what I was doing, she never had access to the account. It wasn't her. I look back up the street. Who then? Cindy? I chuckle. That's ridiculous. She knew even less than Roxanne. Then a thought pops in my mind. Larkin! Someone gave him that note: *"Scott Lyon is a liar. Don't believe anything he tells you."* But who wrote it?

I look down the street and see the Des Moines Public Library sign and get another idea. I walk several blocks, following the signs until I see a building that looks like a library. Modern library buildings have an artistic flare that sets them apart. It's a rectangular glass building with some kind of brown shade behind the glass. From far away, it gives the illusion that the building is brown. But as you grow closer, you see it's a facade. It's clear glass. In front of the building is a statue of a white bunny, and I can only think of Alice in Wonderland. Am I chasing the white rabbit? I walk up the stairs and enter the building.

Inside there's a large desk at the front, with an elderly woman sitting behind it. Behind her are rows and rows of bookshelves. She's looking down and doesn't see me walk past. I walk around the library, looking for computers. When I find them, I step up and see they require a library account. I head back to the front and approach the old woman. She still hasn't noticed me as I stand directly in front of her. I clear my throat, and she still doesn't react.

"Hello," I say.

She looks up, startled. She doesn't greet me as she peers at me through thick glasses.

"What's a guy got to do to get a library card around here?"

She sighs and closes the book she's working on, then shuffles away. After a few seconds, she returns and hands me a form. "Fill this out."

I step further down the desk and start filling in personal information. When I'm done, I hand it back to her, and she looks it over.

"Okay, Joshua. Your card will be mailed to you in a couple of weeks."

"A couple weeks?"

"Yes."

I look around and then back at her. "I was hoping I could get a couple of books now."

She shakes her head. "Sorry, those are the rules."

"What about the computers? Do I have to wait on those also?"

She eyes me suspiciously. "What do you want to do on the computer?"

I shrug. "Maybe read the news. Do some research."

"Is that all?"

I'm taken aback. "Yes..."

She watches me. "Don't you let me catch you looking at the naked girls on the internet."

I can't help myself and chuckle. She frowns and shoots daggers at me with her eyes. I hold up my hands. "I swear, I just want to read the news. No naked girls."

She grunts. "No naked men either."

I laugh again, and she eyes me, then steps away from the desk. She's halfway down the hall before she turns back to me. "Are you coming or not?"

I hustle to catch up. She walks me to the back of the library to the computer station. She leans over one and types in the required information. The password screen fades away, and two icons appear on the dashboard. She motions for me to sit down. I grab the mouse and double-click on the Internet Explorer icon and type in the homepage for the *New York Times*. She remains standing over me, hands on her hips. After several seconds, she walks away.

I spend thirty minutes reading everything I can about the terrorist attacks in New York City. Next, I pull up a search engine and type in my name. Lots of results populate. I add my company name, Sound Security Title. My photo comes up, and I look around, making sure nobody else sees it. I'm listed as missing after the collapse of the buildings. They think I'm dead.

I continue searching my name for another fifteen minutes, but nothing interesting comes up. I'm about to leave when I get one more idea. I search the name of my wife. An article comes up in our local Port Washington newspaper. It mentions my presumed death in the attacks, but it's the last paragraph in the article that holds my attention.

"Mr. Lyon was under investigation by the New York Insurance Commission for insurance fraud. He owned a company named Sound Security Title. He is accused of stealing millions from real estate clients. Mrs. Lyon is now being held responsible for his misdeeds."

I was under investigation? If I was, nobody told me. A sinking feeling hits. Larkin. What if he got out? What if he lived? I quickly type his name into the search engine. Within seconds, I find him. He's missing as well. Presumed dead. His wife hasn't seen him since that morning but that doesn't mean anything. I'm presumed dead too.

I lean back and stare at the ceiling. If I was under investigation, maybe that's where the money went. Maybe the insurance commission found it. Maybe they froze my accounts when I "died." If that's true, the money isn't gone, it's being held. I search for more information on the accusations against me. I only find that singular mention. I look at the clock and realize I've been here for over two hours. I stand from the computer and walk out of the library.

As I walk past the bunny, I consider the implications of what I just learned. If the insurance commission took the money, I'm screwed. There's nothing I can do. But if they took the money, wouldn't they have come after me by now? At least looked in the apartment? The bank account was registered to my new name, Joshua Staples. I gave my apartment address here in Des Moines. They'd have all that information. It would be easy to break into the apartment. Then again, what's the rush on their end? If I'm dead, they can take their time.

In either case, my apartment isn't safe anymore. I can't take the risk of going back there. My situation has gone from bad to worse. I've got seventeen dollars and nowhere to live. As I walk, wondering what to do next, another thought hits me. The ID cards I left in the vent. They'll identify me. Wait...who cares? If they took the money, they know it was me. But why would those cards be in the heating vent? Why wouldn't they have been on me when I died in the building? No, if they search the apartment, they'll find the cards and ID. They'll know I used the cards last week in New York. They couldn't be here unless I'm alive and brought them.

I make a turn and head back toward Locust Street. I've got no choice. I've got to return to the apartment.

Chapter 14

Peter

Peter looks at his watch as he and Zsuzsa exit the train. It took forty-seven minutes from Penn Station to Port Washington. Not nearly as long as he thought it should. Port Washington is the cozy hometown of Scott and Cindy Lyon. The port is on the north shore of Long Island. It's quiet and peaceful. A perfect spot to raise a family. Far enough away from Manhattan to feel rural but close enough to commute.

After looking around, Peter gets his bearings and guides Zsuzsa down the platform. It's his first time here, and when they reach the street, he regrets waiting so long. The town is charming. With mature trees, a cozy downtown, and friendly smiles. Cindy Lyon's home is only a half mile away, and they decide to walk.

"This is what I've always pictured when I've imagined America," Zsuzsa says. They pass below a maple tree outside a two-story home with a white-picket fence. It looks like it belongs on the cover of *Better Homes and Gardens*.

Peter smiles. "Not New York City?"

"Well...that's different."

A dog barks behind the backyard fence in the next yard and Zsuzsa jumps.

"I think that's one thing that surprises people who come to America. They don't realize how large and diverse it is. And I don't mean just culturally."

She nods, but he can tell by her expression she's not sure what he means.

"Believe it or not, this town is extremely old by American standards."

Zsuzsa gives him a look.

"I'm serious. Think about it. European settlers have been here since maybe the sixteenth century. Could be longer. In the US, that's an eternity. Consider the West Coast, like California. The gold rush in the nineteenth century brought pioneers. Before that, only Native Americans inhabited those states. We Magyars have been in Hungary since the ninth century, but this continent was largely uninhabited for six hundred more years."

She grins at him and squeezes his hand. "Is that weird for you?"

He frowns. "I know I'm older than you, but you don't really believe I was around in the seventeenth century, do you?"

She laughs. "That's not what I meant."

"What then?"

"Is it weird for you to be both Hungarian and American? You talk about both places like they're home."

He chuckles. "It's not something I really think about. Both are my home." Peter stops and peers at the base of the tree on the side of the road. There's a sign taped to the bark. That's not unusual. He's seen signs like this all over Manhattan. What captures his attention is the man in the photo. He recognizes him. Below the photo is a question: "Have you seen my daddy?" Peter points to the house. "Looks like we've made it."

They move up the curved concrete walk toward the home and climb the five steps onto the covered deck surrounding the house. A white porch swing is in the corner. There's a small children's play set on the north side of the house with kid toys surrounding it.

Peter watches Zsuzsa before knocking on the door. "Are you sure you want to do this?"

Her eyes are on the toys before they return to him. "Peter, she needs us."

"It's going to be a lot of English."

She cocks her head to the side, her long blond hair sliding over her shoulders. "I'll be fine. It'll be good practice." She steps past him and knocks loudly, then looks at him defiantly.

Moments later, they hear light feet descending the stairs before the door opens. Cindy Lyon stands in the doorframe. Her blue eyes are bright against her white blouse.

"Hi, Peter," she says and extends her hand. "Thank you for coming."

Peter takes her hand and releases it. Then he motions to Zsuzsa. "Mrs. Lyon, this is my wife, Zsuzsa."

The women exchange a smile, shaking hands. "Pleased to meet you," Cindy says.

"Thank you," Zsuzsa responds. Her *th* sounds more like a *t*.

"Please, come in," Cindy says, extending her arm.

They follow her into the living room area. It's a nicely decorated room with a floral-print couch, two wingback chairs, a piano, and a stylish, green carpet. The walls feature a chair rail and floral-print wallpaper. Peter and Zsuzsa sit on the couch while Cindy sits opposite them in a wingback chair.

"I hope you don't mind me saying how lovely you are," Cindy says to Zsuzsa.

Zsuzsa hesitates, then says, "Thank you." Peter wonders if she knows what Cindy said, but before he can ask, she turns to him and says, "How do I say you are too?"

Peter tells her, and after she says it, Cindy smiles and says to Peter, "She's not from here?"

He shakes his head. "It's her first time out of Hungary. We came for our honeymoon. I wanted to show her New York, and then the attacks happened."

Cindy's eyes go wide, and she turns back to Zsuzsa. "I'm so sorry for asking your husband to help me. I feel awful." Her eyes move back to Peter. "You could've said no."

Peter chuckles. "I would have. She wouldn't let me."

Tears appear in Cindy's eyes, and she crosses the room to Zsuzsa. She kneels before her and takes her hand, kissing it. "Thank you."

Zsuzsa watches her, then looks at Peter before thanking Cindy back.

Cindy brushes away a tear, then leans forward and embraces Zsuzsa. Zsuzsa hugs her back but looks at Peter again. He thinks about translating but decides against it. The women seem to communicate just fine without him. Finally, Cindy returns to her chair across the room. She grabs a tissue and dabs at her eyes. "I'm sorry. I just find my emotions so close to the surface right now. When Gary called me and told me you were going to help, I thought it was the first piece of good news I've had in over a week."

"I think you give me too much credit. I'm not sure what I can do for you. I'm a detective and private investigator, not a lawyer. At this point, I think you need that more."

Cindy sighs. "They cost lots of money." She pauses. "I know investigators charge, too. What I mean is, I might need a little time, but I'm going to pay you. Hopefully, we'll be able to find that money. Maybe then they'll unfreeze my accounts."

Peter says, "That seems logical. I don't know if Gary told you, but the detective assigned to the case worked with me before in the NYPD. I talked with him for a few minutes after we met. He confirmed it's the money they're after. If they can repay Scott's clients, this whole thing should go away." Peter leans forward. "Speaking of, do you have any idea where the money is?"

She shakes her head.

"Is it possible Scott already spent it?"

She frowns. "You think so?"

"I don't know. It's a possibility."

She shakes her head. "On what? What could he spend it on? How much did they say it was? Three million?"

Peter nods. "Something like that. He told you nothing about the business?"

She shakes her head. "Never. As far as I knew, the business was doing great. He mentioned having a lot of money in his business bank accounts sometimes. But he always said those were in-and-out transactions. That he was holding the money for his clients."

"Did he buy expensive things? Cars? Property?"

"No. His truck was ten years old, and my car is just an average Chevy Malibu." She bites her cheek. "No way he spent the money."

"If I'm going to help you, I need to know everything about him. I need you to be completely honest with me. Even if that means some information could incriminate you. Okay? I'm on your side."

She nods solemnly.

"You swear to me you knew nothing about Scott's fraud?"

"Nothing."

"You *swear it*?"

She puts her hand over her heart. "I promise you."

Peter sits back in his chair. "Tell me about him. How long have you been married? Where did you meet?"

She raises a leg and tucks it under herself while putting a hand on her cheek. "We met in high school. We lived in a small town in Indiana called Muncie. Have you heard of it?"

Peter shakes his head.

"We went to the same high school. He sat next to me in math class. On the first day of our sophomore year, I looked at him and couldn't look away. It didn't take long for him to notice, and when he looked over, I glanced away. When his eyes returned to the teacher, mine went right back to him." She shakes her head. "I don't know. I just was always drawn to the athletic boys. He played football. He was just so good looking. It went like that for a couple of months. I'd watch him in class and in the halls, while he'd act like I didn't exist.

Finally, we got paired up for a group assignment in math. I think the teacher put us together because he was struggling, and I was getting an A. Or maybe God was answering all my little-girl prayers."

She laughs, and Peter steals a glance at Zsuzsa.

"I need to go to the restroom," Zsuzsa whispers.

Peter nods and turns back to Cindy. "Where's your bathroom?"

"I'll show you," she says to Zsuzsa.

The two women leave the room, and Peter studies the pictures on the walls and mantle.

Cindy returns, and after she sits back down, Peter asks, "Then what?"

Cindy frowns, clearly unsure where she was in her story.

"You said the teacher paired you with Scott."

"Oh, right?" She smiles. "I still kinda think Scott knew how much I liked him. He wouldn't admit it, but everyone in the school knew. Sometimes I'm embarrassed at how obvious I was. But Scott was shy. He'd never make the move. I knew I had to. So, when we were put together, I worked more on learning about him than helping him with the assignments. Eventually, he started to open up. He talked about his struggles in school, and I offered to help with his homework. We started to hang out together after school when he didn't have practice. It might sound crazy, but I was in love with him almost from the start. He was my first actual boyfriend and everything to me." She shuffles in her seat. "The more I got to know him, the more his true self came out. He was far more confident than he ever showed in class. He had big dreams and believed he was going to do incredible things. When he'd talk, I'd feel it too. He just has this way about him. People trusted him." She stops and cocks her head. "The more I was around him, the more I wanted him all the time. He was always in my thoughts. Then, one day, he stopped coming to school."

Peter raises an eyebrow. "Stopped coming to school? Why?"

She rubs her arms. "He always had these bruises on him. On his arms and sides. He was sensitive about them when I asked. He never wanted to talk about it. I thought they were from football." She shakes her head. "They were from his father. His dad got physical with him. He'd beat his mom, and when Scott would try to stop him..." She looks down at her arms and then back up. "One night it got so bad that his dad killed his mom. He hit her, and she fell into the brick fireplace. She hit her head. Blood was everywhere. When his father realized just how far he'd gone, he took out a gun and shot himself. Scott was upstairs in his room, headphones on, trying not to listen. He heard the gun and went down. He's the one who found them."

Silence hangs over the room.

Zsuzsa hasn't returned, and Peter wonders if she's okay. "What happened to Scott, then?"

"They put him in foster care. He was placed with a family in Daleville. It was only a few miles away but a different high school."

"Why not with family?"

She shakes her head. "He didn't have any. His mom had one sister, but she was a drug addict. She'd lost custody of her children. Three boys. Really sad family. All of them are dead now. Even the youngest, Josh, who was Scott's age. He died a few years ago."

"How did he die?"

"Drugs...same as his mom. All the boys. Well...one died of suicide. I don't remember the older boy's name. Chris, maybe? Scott's the only member of his family left." She stops and tears well up in her eyes. "*Was* the only one left..."

Peter watches her as she dabs at her eyes. He waits for her eyes to refocus on him. "The detective working your case, Kramer. He said they don't want to take your house. But he said they may have no choice if they can't find the money."

She swallows, clutching the tissue on her lap, her eyes down.

Peter waits until she looks back up at him. "Cindy, we've got to find that money. That's the only way you and your children can stay in your home."

She nods.

"Do you have any ideas? Anywhere you think he might have put it?"

She shakes her head.

"Any clues? Anything I can work with?"

She puts her fingers to her lips, and her eyes get a faraway look. "Once, a few weeks ago, he asked me a weird question. I thought nothing of it at the time. But now..."

"What was it?"

She puts her hand up, palm extended. "We were talking about his parents. He never enjoyed talking about them, but that day, he told me more about them than he ever had. He said he'd hated his father."

Peter frowns.

"I know, I know. But it was *why* he hated his father that stood out to me. He said it was because his father had given up. After killing Scott's mother, he shot himself. Scott got this look on his face. Like he was disgusted. Not from the killing, but from his dad giving up. He said he'd never do that. Even if he killed someone, he'd run. He'd never let someone take him." Cindy looks out the window behind Peter. "I keep thinking about that. I don't know, maybe it's just me, but I keep wondering, what if he didn't die? What if he made it out of the building? What if he's still alive?"

Peter chews on his lip. He doesn't want to give her false hope.

"Is that crazy?"

"Probably. But let's say he made it out. Where would he go?"

She shakes her head. "I really don't know."

Zsuzsa walks back into the room, and Peter stands.

"Are you okay?" Peter asks her in Hungarian.

She nods.

Peter turns back to Cindy. "I think that's enough for today. I'll call you if I think of anything else."

Cindy walks them to the door. Zsuzsa steps out first, and Cindy grabs Peter by the arm. "Peter, what am I going to do?"

"What do you mean?"

"Without him? How am I supposed to go on?"

Peter watches her, knowing exactly what she's feeling. He felt the same way when he learned of his wife's murder. "You said it yourself. Maybe he's still alive. If he were, there has to be a reason he's not coming home. Why?"

She grits her teeth, and fire lights in her eyes. "Shame. That's all I can figure. But you know what? If he ever came back home, I'd kill him myself for what he's done to us."

Chapter 15

Scott

I stand on the corner of Locust Street and watch my apartment building. This seems impossible. I don't even know what I'm looking for. Maybe a big FBI sign on a van parked out front? Maybe guys walking around in navy-blue jackets with yellow lettering?

I don't see any of that. It's a quiet sunny day in the Midwest. Nothing out of the ordinary. I wait for several minutes, then cross the street and enter the building. I go up the stairs rather than use the elevator. My anxiety is high, and I listen for any movement but hear none. When I reach the floor below mine, I stop and listen. I can hear a TV blaring behind one door below my apartment. I take several steps up the stairwell and peek around the corner. I can see my door. It looks just like I left it this morning. The hallway is deserted. But then I hear something, and without delay, I descend the stairs to the level below. I wait, listening. I can make out the bing of the elevator. I creep back up the stairs and look. The hallway is empty again, except this time I see a white paper in the crack of my door. Was that there before? Did I just miss it?

Curious, I climb the rest of the steps and tiptoe down the hallway. When I reach the door, I can see only the corner of the paper sticking out. I look down both sides of the hall, then put my ear to the door. I can't hear anything inside. It's silent. I take a breath and put the key in the lock and turn the knob. When I push open the door, I expect to hear a voice tell me to put my hands up. But instead, the only noise is the white paper dropping to the floor. I pick it up and step inside. It's a typed note addressed to me. It's from my landlord. It says they informed me a few weeks ago that they were going to change out some of the furniture in the apartment. Today they did.

My heart rate quickens as I walk inside and look around. There's a new bed set. The couch and chair are also new. I look at the heating vent and peer inside. I don't see anything. I get the butter knife and loosen the screw. After I take off the vent cover, I feel around. Nothing. My credit cards and ID are gone. I drop to my knees and look under the box springs. I crawl around the room, searching for my property. Nothing. I can't find any sign of them. I walk into the kitchen and see the saucepan still on the stove and the coffee cup in the sink. Everything is just as I left it, other than the furniture.

I walk into the bathroom and look around. Same as I left it. Nothing moved. What is this? What are the chances the landlord changed the furniture today? And if he did, why would he take my cards and ID? It wasn't the landlord. Someone broke in and took them. My eyes dart around the bedroom. Someone's watching me. They know I'm alive. They stole my money and have my ID and credit cards. Who is it, and what are they planning?

Chapter 16

Scott

I stay in the apartment, sitting at the kitchen table. It can't be the police. They wouldn't take my furniture, credit cards, and ID. They'd break down the door. Arrest me. Take me into custody and start asking questions. They wouldn't play games. That's what this is, right? Someone's messing with me? Maybe it's more than one somebody. That knowledge is strangely comforting. Sure, I'm being watched. Hunted. But that's better than the alternative. I have to stay off the cops' radar.

I rest my hand on my cheek and stare. Who would do this? I consider the question. They stole my money, and they know I'm still alive. They haven't turned me in. Why? They don't want attention brought to them. They don't want me arrested. Did they take my ID and credit cards for leverage? What do they still want from me?

I stand from the table and open the pantry. I'm hungry and broke. I scowl at the cupboard. All I've got is some canned stew. I look through the drawers and can't find the can opener I used yesterday. Did they steal it too? Another mind game? My patience is waning as I slam drawer after drawer. Finally, I grab a knife and jab it into the top of the can. The can slips, and I cut my hand. A stream of obscenities flies from my tongue as I run my hand under cold water. When the bleeding has mostly stopped, I growl at the knife, picking it back up. I consider throwing it across the room but stop myself, taking long, slow breaths. I pry open the lid with the back of a butter knife and empty the stew into a saucepan. The hole in the top is small, and it takes several seconds before I empty the contents.

I stand stirring the stew occasionally, staring at the stove. Whoever is doing this to me has the upper hand. They know where I am, and they have my money. I've got to flip the script. Put them on their heels. Do something unexpected.

I pull the pan off the stove and walk back to the table. I don't bother dirtying a bowl and eat the stew right from the pan. There's a pencil and paper on the table. I write three names on a sheet of paper, then put it in the bottom of the trash can. I make it visible, hoping they'll find it. When I finish, I can feel my mood improve. I'm thinking clearer now. They screwed with the wrong man. I'm going to make it my mission to find them and make them pay.

I finish the stew, put the pan in the sink, and scrutinize the apartment. If I never come back again, what will I need? I pile several items on the kitchen table. Nothing big, a few cans of food, toothpaste, deodorant, a toothbrush, and a bottle of water. I look around the apartment one more time, making sure there isn't anything else that can link me to being here since the terrorist attacks in New York. I walk out the front door, but instead of going to the front entrance, I go to the parking garage. I don't have a car, and if someone is watching the building, they'd never expect me to exit the garage. I sneak out one of the side doors, just in case. I climb the back fence, and instead of going down Locus Street, I head along Third until I reach Grand. I walk along Grand toward Iowa State Bank.

When I reach the bank, I stash my bag of supplies in the bushes across the street and enter the redbrick building. I look to my left and see her. She sits behind her desk, eyes on her computer screen. A new teller sees me and calls out, but I ignore her. I walk over to the manager with the long blond hair and bright-pink nails with matching lips and dress.

"Excuse me," I say, standing in front of her. I notice two picture frames on her desk. A boy and a girl. They're similar ages to mine.

She looks up over her screen, and I can tell she recognizes me. "Yes, may I help you?"

I sit in the seat opposite her desk. Glancing at her left hand, I see I'm correct—no ring. "Are you the manager?"

She smiles. "Assistant manager." She points to the plaque on her desk. It includes her title and name, Ms. Tomlin.

"My name's Joshua Staples. I'm a new customer. I was in earlier today. I noticed you."

She eyes me and brushes her long hair. She has striking blue eyes. If she lost twenty pounds, I might be interested. She smiles. "Yes, Mr. Staples. I remember."

I extend my hand. "Call me Josh." She takes it. She has smooth skin. Her handshake is soft and firm. She tries to release my hand, but I don't let her. "What's your name?"

She inclines her head toward the plaque. "Ms. Tomlin."

I give her a sly smile. "You want me to call you Ms. Tomlin?"

She looks down and smiles. "Stacey."

I release her hand and note her lavender scent. "Stacey, what a lovely name. It suits you."

She lowers her long eyelashes. She's wearing more makeup than I like, but she's applied it well. Some women cake it on like it's mud from a dry waller's trowel. She looks over at the two tellers behind the desks. I can't see them, my back is to them, but her eyes are more serious when they return to me. "How can I help you, Mister...Josh?"

"Stacey, I thought you'd never ask. Have you ever heard of a REIT?"

She frowns, and a vertical line appears on her forehead. "No."

I lean back in my chair, raise my foot, cross it over my other leg, and lean forward. "It's a company that invests in real estate. But not in small portions. These companies invest in lots and lots of rental real estate. They buy income-producing properties, operate them for profit, then trade their shares on the stock exchange. They promise a good return for investors, and the investors eat it up."

She's following me, but I can also tell I better get to the point or I'm going to lose her.

"Stacey, I work for one of these REITs. A big one in New York City. My company has sent me here to look for property in Des Moines."

She nods, obviously wondering why I'm talking to her.

"That brings me to you. Do you know of any rental properties I should look to buy while I'm here?"

Her plump hands return to her keyboard. "This is a bank. Shouldn't you be talking to a realtor? Maybe one who does commercial properties?"

"Of course. And I am. But I've been sent all over the country looking for property. Believe it or not, I've had the most success with banks. I looked up Iowa State Bank. You all have a lot of money loaned out in commercial property. Maybe you know of a property that's struggling. They might sell for the right price. Or maybe you've foreclosed on property that you'd like to liquidate."

A light pops in her eyes. "Oh, I do know of one, actually. It's a building over on Pennsylvania. It's close to here, only a few blocks away. The owner defaulted on the loan." She rises from her chair. She's a little taller than I thought she'd be. Maybe five foot eight. "Mr. Reacher, our bank manager, could show you the property." She holds up a hand. "Wait one second." She begins to walk away, but I reach out and grab her arm. She's startled and instinctively pulls away, but stops when she sees I'm looking into her eyes.

"I'd rather it be you who shows me."

Her cheeks flush, and she looks down. "Mr. Reacher usually handles things like this."

I continue to hold her arm. She tries to pull back, but again I resist. She looks back up at me. "I want you to show me, Stacey."

I can see she's holding her breath, but finally smiles. "Okay, let me talk to him."

I release her, and she walks behind the teller stations to the other side of the lobby. One teller is helping a customer. The other was watching us and looks away when she sees me look at her. I sit back down and turn the pictures on the desk. It's obvious the children are Stacey's. They have the same blue eyes and ruddy cheeks. Both have smooth skin like their mother. She has nothing else on the desk that's personal other than a glass vase with white daisies.

She returns after several minutes with a set of keys, and the bank manager stands behind her. He's a small man, in his mid-fifties, with gray hair and glasses. He has a sizeable paunch, and it prevents his tie from reaching his belt. He steps around Stacey. "Mr. Staples. It's an honor to have you in our bank today, sir." I take his outstretched hand. "I understand you're interested in looking at commercial property."

"I am. Ms. Tomlin told me about a spot on Pennsylvania. I'm looking forward to seeing it."

"It's a very nice property with six current tenants and room for plenty more. The previous owner defaulted on the loan." He leans closer to me and drops his voice. "Between you and me, they were in over their heads. Didn't know what they were doing." He straightens. "But a man like you could get that property into great shape."

I always wonder about bankers who run down their current or past clients. If you loaned them the money, and they failed to repay it, doesn't that say something about you also? Kind of like when sports teams denigrate their opponents after beating them. Wouldn't it make more sense to praise them? If you beat them, and they were good, that just makes you look better.

"Well, I'm excited to see it." I turn toward the exit doors and see both bankers are following me. I stop. "Mr. Reacher, is it?"

"Yes."

"You seem like a busy man, running the bank here. Why don't you let Ms. Tomlin handle this one? We can come back afterward, and you can answer any questions I might have."

He looks at me and then at Stacey. Her cheeks redden, and she looks at the floor.

"I...I'd love to be there to answer any questions you might have..."

I keep my voice low. "Mr. Reacher, I appreciate that. But I'd prefer it only be Ms. Tomlin and myself."

He frowns and looks at her again. She shakes her head and shrugs while laughing nervously. He pauses and then extends his hand, offering a fake smile. "Mr. Staples, I hope you enjoy the property. I think I have too much here to leave right now. Ms. Tomlin will take good care of you. Please reach out with any further questions."

I take his hand, thank him, and then hold the door for Stacey.

Once we're outside, she looks up at me, giggling. I wink and smile.

Chapter 17

Zsuzsa

"Did you find anything interesting?"

I look away from the window and back at him in mock surprise. Peter sits beside me on the train back to Manhattan. Since leaving Cindy's house, Peter's been doing all the talking, bringing me up to speed on his conversation with Cindy.

"What do you mean?"

He rolls his eyes and smirks. "You weren't in that bathroom the whole time."

I shrug. "Maybe not."

"So..."

"So what?"

He raises an eyebrow. "Zsuzsa..."

I look back out the window. "Not really. It seemed like what I imagined a basic American house to be. You two were too close to the kitchen, so I didn't go in there, but I looked around the bedrooms."

"Nothing interesting?"

"Nope. The girl likes Barbies and teddy bears. The boy likes cars and trucks. He also had one of those American footballs. It was plastic and blue and had a word written on it. I think it means big or huge."

"Giants?"

"Yes, that's it. By the way, why is the ball shaped like that?"

Peter shakes his head. "I don't know. Another name for it is 'pigskin.' Maybe it's related."

I shake my head. "I bet it was a mistake. Someone was trying to make a round ball, and it came out looking more like an egg."

Peter smiles and squeezes my hand. "What about Scott and Cindy's room? Did you go in there?"

"I peeked in."

"Nothing?"

"At first, I wondered if it was another girl's room. Older, though. I didn't see a single thing that would show a man ever lived in there."

"What do you mean?"

"I mean, it was kind of like the living room area we met her in. The bedroom was all flowers and pastel colors. The bed was frilly. It was girl, through and through. But then I opened the closet and saw Scott's clothes. There were two dressers, but only two of the drawers had his clothes. The rest were all hers."

Peter stares at the chair in front of him and raises his hand to rub at his beard. He always does that when he's thinking about something.

"What?" I ask. He doesn't hear me, so I have to squeeze his hand. Now he looks at me. "Peter. What are you thinking?"

"Nothing."

"No, that isn't how this is going to work. I'm fine sitting and listening to you drone on with people in English. But when it's us, you tell me what's on your mind."

He looks at me, and a sly smile plays on his lips. "When did you get so bossy?"

"When you put a ring on my finger." I hold it up to show him.

He chuckles. "I was just thinking. I'm not sure that's unusual."

"What do you mean?"

"Well, I've been in a few different bedrooms while investigating crimes. The wife or girlfriend decorates most. They often look like that."

I consider that. "But nothing? Only his clothes?"

Peter rests his head against the headrest. "True. Usually, there's at least a nightstand with some of his personal effects. Maybe a book or magazine. Something. Then again, maybe there was, and after he didn't come home, it was too painful for her. She put them out of sight."

We fall silent considering that.

"What did you think of her?" I ask.

Peter looks at me. "How do you mean?"

"You've interviewed a lot of criminals, victims of crime, and family members hurt by those who've committed crimes. How did she seem to you?"

He considers it for a moment. "Genuine. Her emotions were all over the place. At first, she was sad and hurt. Then, when she thought Scott might still be alive, that seemed understandable. When a loved one dies, it doesn't seem real."

"What about her anger at the end? When she was talking about Scott doing that to her?"

His eyebrows raise. "You caught that?"

"I understood bits and pieces."

He smiles. "Again, reasonable. I can't blame her for being angry with him. I'm sure she misses him, but she also sees him in a whole new light now."

I shake my head. "I'd never forgive him."

Peter looks at me but says nothing.

We fall silent again.

Finally, I ask, "So, what now?"

He watches me, and his green eyes grow intense. "He had an assistant in the business. I think we need to find her. Maybe she can give us something more. We've got to find that money."

"What if Cindy's right?"

"About what?"

"What if he is alive?"

He gives me a look. "You saw those buildings. If he was inside, he's dead."

"What if he wasn't inside? What if he got out? If he knew he was being investigated, it would make sense he would run. Wouldn't it?"

Peter nods. "Sure. But that's a big if."

He's right. Still, I can't explain this feeling I have. Something isn't sitting well. We're missing something.

"What I still can't figure is why he withdrew the money four days before the attacks. The money sat in his escrow account until then. He didn't pay off the mortgages but left the money in the account.

Why four days before he died? What spooked him? Or was that the plan all along?"

I look at him but don't respond. He's feeling the same way I am. There's something we're missing.

"Tomorrow, let's go talk to his assistant, Roxanne. Maybe she has some answers."

I rest my head against his shoulder. I've never felt more comfortable around anyone in my life. There's never an awkward silence. I don't want to disrupt the moment. I know he's thinking, but I have something else I've always wanted to ask him.

"Peter?"

"Hmm?"

I'm not sure he's paying attention. I take my head from his shoulder and look at him. I wait until his eyes meet mine.

"Have you ever shot anyone?"

He frowns. "You know I have."

I think back to Budapest. "Right. I mean, have you ever killed anyone?"

He raises an eyebrow. "Why?"

I shrug. "Curious, I guess."

He shakes his head. "Thankfully, no. I'm not sure I could ever forgive myself. No matter how bad they were."

Chapter 18

Peter

Peter quietly descends the stairs of Gary and Becky's house and exits the front door. He leaves Zsuzsa still in bed. Last night was a late one. They went to Little Italy and ate at his favorite restaurant on Mulberry Street. It was the first night of reopening after the 9/11 attacks, and patrons were showing their support. The street was packed, and the wait for a table was two hours. When he woke, Zsuzsa was snoring softly, and he didn't want to wake her. Plus, this was a meeting he preferred to handle alone.

Since leaving Cindy's house, the uneasy feeling in his gut hasn't subsided. He knows he's missing something but can't determine what it is. He's hoping this meeting might shed some light. He walks six blocks, crosses the street, and enters the small café at the corner of Twenty-Eighth and Madison. He makes eye contact with the man sitting in the far corner and heads to the counter. He orders tea and a muffin, then joins the man at the table.

"You're early," Peter says.

Detective Eric Kramer looks at him. "My father always said if you aren't early, you're late."

Peter nods. "I remember him saying that. How's the old guy, anyway?"

"Dead."

Peter raises his cup to his mouth and hesitates. "Oh, Eric, I didn't know. I'm sorry."

Kramer shrugs. "The dang old belcher had it coming. Forty years of cancer sticks will do that to you."

"Dang old belcher?"

Kramer shrugs. "My doctor tells me my blood pressure is too high. Wants to put me on medication. I read somewhere that cursing raises it. I'm testing it out."

Peter chuckles. "How's it going?"

"At first, it was really hard. Now I'm getting better at it, even if I do sound ridiculous."

Peter figures there's no advantage to pointing out the carton of cigarettes Kramer has tucked away in his shirt pocket. Maybe swearing is easier to quit. "My condolences to you and your family."

Kramer nods and gulps his coffee. "Yeah, well...I never thought I'd see you again. I heard about the last time you was here. You're a lucky son of a gun."

Peter nods.

"Why'd you come back? I almost dropped a load in my pants when I walked in and saw you sitting there. Looking to get back on the force? With these attacks, we could use the help. Did you see Bush was here yesterday?"

"I did. I'm only visiting. It was supposed to be temporary, but..."

"You couldn't go back?"

"Not right away."

Kramer nods and looks over the café, cursing under his breath, then stopping himself. "Do you remember Lyndsay?"

"Ralph?"

Kramer nods. "He died in Tower Two."

"No..."

Kramer grits his teeth. "There better be a warm seat right next to the devil for those fudging cowards on those planes."

Neither man speaks, looking down at their beverages.

"So, Peter, what's this about? Why'd you want to talk?"

"Cindy Lyon."

Kramer frowns. "What's she to you?"

"You know Gary, the attorney who was helping her?"

"The State Department guy?"

"Yes."

"Yeah."

"He's my brother-in-law."

"Hmm."

"Mrs. Lyon is his wife's cousin."

"Ah-ha." Kramer shakes his head. "I don't think she was involved, but I don't think it matters."

"How's that?"

"Come on, man. Think about it. There's only one of her and multiple wronged clients. Even if she's a victim, like she claims, we've got to blame somebody."

"For what?"

"You know as well as I do, she knew what her husband was up to."

"How do you figure?"

"Oh, come on. She knew he stole that money. Maybe she was even in on it."

Peter eyes him, sipping his tea.

Kramer lays his palm flat on the table. "You were married, right?"

"Yes?"

"How long?"

"Twenty years."

Kramer nods. "Think about it. You were a cop, a detective. You were investigating confidential matters. Stuff you couldn't talk about. You were a good cop. Probably kept it to yourself. Didn't even tell your wife." Peter shrugs. Kramer points at Peter. "But did she know?"

"Know what?"

"What you were investigating? I'm not talking specifics. I'm talking in general. Did she know when you were working on a tough case? When you were under pressure? Did you ever take your work home with you?"

Peter eyes him.

"You know what I'm talking about. Call it gosh-dang woman's intuition, but she knew."

Peter watches him, rubbing his beard.

"You know I'm right."

"So, what's your point?"

Kramer leans forward and picks up his coffee cup. "My point is that she knew something. And if I can prove it, I'm going to bury her." He looks across the café. A striking blond in a blue skirt is ordering a coffee. He watches her for several seconds before turning back. His dark eyes are cold. "I can't get those attacks out of my mind, Peter. I knew cops, firefighters, good people who lost their lives in those buildings. Her husband stole the money, and if she knew, she's just like those masterminds behind the attacks. They didn't fly the planes, but they were involved. I have no patience for that. She's going to pay for what she knew."

Peter grimaces. "So, you think she has the money?"

Kramer looks away.

"Yes or no?"

He shakes his head. "No."

Peter sees something in his eyes. "What is it, Eric?"

Kramer bites his cheek.

"Tell me."

Kramer closes his eyes and rubs his forehead. "Lyon had an assistant."

"Yeah?"

"The assistant has a prior."

"What kind?"

"Theft...from an employer..."

"Really?"

He nods and gulps coffee. "It was years ago, but she stole from her previous employer."

"How much?"

Kramer shakes his head. "A thousand bucks. Not much."

Peter scoffs. "Three million is a big difference."

Kramer glares at him. "Maybe she saw an opportunity and took it. Anyway, we'll know soon enough. All the company's documents were lost in the tower. It's going to take longer than normal, but we'll figure it out. We're gathering the bank statements now. After the financial-forensics guys go through it, we'll know where to look for the money. When we find it, I'm coming after whoever's responsible." He stops and pounds the table. "And whoever knew. That includes your client."

Chapter 19

Scott

Stacey's car is exactly what I expected, complete with the bedazzled *Playboy*-bunny sticker on the back window and the pink dice hanging from the rearview mirror. Her seat covers match the sticker on the back. The vehicle is one of those new SUVs that makes a Toyota Corolla seem large. I'm not a tall man, just shy of six feet, but this car makes me feel claustrophobic. My shoulders are too wide for the seat, and my arm rubs against the door. She starts the car, and the radio blasts with something she might consider music. She pulls out of the parking lot, nearly hitting a car as we pull onto the road. We drive one mile to the commercial building on Pennsylvania, and I'm praying I survive the whole time. When we're stopped at a red light, I motion to the back. "Maybe we should have brought Mr. Reacher along. He could have sat on the booster seat. He's about that tall."

She looks over and bursts into a chorus of giggles.

"Do you enjoy working for him?"

She looks at me but doesn't respond.

"Oh, come on. It's not like I'm going to say anything to him. Tell me."

"He's okay. Kind of seems like he's got a stick up his butt most of the time."

I cringe. "Sounds painful."

She giggles again and then points to a brown building across the street. "That's it."

I look at the building and then around the neighborhood, feigning interest. She pulls the car into the parking garage, and I notice only a quarter of all the reserved spaces are occupied. We get out of the car, walk into the elevator, and go to the ground level. The lobby is an elegant space with high ceilings and marble floors. Each tenant suite has glass walls, and all but one has a For Lease sign. It's a lovely building.

"What's the sales price?"

She looks down at the realtor sheet, then hands it to me. Having worked in New York City for so many years, I forget how much cheaper the rest of the country is. The price looks like a steal, especially considering the square footage.

"Would you like to see inside any of the office suites? I can ask the tenants."

I look around, then reexamine the sheet. "How many levels? Five?"

"I think so. Yes."

I nod. "Is each level occupied?"

"About like this. Not the top floor. It's empty."

Perfect. "Can we see that floor?"

She nods, and we ride the elevator to the top. When the doors open on the fifth floor, I can see why it's unoccupied. The entire level appears to be under construction. Its bare floors, metal framing, and exposed ductwork.

"What happened here?" I ask. I notice without furnishings and carpet my voice echoes in the hollow space.

She drops her voice to a whisper. "I think this is why the previous owner lost the building."

"Oh?"

She nods, her blond hair sliding along her shoulders. "They were renovating this level for a tenant. A law firm. You've heard of Keith Baron and Associates?"

I shake my head.

She waves a hand. "Oh, yeah, I forget, you aren't from around here. If you were, you'd know the name. He was all over the radio and TV. He spent a fortune on advertising. Well, turns out he was having an affair." She pauses as if she just let me in on top-secret information. "So, it turns out, his wife learned about it and took him to the cleaners. She took everything." I wonder how that could be possible. Maybe she took half, but I doubt she got all his money. Then again, the hit to his reputation may have been more than he could take. "His firm was supposed to move into this suite. But when he went out of business, the whole thing fell apart. The landlord lost not only the money they paid for the demolition but also the expected rent. They were over-leveraged and defaulted on the loan. That's how we got it."

I exaggerate my surprise. "Wow! That's awful."

She nods, and I walk toward the large window in the corner of the office suite. I look out at the city below as she comes over to join me. "Are you married, Stacey?" I ask without looking at her.

"Divorced."

"How long?"

"Just over a year."

"And you have two kids?"

She hesitates.

"I saw the pictures on your desk."

"Oh, yes. A boy and a girl."

I turn and look at her, stepping closer. I can smell the scent of lavender again and wonder if it's perfume or lotion. She looks up at me, making eye contact. It's not even a question that she wants this. I wait. Not because I'm uncertain, but because I want her anticipation to grow. We face each other for several seconds. I can see she's holding her breath. She wants me to kiss her. She tentatively smiles, but I don't return it. I stare into her eyes before taking her in my arms. I kiss her gently at first, then more passionately. There's no hesitation on her part.

After several seconds, I release my lips from hers and stare into her eyes. "What are you doing tonight?"

She frowns. "I have my kids."

She remains in my arms, and I stare into her eyes. "Can you get someone to watch them?"

She shakes her head. "I don't think so."

I lean forward and kiss her again. After several seconds, I pull back and look into her eyes. "Are you sure you can't find someone else to stay with them?"

She watches me, debating. Finally, she says, "Why don't you come over around ten? They'll be asleep."

Chapter 20

Peter

Scott's assistant, Roxanne, lives across the river in Brooklyn. Her apartment is on the fifth floor of a twelve-story building with an intercom system. Peter and Zsuzsa arrive at the building and see they have to ring and ask permission before the door will open. Peter steps to the buzzer, pushes the button, then waits for a reply.

"Yes?"

"Roxanne Stanley?"

"Yes."

"Hello, my name is Peter Andrassy. I'm working for the wife of your boss, Scott Lyon. Can I come up and talk to you for a few minutes?"

"What about?"

Peter leans closer to the microphone. "Just a few questions about Scott's business dealings."

A long pause on the other side of the receiver.

"I'd like to be left alone," she says, and the speaker clicks off.

Peter sighs and frowns before turning back to Zsuzsa.

"She doesn't want to talk?" Zsuzsa asks.

Peter shakes his head.

They stand in front of the building for several seconds when Zsuzsa says, "Walk away."

Peter looks at her with surprise.

"I mean it. Say something to me in English, then wave and walk away. Hurry."

Peter looks down the walk, sees a man approaching, then raises a hand and tells her goodbye while walking off. When he's several steps past, but still within earshot, he turns and watches. The man reaches Zsuzsa, and she smiles at him. He's thirty-something with dark, curly hair and a tight V-neck T-shirt.

"Hi," Zsuzsa says.

The man looks at her and smiles. "Hi."

He walks to the front door and opens it, then looks back at her. "Did you need to get in?"

She nods, saying nothing, then follows him inside. Peter stands partway down the street, waiting. After several seconds, he walks back to the front entrance. He presses his face to the glass and surveys the lobby. It's empty other than a row of mailboxes. He stands there for several minutes until, finally, the elevator door opens, and a woman exits, followed by Zsuzsa. The woman walks in front of her and leaves the building while Zsuzsa holds the door open for him.

"Did you get lost?" he asks.

She laughs. "He asked me something. I wasn't sure what it was, but then he waved his hand. I followed him and got on the elevator. He pushed number six, and I pushed eight. He tried to talk to me in the elevator, but I didn't respond. He didn't get the hint, still smiling and flirting. Finally, I just started speaking Hungarian to him."

Peter chuckles. "What did he do?"

"He got this funny look on his face and shook his head, then looked away. He got off on his floor, and I went up to eight. I didn't get off. The elevator went up to the top floor and got the woman you saw. Sorry it took me so long."

Peter smiles. "You got us in the building. I'd say you did a good job."

She smiles and follows him to the elevator. They reach the fifth floor, Roxanne's floor, and find her door but keep their distance.

"How are you going to get her to talk to you?" Zsuzsa asks.

Peter shakes his head. "I'm not sure. I'm open to ideas."

They stand in the hallway looking down, thinking.

"I wish I spoke better English."

"If you did, what would you say?"

"I'm not sure. But I'm less intimidating than you." She grins at him, and he rolls his eyes.

"Maybe we should play that to our advantage."

"What do you mean?" she asks.

"She heard my voice on the buzzer. If you're standing at her door when she looks out the peephole, maybe she'll answer." She nods, and Peter holds up a finger. "You could say something that might intrigue her."

"Like what?"

"Like Scott Lyon is alive."

"But he's not."

"Are you sure?"

"No. But...so you want to lie to her?"

"I didn't say that. We just have to get her to talk to us. Get the conversation started."

"I don't know how to say that."

Peter smiles. "But I do. Let's do some practice."

They take five minutes reviewing what Roxanne might say and what Zsuzsa should say in response. When Peter is confident in Zsuzsa's pronunciation, he tells her to step up to the door. Peter positions himself against the wall, out of sight. Zsuzsa knocks and waits. After several seconds, they hear footsteps behind the door.

"Who is it?" the voice calls from behind the door.

"My name is Zsuzsa," she says, doing her best to sound natural, but her voice is heavily accented.

"What do you want?"

Peter nods, and Zsuzsa says, "Scott Lyon is alive."

The door opens, and a striking, dark-haired woman stands in the doorframe. She frowns at Zsuzsa. "What did you say?"

Zsuzsa doesn't respond, and Peter moves to stand beside her. "She said Scott Lyon is alive. My name's Peter. I'm a private investigator and formally a New York City detective. We're working for Cindy Lyon. She's in a lot of trouble because of her husband."

Roxanne watches him. "Where's Scott?"

"We were hoping you could tell us."

She frowns. "You said he's alive. How do you know?"

"We think he could be. We aren't sure."

She glares at him and closes the door halfway, but doesn't shut it. "I don't want to be mixed up in anything. I just want to be left alone."

Peter takes a chance. "This isn't about you and Scott. That's not why we're here."

The statement stops her, and she watches him with obvious questions in her eyes.

"Scott was involved in some illegal business practices, and now his wife is in a lot of trouble. We want to ask you some questions. Nobody will know you talked to us. We aren't the police. We're just trying to help Cindy Lyon."

"Is Scott alive or not?"

Peter shakes his head. "Probably not."

She looks back at Zsuzsa. "You said he was alive."

Zsuzsa doesn't respond.

"She only said that because we thought it would get you to open the door."

Roxanne glares at him, debating. Finally, she says, "You aren't with the police?"

"No."

She opens the door wider. "Come in. I'll give you five minutes."

Peter waits for Zsuzsa, and they follow Roxanne inside. The apartment is small—Peter would guess no larger than three hundred square feet. The room they enter is a living area that also serves as the kitchen. There's a couch with a TV, a small refrigerator, a microwave, and a sink. Roxanne has no kitchen table. Two doors lead out of the room—probably a bathroom and a small bedroom.

"You can sit on the couch," Roxanne says.

Peter and Zsuzsa sit side by side while Roxanne pulls a small step stool from beside the counter and positions it across from them. She looks at Zsuzsa first, then Peter. "She doesn't speak English?"

"Not much."

She scrutinizes them for several seconds, then says, "She's your wife?"

"Yes. It's her first time in America."

"Where are you from?"

"Budapest."

"Wow. I've never been to Europe. You said you used to work in the NYPD."

"I did. I was a detective for twenty years."

She nods. "How do you know Scott's wife?"

"She's my sister-in-law's cousin. My wife and I were visiting during our honeymoon and couldn't go back home because of the attacks. They asked me if I would help Cindy."

"Help her with what?"

Peter rubs his knees. "It seems likely that Scott was involved in fraud."

Roxanne frowns. "How do you know that?"

Peter wonders about her phrasing, but doesn't point it out. "Scott was being investigated by the insurance commission for theft of client funds."

Roxanne watches him but doesn't respond.

"You don't seem surprised?"

Roxanne sighs and clasps her hands together. "I didn't know that. It doesn't surprise me, but I didn't know. Scott had been...different lately."

"How?"

She puts her hands on her jeans and looks away. "He just acted strangely at times. There were these deposits he'd make. They went into a different account. It wasn't the operating account or the trust account. I knew nothing about it. Never even saw the deposit book. I asked him about it once. He just passed it off as an investment account. Said it was personal."

"Did you normally maintain the deposit book?"

She nods. "On the other accounts, I did."

"Did you see any of these unusual deposit slips?"

She shakes her head. "Never. They were always in sealed envelopes. He'd have me drop the deposits in the overnight deposit box. He never wanted me to go to the teller." She looks him in the eye. "I almost opened an envelope once. I was burning with curiosity. I would have too. But I didn't have another envelope with me to reseal it."

"Did you think he was doing something illegal?"

"I don't know. But when Mr. Larkin came in, that really got me wondering."

"Mr. Larkin?"

"Yeah, he was a customer. We did a closing for him a few months ago. He sold one of his homes, and we were the title company that transacted it."

"What was different about him?"

She sighs. "Nothing at the closing. Everything was normal. But then, a few days before the planes hit the towers, he came into our office. Scott wasn't there. He was at the gym. Larkin came in super angry. Angrier than I've ever seen a customer. He demanded to speak to Scott and wouldn't leave until he did."

"What did Scott do?"

"I called him and told him." She stops and frowns. "He seemed surprised, but not. I don't know if that makes sense. It was like he expected the call, but not when it came."

Peter looks over at Zsuzsa. She's watching Roxanne, and he wonders if she's following any of this. "Did Scott come talk to him?"

"He did. They went into the office. I could hear Larkin yelling at first, but after several minutes, he came out and left. Scott walked him out. It seemed fine. Like it was just a misunderstanding."

"So, you think it was resolved?"

She shrugs. "I don't know. I guess."

"You aren't sure?"

"The morning the planes hit the towers, when I was leaving, I thought I saw Larkin."

"Entering the building?"

"Yeah. But I'm not sure it was him. He was on the other end of the lobby. I didn't even think about it until I was already outside."

"Do you have any more information on Mr. Larkin? His name? Physical description? Address? Phone number?"

She shakes her head. "I don't have any contact information. Everything was lost in the tower." Her voice lowers, and she looks away.

"What about his first name?"

She puts her finger to her lips. "Shane, I think. I don't know if that's right, but that's the name that comes to mind. I'm probably wrong."

"Do you remember where his property was?"

"Somewhere in the Bronx. I can't remember where. It was an apartment complex."

"You said you were leaving the building. Where were you going?"

"Scott asked me to make a bank run for him. It was early, the banks weren't open yet. I stopped and checked the mail first. I was at the bank when the towers were hit."

"Scott was there? He was already at work that morning?"

"Yes."

"Was that unusual?"

She cocks her head to the side. "Now that you mention it, yes."

"Was he alone?"

"Yes."

Peter looks at Zsuzsa and can see her eyes drooping. She notices him looking at her and pushes her eyes open, smiling. He reaches out and takes her hand, then looks back at Roxanne.

"Just a couple more questions, and we'll leave you."

She nods.

"How long did you work for Scott?"

"Two years."

"What did you do before that?"

"I worked for a doctor's office in their accounting department."

"Here, in New York?"

"No, in my hometown of Cincinnati."

Peter looks her in the eye. "How long after you started working for Scott did you sleep with him?"

Her face colors, and she shakes her head. "I didn't sleep with him."

Peter says nothing, watching her. Finally, she looks down.

"Who says I was sleeping with him?"

"Remember that part about being a detective with the NYPD for twenty years?"

She stares at him, then looks away. "About six months."

Peter nods. "So, you were having an affair with him for a year and a half?"

She returns her gaze to him. He's surprised to see tears in her eyes. She swallows and nods.

"Have you seen Scott since the attack?"

She shakes her head, looking down.

"Roxanne, look at me."

Roxanne brushes at her eyes and looks back up. "Is Scott still alive?"

A sob escapes, and the tears stream down her face. She shakes her head.

"You're sure?"

She nods, holding her hand over her mouth.

Peter rubs his beard, then stands from the couch, pulling Zsuzsa up with him. He takes a few steps toward the door, then stops. Roxanne remains on the stool, her long, dark hair covering her face. He puts his hand on the doorknob but doesn't open it. He looks down at her.

"The police know about your past. They know you stole money from your employer in Cincinnati."

She doesn't react, her face still in her hands.

"If they haven't yet, they'll be coming to talk to you. They think you might have been working with Scott to steal the money."

She pulls her head from her hands and looks at him. Her eyes are puffy and red.

"We appreciate you taking the time to talk to us." He opens the door, and he and Zsuzsa step out, closing it behind them.

Chapter 21

Scott

I stand at the front door, knock, and look around as I wait. It's a simple house, no bigger than fifteen hundred square feet. The yard's been neglected. It's overgrown. A small dog yaps from inside the home. Seconds later, I hear footsteps, and the door opens. Stacey stands in the entry, smiling at me. She looks even more done up than she did earlier today. If that's possible. Her hair is big and curly. She's wearing a pair of jeans and a red, silky blouse with a plunging neckline. I smile back, then dart a glance at the generous amount of cleavage. Her feet are bare, and I can see her toenails match her blouse. Her fingernails have also changed color.

"Hey," she says, motioning for me to come in. She holds the door open, and I step inside. She shuts the door and brushes past me. Her lavender scent is noticeable, but not as strong as earlier. She takes my hand and leads me to the kitchen. "Want a beer?"

"Sure."

She points to a chair at the kitchen table, and I sit down while she goes to the fridge. The house is clean. The kitchen is nicely decorated. If you like glitter-speckled picture frames with expressions

Aretha Franklin might sing. The refrigerator is plastered with photos of family. Stacey opens both bottles and hands one to me. She sits across the table. Something's different. She's more cautious than earlier. She seems guarded. This might not be as easy as I thought.

"Did you have any trouble finding the place?"

I shake my head and lean back in the wooden chair. "Nah, your instructions were perfect."

She smiles. She wears large hooped earrings that swing from side to side when her head moves. She's a woman who loves jewelry. She's wearing a bracelet, a necklace, and earrings. "You should have come back to the office with me. Mr. Reacher was disappointed. He was hoping you'd have more questions for him about the property."

I shrug. "I had a few other things I had to do today. My broker wanted to show me some other properties."

"Oh? Who's your broker?"

She says it as if she's only making conversation, but her focused eyes tell me it's a test. She wants to know if I'm legit. Maybe since we parted earlier today, she's been having second thoughts. That might be true, but I remind myself she opened the door, and the blouse and pushup bra send an obvious message.

"Ryan Little." I saw his name on a listing downtown.

"Oh, I've heard of him." She relaxes as she takes a drink from her bottle. "Find anything you liked?"

"One, actually. I even liked it more than your building."

"Oh?"

I flash her a sly grin. "Your building was more fun, though."

Her cheeks color. "How long are you here?"

I shrug. "Not sure. I was only supposed to stay until tomorrow. But I could see staying a little longer."

She smiles and lowers her eyelashes. She wants me. It's as obvious as it was at the bank. She's just doing her due diligence. Telling herself she's got to know me before giving herself over. "Are you going back to New York City?"

I shake my head. "No, Texas."

Her eyes light up. "Really? What part?"

She's eager. Texas has some significance to her. I've never been there and don't have the first clue. I've got to tread lightly. I name the only city I can think of. "Houston."

She nearly bounces with glee. "No?! That's where I'm from."

"Wow! How about that? It'll be my first time."

"What part are you visiting?"

"What part of Houston?" She bobs her head. "I'm not sure. My company has a few things for me to check out. They're back in my apartment."

She raises the bottle to her lips but pauses. "You have an apartment?"

"Hotel...I meant hotel. I have an apartment in New York City."

"Which hotel are you staying in?"

I can only think of one hotel chain and figure there's got to be one here. "The Hilton."

"Oh, the one downtown?"

"Yes."

She nods. I can't tell if that was a test. Is there a Hilton downtown?

"I'm from Sugarland."

"Huh?"

"In Houston. I'm not technically from Houston. I grew up in Sugarland." She says it as if that should mean something to me.

I take a drink of beer, then say something I regret. "Maybe you should come with me."

Her eyes sparkle. "Really?"

No, not really. What is wrong with me? "Sure. Do you think you could? What about your kids?"

Her face falls. She looks down at her beer and scratches at the bottle. "Yeah, they just started school. I probably can't get away." She looks back up. "Oh, I wish I could, though. It's been a long time. Maybe next time."

I reach across the table and take her hand. "For sure. Let's plan it."

"You mean it?"

"Absolutely."

"I'd love to go back. It's been so long."

For the next five minutes, she answers questions about her life. She tells me about meeting her ex in Houston and following him here. She tells me about getting pregnant and his awful family and how she got the job at the bank.

"Why do you stay? Why not go back to Houston?"

She shrugs. "This is home for my kids. They have friends. I have a job and a house here. I don't want to start over."

I nod, and she gives me a curious look.

"Were you in New York when it happened?"

"The towers?"

"Yeah."

I shake my head. "Cleveland. Traveling for work."

"What I've seen on TV is so sad. So many missing people. Do you know any?"

This is the opportunity I've been looking for. "A friend of mine is still missing," I say and look down.

She covers her mouth. "What? Are you serious?"

I shrug with a pained expression.

"Is he...dead?"

The question catches me off guard, and I frown. She realizes what she's said.

"I mean...that's awful. I'm so sorry."

I shrug, keeping my eyes down.

"What's his name?"

"Scott."

She places a hand over her chest and looks at me with a sympathetic expression. I sigh and pretend to be overcome with emotion as I place my head in my hands. I hear her chair move, and then she's beside me, rubbing my arm. I keep my head down, working up tears that won't seem to come. How do actors do it? Don't they say they think of their dead dog? That won't help. I never had one. Maybe something else? Maybe all the money I lost. When I finally look at her, I hope my eyes are misty. They certainly must look sad.

She looks at me with pity, then reaches forward and pulls me to her. Her chest is pressed against my arm, and I notice how soft her skin feels. She holds me for several seconds, then pulls back, looking into my eyes. We hold that pose for a moment, and then she comes forward and kisses me. Before long, we're making out. Our hands all over each other. We go on for several minutes until she pulls away and stands from her chair. She reaches for my hand and pulls me with her as we head down the hallway to her bedroom.

Thirty minutes later, we lie naked in bed in the dark room. My back is propped against the headboard. She's turned into me; her leg over mine. She's resting her head against my shoulder, tracing circles on my chest. I can only see the outline of her face. It's too dark.

"Can I ask you something?" she says.

"Sure."

"When you first came into the bank..."

"Yeah?"

"You seemed pretty upset."

I wait to see if she'll say anything else. "Is that a question?"

She hesitates.

"What do you want to know?"

"Did someone steal money from you?"

All day I've been wondering how I'd get to this point in our conversation. I never dreamed she'd be the one to initiate it. I sigh. "Yes."

"Who?"

"That's a good question."

She sits up on her knees. I can see the outline of her face in the moonlight. She looks at me with concern. "You don't know?"

I shake my head. "All I can see on the bank statements is the money transferred out. I can't see where it went." I look away from her and stare at the window. I can feel her eyes on me.

"I could find out."

I turn back to her. "You could?"

"I think so. It might take some digging, but I can find out where the money went."

I lean forward and kiss her. "You don't know how much that would mean to me."

She smiles. "Show me..."

Chapter 22

Zsuzsa

After leaving Roxanne's apartment, we ride the elevator and exit through the main doors. Once on the street, Peter points to a sandwich place and asks, "Hungry?"

I shrug, and we cross the street, hand in hand. Once inside, we walk to the front counter and look at the menu on the big white sign above us. It's all in English. I only recognize a few words. There aren't even any pictures. A handsome young man stands behind the counter wearing a white apron. He smiles at me, then says something to Peter. Peter holds up an index finger. The guy watches me as he holds a pen bent over a notepad on the counter.

"What would you like?" Peter asks, without taking his eyes from the board above.

"How about some soup?"

He looks to the far side of the sign. "Looks like they have Italian-wedding soup, Stracciatella, and lentil." I don't recognize any of those names and say nothing. Peter stares at the board for a few seconds, then looks at me. "Did you decide?"

I shrug. "I don't care."

"How about the lentil?"

"Fine."

My irritation is growing, but he doesn't see it. He turns back to the guy and places our order. He hands him cash, then we walk to the opposite side of the room. Peter insists on the counter with barstools against the window. I sit down while he takes the empty cups to the soda machine. When he returns, he's got water for us. His has ice. He smiles and says something about how much he likes this place as he looks around. I stare out the window.

"Is something wrong?"

I shake my head. I can see he's watching me, but I don't look at him.

"Zsuzsa...what is it? Did you want to go somewhere else?"

I stare out the window. Roxanne's building is across the street. From here, I can see the front door.

"Zsuzsa?"

I continue staring ahead as my frustration rises. Tears spring to my eyes, and I fight them back. He reaches out and holds my hand. I pick up a napkin and dab at the corners of my eyes.

After a minute, the guy behind the counter calls Peter's name, and he retrieves our food. He sits down and places the soup in front of me. I still don't look at him. He unwraps his sandwich, and right before he takes a bite, I mutter, "I just wish I could help you."

He sets down his sandwich. I see he's looking at me from the corner of my eye. "What do you mean, 'help me more?'"

I turn and shake my head. "This." I motion around us. "Going into places and not being able to even order soup. Not being able to read the menu. Afraid someone might talk to me because I can't talk back. Sit in long meetings while you talk to people, and I can't understand more than a few words. Fight not to fall asleep. I just feel useless. Like I'm a burden to you."

He stares at me, expressionless. After what seems like a minute, he says, "Being in a foreign country is hard," then turns back to his sandwich and takes a bite.

I stare at him. "Yeah, really hard." That's really all he's going to say? I turn back to my soup and pick up my spoon. "It's fine. You can't relate. You speak English and Hungarian like it's nothing. You're fluent in both. You don't know how hard it is." I take a spoonful of soup and slide it into my mouth. It's warm and has a delicate flavor. It's fantastic, and it helps.

Peter stares out the window. I eat more of my soup, trying to process his reaction. Do I even know this man? Two minutes pass, and he still doesn't reply. Finally, I can't stand it anymore. I turn back to him. "That's it?"

He looks at me and chuckles. "What?"

"You aren't going to say anything else?"

"Like what?"

"Am I a burden to you? Should I just wait for you at Gary and Becky's? Say something. Tell me what you're feeling. I know you can't relate because you're so smart and a language savant. But this isn't easy for me. I just want you to understand and care."

He looks at me, and for the life of me, I don't know what he's going to say. Maybe he won't say anything at all. "Can I tell you a story?"

I frown but nod.

"When I was sixteen, I left Hungary to come here. That was almost twenty-eight years ago. I was with a friend in Budapest. He convinced me we should go to America. He claimed it was the land of opportunity. I was unhappy in Hungary, and I believed him. We rode a train to Sopron, then snuck across the Austrian border and walked to Vienna. After we arrived, he got passage to America almost immediately. I had to wait. I almost turned back and went home, but knew I couldn't. I had nothing to go home to. For several weeks, I stayed in a camp in Vienna."

He takes a bite of his sandwich and looks back at the building across from us. "Finally, I was able to go to America. I got to France and boarded a ship. Nobody around me spoke Hungarian. Not a single person." He stops and squints with the memory. "I was alone. I knew almost no English, French, or German. Maybe a word here and there, but nothing significant. I sat on that ship for days without a soul to talk to. I couldn't communicate what I wanted or anything about me. I had a terrible bout of seasickness and was so incredibly lonely." He points out the window. "Remember when we first came? We could see the Statue of Liberty from Manhattan?"

"Yes."

"I'll never forget the moment I saw it. I was excited to be in America. But, mostly, I was ready to get off that ship. We docked not too far away here in Manhattan. I was excited but scared. I knew they could deny me entry and send me back. That wouldn't have been so bad if not for the ship ride. I couldn't have made it." He turns back and looks at me. "There were hundreds of us immigrants on the ship. We were marched into a building where we were examined for disease and physical ailments. They spoke English, and I had to guess what they wanted. Finally, they asked for my name. When I told them, I said it backward. I said it like we would say it. Surname first, Andrassy Peter. The inspections man looked at me, then called someone over. It was a boy not much older than me. He spoke to me in Hungarian." Peter smiles. "It was the first time I'd heard our language in weeks. It was incredible. I could speak again. Tears ran down my cheeks and I hugged him." He stops and looks me deep in the eyes. His green eyes remind me of the trees around the Balaton. "Zsuzsa, I may not understand exactly what you're going through, but I know what it's like not to be able to speak and not understand."

I look at him, and tears fill my eyes and run down my cheeks. I'm overwhelmed with shame. How could I not think of that? How could I not realize he's been through way more than I have? He's here with me. He had nobody. I cover my face with my hands.

"I'm sorry," I mumble, blubbering into my palms.

He chuckles and wraps his arms around me. He kisses my head. "I don't want you to be sorry. I know it's hard. We can go back. We don't have to stay."

I sit on the barstool, letting him hold me. After a minute, he pulls back and kisses me. We look into each other's eyes.

"I want to stay."

"You're sure?"

"Yes. The soup is excellent, by the way," I say, smiling.

He laughs. "I'm glad. So's my sandwich."

"How did you know about this place? Have you been here before?"

He shakes his head. "Nope. I liked the location."

I look out at the street before us. There's nothing but apartment buildings. They aren't even charming.

"Did you understand any of my conversation with Roxanne?"

I sigh. "Not really. Did I hear right at the end, though? Did you tell her the police were looking for her?"

"No. I told her they knew about her stealing money before. I might have implied they think she was involved with Scott's theft."

"Why would you tell her that? Do you think she was?"

"I'm not sure. But if she is, it might make her react. Maybe she'll do something."

"Like what?"

A movement across the street catches our attention. Roxanne walks out the front door of her apartment building. She has a rolling bag behind her.

Peter points in her direction. "Like that."

Chapter 23

Scott

I look at my watch as I stand on the sidewalk opposite the Iowa State Bank. I've been standing here for ten minutes. We were supposed to meet at noon. What's taking her so long?

I haven't seen her since early this morning. Last night, after we had sex for the second time, she admitted her kids weren't home. She had arranged for a friend to take them overnight. She left me early in the morning to get them while I showered, ate food from her pantry, and left before they came back. I've been walking around Des Moines since. I was tempted to go back to my apartment but fought the urge, counting down the minutes until noon.

The front door to the bank opens and Stacey exits. Our eyes lock, and she motions with her head up the street. I walk opposite her, matching her pace until we travel one block. When we're out of sight of the bank, she finally crosses.

"I only have an hour until I have to be back," she says. "There's a small Greek place around the corner. It's close and quick. Can we go there?"

"Sure."

We travel half a block, enter the restaurant, and sit in a booth along the wall. The server greets us, and Stacey orders a Diet Coke while I request water.

When we're alone, I ask, "Did you find out anything?"

She nods and pulls a sheet of paper from her purse and hands it to me. It's a list of transactions from my bank account, but this time there's more information. The withdrawals show where the money went. The transfers were to a bank account with Washington Mutual. Even the bank account numbers are listed, though it doesn't say who the owner is. It's less than what I'd hoped, but it's a start.

She watches me as I examine the page. "I have a friend who works for Washington Mutual," she says.

I look up from the paper.

"I called her."

She knows something. I can see it in her eyes.

The server comes back, and Stacey orders a salad. I shake my head and say I'm not hungry. When the server leaves, Stacey says, "The money was transferred to an LLC. The name of the LLC is Rosenberg's Bomb."

I frown, leaning forward. "What?"

"That's the account holder. A company named Rosenberg's Bomb."

I lean back in my chair and look up at the ceiling.

"Does that mean anything to you?"

I shake my head.

"I was curious, so I did some digging. The LLC was created in New York. There was no physical address for the company. The mailing address was a PO box."

"What was the zip code?"

"I don't remember. Somewhere in Brooklyn."

The server returns with Stacey's salad. She begins to eat while I stare out the window.

"I couldn't find anything else about the LLC. I don't know who set it up or who owns it. I called my friend back and asked her, but she couldn't tell me."

I rub my hands back and forth, my mind working.

"She told me one other thing, though."

"What?"

"The LLC's bank account is empty. The money's gone."

"Where did it go?"

"She couldn't say."

I take a deep breath, trying to control my anger. I look at her salad. I'm hungry.

She finishes, and the server returns.

"Are you sure you don't want anything?" Stacey asks.

I shake my head. Stacey opens her purse, then starts rummaging through it. When she looks up, her cheeks have colored. "Josh?"

"Yeah."

"Would you mind paying for the salad? I left my wallet back at the bank."

I pick up the bill. It's thirteen dollars without the tip. I know I only have twelve in my wallet. I reach behind me and make a motion of feeling for my wallet. My face drops. "I don't have mine either."

"What?"

I shrug. "I guess I forgot it in my hotel room."

Her eyes narrow, then she goes through her purse again. "Oh," she says. "Here it is. I guess I do have it." She takes out a twenty and puts in on the tray the bill was presented on. The server comes back and takes it and brings her change. She leaves three dollars, and we exit.

I look down at my watch. "What time do you have to be back?"

"One."

"You have five minutes."

"Will you walk me?"

I nod and turn. Then I feel her reach behind me and pull my wallet from my back pocket.

"What are you doing?"

She holds up the wallet, opens it, and pulls out the twelve dollars. She flips to the ID in the front and examines it. "You had your wallet the whole time. You lied to me."

"So did you."

Her eyes register surprise. "What?"

"You think I bought that whole game of looking in your purse?" I put my hands to my cheeks. "Oh no, I don't have any money." I drop my hands. "You knew you had money the whole time. You were testing me."

She doesn't react. She knows I'm right. "Why did you lie to me?"

"Why did you?"

"I asked first."

I smirk and start walking.

She calls out, "Because I think there's more to your story than you're telling me."

I turn back. "If you thought that, why didn't you just ask?"

She walks up to me. "So, is there more to your story? What's really going on?"

I look down. "I'm not here for work. I was planning to move here." I look back up as her eyes widen. "That money in my account was supposed to help me start a business. It's all I had. Someone stole it. I think I know who. But they left me flat broke. I've got nothing. Everything I had was in that account. That twelve dollars is all the money I have in the world."

She puts the money back in my wallet and hands it to me. "Who stole it?"

"I had a real estate business back in New York. When I closed it to move here, someone got really upset."

"Your wife? Are you married?"

I shake my head. "No, of course not. She was an employee. When I closed the real estate business, she lost her job."

"Why did you close it?"

I shake my head and start walking back toward the bank. She falls in beside me. I sigh. "Have you ever been to New York?"

She shakes her head.

"It's a lot. I got tired of it. I wanted something new. Something slower. I was successful in my real estate business. I made a lot of money. I didn't want the pressure anymore. I came out here and loved it. So I sold the business. That employee wasn't happy. She told me she'd get even. I thought it was a figure of speech."

"So, if you think she stole the money, why don't you go to the police? We can help you at the bank. Let's call the police and bring them over."

I stop walking. "Believe me. I'd love to go to the police. But I can't."

"Why not?"

"Have you ever heard of the Bonanno family?"

She shakes her head.

"They're a crime family in New York. They were a client of mine. I did work for them. Some of that work wasn't exactly kosher."

She starts backing away, and I come forward, grabbing her hand.

"I had to get out of there. I came here to restart my life. Get a clean break. I want to be here. I want to be with you. Can you help me?"

Her eyes look into mine, and I can see them soften. "What do you need?"

"Just some money. I've got to go back to New York. Find my money before it's too late."

"For how long?" I see concern in her eyes.

"Not long. I've got to find her."

"I don't have much I can give you."

"Anything you can spare would mean a lot."

She watches me for several seconds, then says, "Stay here."

She walks across the street to the bank. When she comes back, she's holding an envelope. "It's five hundred dollars. That's all I have."

I nod and reach for it.

She pulls back, keeping it from me. "I need it paid back. This is only a loan."

I nod. "Believe me. When I get my money back, I'll pay you back and then some. I won't forget what you did for me."

Chapter 24

Peter

"Any movement?"

Peter sits across the table from Zsuzsa at Truman's KC Pizza Tavern in Des Moines. After watching Roxanne leave her apartment building in Brooklyn with luggage, they followed her. She went to the train station and booked a ticket to Chicago, then here to Des Moines. Not wanting to lose her, they did the same. After the two-day trip, they arrived a few hours ago and followed Roxanne to the apartment building across the street.

Zsuzsa shakes her head, checking the building one more time. "She hasn't moved." Peter nods and picks up a slice of pepperoni pizza. He slides a plastic bag across the table toward Zsuzsa. She picks it up and looks inside. There's a change of clothes and toiletries. She holds the sweater against her body. "Hmm."

"What?"

She shakes her head. The shirt is way too big. "Should I read anything into this?"

Peter gives her a look. "The other option would have fit a ten-year-old girl."

She smiles. "Better to guess too small than too big."

"But this you can at least wear. Even if it doesn't fit right."

"And every time I do, I'll be reminded my husband thinks I'm two sizes bigger than I am." She laughs at his expression. "Thanks for going. Next time, it'll be my turn."

"You don't know what size I wear."

She rolls her eyes.

"You do?"

"Of course."

"How?"

"I picked out your tuxedo at the wedding. Remember?"

"Yes, but that's a tuxedo. Casual clothes are different."

She shakes her head. "Nope. Plus, women are just better at that than men."

"Well, if they are, it's only because men's sizes make way more sense. Women's sizes are nonsensical. What does size two or size six even mean? How can a woman six feet tall and a woman five feet tall both be size six?"

"Aren't you supposed to be a detective?"

He glares at her. "That was below the belt."

She smiles. "No, it wasn't. If it was, you'd like it."

Peter bursts out laughing, and several people in the restaurant turn and look at them.

Zsuzsa motions to the window. "Do you think she's in for the night?"

Peter turns his attention to the building. "Hard to say. Who do you think lives there?"

Zsuzsa shrugs. "Family?"

"Maybe."

Peter reaches in his pocket and withdraws a mobile phone and hands it to Zsuzsa. "I almost forgot. I picked up two burner phones. If we get separated, we can call each other."

She smiles, taking it from him. "Good thinking. That almost makes up for the sweater."

Peter gives her a look, then turns back to the window. "What if I go over there?"

"And do what?"

"Just check it out. Maybe see who she's visiting."

"How are you going to know?"

"I'm a detective. Remember?"

She holds up the sweater and looks at it.

"I hate you."

Now it's her turn to laugh. "What if she sees you?"

"She won't."

"But what if she does?"

Peter stands from the table, taking a gulp of water. "I won't be long. Maybe ten minutes." He holds up his phone. "If you see her..."

"What's your number?"

He winks. "I programmed it into the phone." She smiles, and he leans over, kissing her. "Be right back."

Peter walks out of the restaurant and crosses the street. When he approaches the apartment building, he looks around for a buzzer but doesn't see one. He tries the front door and it opens. He walks into the lobby and sees a row of mailboxes. He examines each, taking out his notepad and writing every name he sees. When he's two from the end, a bell rings behind him, indicating the elevator has arrived. He ducks out of sight behind a candy machine. A woman exits, and he recognizes her. She doesn't see him, turning to her left toward the front door. She's carrying only her purse. Peter leans out from behind the machine. When she reaches the door, she stops. She opens her purse, shakes her head, and turns back. He ducks back behind the machine. She walks back by the elevator, and just when he thinks she's going to confront him, she pushes the call button. The elevator opens, and she steps inside.

When he hears it close, Peter opens the stairwell door and runs up to the second floor. He opens the door and sticks his head out. Not seeing her, he runs up to the third floor. He repeats the process and sees her on the opposite side of the building, entering an apartment. Peter looks around the hallway. Rather than venture out, he stays in the stairwell with the door slightly propped. After only thirty seconds, he sees movement and knows she's coming out. He stands still, one eye on her. She walks to the elevator, gets inside, and he pulls out his phone. He dials Zsuzsa. After one ring, she answers.

"She's coming out the front."

"Are you going to follow her?"

"I saw what apartment she came out of."

"So?"

"Listen, she didn't have her suitcase with her."

"So...oh, here she is. She's leaving the building."

"Stay there. Keep an eye out for her return. I'm going to go check in the apartment."

"What? Peter..."

"I just want to see who she's with."

"What if they see you?"

"They won't. I'll be fine. Call me if I'm not out when she comes back."

Peter ends the call and walks down the hallway. When he reaches the door, he looks for a name but sees nothing. He makes a note of the apartment number, then puts his ear to the door. It's silent. He knocks and steps back. Nothing. Curious, he listens one more time with his ear pressed against the door. Silence. He looks around the hall, sees he's alone, then takes out his knife. He picks the lock and enters the apartment, closing the door behind him.

It's sparsely furnished. There's a small kitchen table, a refrigerator, a garbage can, and three cabinets in the kitchen. It's a studio apartment with a bedroom connected to the kitchen with a set of double doors separating. The room has a bed, but nothing on the walls. Roxanne's suitcase is on the side of the bed, open. He looks at it but doesn't go through it. He checks the closet and the bathroom. Both are nearly empty. Nobody lives here.

He walks back to the kitchen and looks around. He opens the fridge and sees it's empty. He opens the freezer and finds instant coffee. In the sink are a saucepan and mug that have been washed out but aren't clean. There's a small amount of orange residue on the edge of the saucepan. He opens the cabinets and finds a can of stew and a box of crackers.

He walks back to the bedroom, looks around one more time, and just as he's about to exit, he looks at the garbage can. He opens it and finds a sheet of paper. Three names are written on the sheet. The handwriting is male. At the top of the list is the name Shane Larkin. That's the name of the man Roxanne said visited several days before the terrorist attacks. The angry client. Peter folds the paper and puts it in his pocket. He exits the apartment, walks down the stairs to the ground floor, and exits the building. He crosses the street and reenters the pizza place. When he does, the server stops him. "I'm glad you came back, man."

"Yeah, we'll leave. Sorry, we've been here so long."

He gives Peter a curious look. "Dude, I thought you were stiffing me."

"What?"

"I thought you were skipping out on the bill."

"No." Peter looks at the booth where he'd left Zsuzsa. The table is cleared and she's gone. "Where's my wife?"

"I don't know. I went to the bathroom, and when I came out, she was gone. That's why I thought you'd bounced."

Peter approaches the other occupied tables, asking if they saw her leave. Both shake their heads. Peter goes back to the server. "Here's your bill, man."

Peter looks at it, hands him enough cash to cover it and the tip, then walks out. He dials Zsuzsa and waits for her to pick up. The phone rings several times and then ends. He tries again, and this time the ringing stops immediately. Peter looks at the building across the street and remembers Zsuzsa saying Roxanne had turned right. He tears off in that direction.

Chapter 25

Scott

My anxiety is at an all-time high as I enter New York City. When I left last week, I never thought I'd be back. When my money was stolen and I learned Roxanne was behind it, I knew I had no choice. Although I don't think anyone would recognize me, you can never be too careful. I'm not the same man who walked out of here after the terrorist attacks. My light-brown hair is nearly black, and my facial hair has come in nicely. My beard isn't thick, but it's adequate.

At Penn Station, I take the Five train to Winthrop and exit. All around me, people were talking about the attacks. I heard all kinds of theories and stories about people they knew who were killed in the towers. It's midday, and although it's getting later in September, it feels like summer as I climb the steps out of the underground. The sun is shining, and I regret the hoodie I'm wearing. It's meant to disguise me, but I wonder if it might bring too much attention in this heat. I walk along Winthrop and fill my lungs with urban air. I decide to cut through Prospect Park. There's a sampling of people out walking their dogs or pushing kids in strollers.

When I reach a large open area, there's a smattering of people lying on blankets, partaking in a picnic, or simply basking in the warm weather. A sign on one of the light poles gets my attention. It's a photo of a man with "Missing" written in block letters. He's wearing a suit in the photo. I keep walking and see another. It's a different person this time. The woman is laughing while holding a drink. She's at some kind of party. She's in her mid-thirties. Beneath her, the caption reads: "Have you seen my sister?" I keep walking, seeing similar signs and posters before exiting the park.

It's another five minutes until I reach Roxanne's building. A woman exits as I approach. She sees me and holds the door while smiling. I haven't been in the city long, but I notice a change in the people. New York is known for anxious, hard-charging folks. But the opposite seems true now. They're friendlier. There's a comradery I've never felt before. I thank her and slip past her toward the elevators. I consider taking the stairs, but when I push the button, the doors open to an empty lift. I enter, push the button to Roxanne's floor, and ride up. When I reach Roxanne's level, I exit and walk several paces to her apartment door. I look around, making sure I'm alone, then test the handle. It's locked. I check my surroundings again, then knock. I step to the side, making myself invisible to someone looking through the peephole. I listen for movement but hear none. When I'm sure she isn't going to answer, I walk back toward her neighbor's door. I listen and hear silence. I consider knocking but decide against it.

I return to Roxanne's door and take a step back. I kick with all my might, and the door gives but doesn't open. I listen for noise down the hall. Nothing. I step back again and kick. This time, the frame around the lock splinters. It still doesn't open, but it's close. I push against it, but that isn't enough. I kick one more time, and the door smashes open. I step inside. Splintered wood covers the linoleum floor. I close the door, then slide a kitchen chair behind it.

I look around the apartment. There's a dirty mug in the sink and a half-eaten piece of toast on a plate. I spend only a few seconds in the kitchen, then move to the bedroom. The bed is unmade. It's been slept in recently. The closet door is open, and there's a summer dress on a hanger lying on the mattress. A pair of tennis shoes are on the ground beside the bed, and I almost trip over them. Inside the closet, there's a gap near the bottom. I don't know for sure, but the impressions on the carpet make me think something was stored here. Perhaps a suitcase.

I open the bathroom door. There's no toothbrush. She's gone. I stand in the bedroom, looking around. Where would she go? If she has my money, what would she do with it? I lift the mattress, but there's nothing below it. I walk back into the entrance and stare at the couch. There's a window, the only one in the apartment. I walk to it and look out. I can see the Manhattan skyline from here. It's eerie. I've never seen it without the towers. The sight makes my insides churn. My eyes scan the neighborhood, and I see a police car. It pulls up down the street and stops. A Chevy Malibu parks a few seconds later. A short man with graying hair gets out. He's joined by a larger man. A gun is on his hip. He's a cop. They look up at the building and I step back. They know. They've found me.

I slide the chair away from the door and enter the hallway. I look around and see the door to the stairwell. When I open it, I can hear the shuffle of feet below. They're coming. I let the door close and scan the level. Looking for anywhere to hide. A janitor's closet is midway down, and I go to it. I turn the knob, and the door opens. I step inside the dark room and pull the door closed, listening with my ear pressed to it.

Several seconds pass before I hear footsteps. They're opposite me at the stairwell. Nearby, the elevator chimes, and I hear more footsteps. A man calls out to another, and men run down the hallway. When they pass, I consider opening the door and running but decide against it. If they see me, I'm cooked. My only choice is to stay here and hope they think I escaped. Several more seconds pass without a sound. Finally, I hear them back in the hallway. One is talking into a radio. He's calling for more police. They know. They saw the broken door. They're going to spread out and start looking for me. I'm a rat in a cage.

He walks down the hall, and I can't make out the words. He's talking to his partner. Their voices are nothing more than mumbles. Several minutes pass before I hear the elevator chime and more police. One is giving instructions. He's telling them to knock on all the doors. There are multiple voices, including a woman's. I can't tell how many. I hear footsteps pass and the elevator. A knock sounds on a door to my left. They knock again with no answer. I calculate in my mind. How many doors were there? Six?

Two doors are being knocked on simultaneously. I shift my weight and feel something fall beside me. It's almost soundless and is drowned out by the knocking doors. They're coming closer. None of the residents appear to be home. They give up. I look down under the gap in the door. I can see shadows. Footsteps stop in front of my door. A knock surprises me, and I jump but thankfully touch nothing. I don't think I made a sound.

"Hey, that's a janitor's closet," I hear a man explain.

"Oh," says a female voice.

"Check to make sure it's locked."

I grip the doorknob with two hands and lean back with everything I have. It can't move at all. It's got to feel locked to her. I can feel the pressure against the other side of the handle. Then there's a tug outward. I grit my teeth and continue to pull with all my might.

"It's locked," she says.

I can feel the blood pumping through my veins. I take a few deep breaths through my nose. It smells like I knocked over some bleach, and there's liquid on the ground. I just hope there's not enough to run under the door.

They continue down the hallway. Only one person answers and says they don't know anything about the woman who lives at the other end of the hall. They didn't see me or know the apartment was broken into. The two cops call out to the others and say they're going down to the next level. They call the elevator and leave. I breathe deeply, feeling lightheaded. The smell from the cleaning supplies is getting to me. I can't stay in here much longer.

Finally, I hear voices again. The two men are coming down the hallway. They stop at the elevator. "Where do you think she went?"

"I'm not sure."

"Do you think she went to Des Moines?" Hesitation. "You think she's got the money?"

"If she doesn't, who does? You saw that door. Somebody certainly thinks she does."

"Who?"

"Beats me."

The elevator arrives.

"We'll put out a BOLO on her. Call the police in Des Moines and Cincinnati."

The elevator doors close, and the voices are drowned out. My eyes grow cloudy, and I push open the door, panting for breath. I lean over, sucking in gulps of air, looking around. I'm alone. My mind clears, and I turn back to look in the closet. There's bleach. A lot of it. It's puddling under the door. Somehow, they missed it. I close the door, walk to the end of the hall, and look out the window. The men in plain clothes with guns at their belt stand by the car. After several minutes, the other officers join them, and they all leave. I go down the stairs, exit the building, and walk back toward the subway.

Des Moines? Is she in Des Moines? I was right there. Was she coming to find me? I've got to go back just in case. I've got to find her before they do.

Chapter 26

Zsuzsa

I hang up the phone and grab the bag of clothes and toiletries Peter got me. I almost leave the sweater but stuff it in the bag and run out the door. Peter wanted me to stay put, but that's not happening. When I'm out on the street, I see her. She's walking with her purse slung over her wrist. She's wearing a cute skirt and sandals. She has a tight, fit body. Her hair is pulled back in a braid, and she's wearing sunglasses. She's really beautiful. I wonder if I walk like that. Is that something learned or natural? She almost glides as she moves down the street.

I stay on the opposite side, well back from her. For a moment, I doubt myself. Should I have followed Peter's request? But what if he's wrong? What if she's not coming back? We could lose her. Plus, this is my chance to actually *do something*. Not just be sitting in the room while Peter talks. I can contribute. She turns the corner, and I cross the street. Cars pass and occasionally a pedestrian. After several blocks, she stops in front of a redbrick building. She walks up the steps and enters. I walk forward. It's a bank. Is she getting the money? I need to know what she's doing. Do I risk going in there? What if she recognizes me?

I walk to the door and cup my hands over the glass. I can't see much. There are several people in the bank. Two teller stations. Both are occupied. I can't see Roxanne. I make up my mind, take a breath, and step inside. One teller looks at me and smiles, but goes on helping the older woman in front of her. I glance around the lobby and see her. She's sitting in front of a desk near the wall. She's talking to another woman with blond hair. I consider going close, but even if I do, I probably won't understand a word of their conversation. I look over at the teller stations and see they're still occupied. In the corner, beside the front window, are two empty chairs with an end table and magazines. I go over and sit down, picking up a magazine. I raise it high to shield my face. My phone rings, and I reach into my purse. I pull it out and silence it. If I answer and speak Hungarian, she'll recognize me for sure. I don't even look to see if Roxanne saw me. I put the magazine back up and cover my face. I hold the phone and silence it again when Peter calls back. I press the button at the top until the phone turns off.

After a minute, I venture a look beyond the magazine. Roxanne's gone, and the woman she was talking to is approaching.

"Hi," she says. "Can I help you?"

I jump up, startling her. I raise my hands. "No. Sorry." I rush to the door and exit.

When I'm out on the street, I look around frantically. She's gone. Vanished. I pull my phone out of my purse and turn it on and call Peter.

"Where are you?" he asks.

"At the Iowa State Bank."

"What?"

"I followed Roxanne here."

"I told you not to."

"I know. But listen, she saw me. She knows we're here. She lost me. She's gone."

"Stay there. I'm coming."

I cross the street and sit down on the park bench opposite the bank. It's late in the afternoon, and the sun is setting behind the buildings to the west. I look up and down the street, wondering where Roxanne went. I slap the seat beside me. *That was so stupid, Zsuzsa!* Peter's never going to trust me to follow someone on my own. He was right. I should have sat at the pizza place and waited.

Three minutes pass, and Peter comes around the corner. He sees me and walks over. He sits down beside me, saying nothing. I can't stand it. What's he thinking?

"I'm sorry," I say.

He looks at me with an unreadable expression. He's mad. He has every right to be. I look away, ashamed, when he withdraws a paper from his pocket. "I found this in the apartment."

I take the paper, looking into his eyes. His voice is calm. I look down at the paper.

"She didn't write this," I say.

"Right. That's a man's handwriting."

I look into his eyes. "Who did?"

He raises an eyebrow. "Nobody else is living in that apartment. It was empty, other than what she brought with her."

"No way she arranged for an apartment this quickly. She had it already."

Peter shrugs. "Or knew it would be empty."

I frown. "How?"

He puts his arm up on the back of the bench. "What if she knew it belonged to Scott? She'd know it was empty."

I turn away and stare at the bank. If she knew he had this apartment, she also knew about the money. I look down at the sheet of paper and the names written on it. "Scott wrote this."

He nods and points at the name on the top of the sheet. "Recognize that name?" It's an American name and isn't familiar to me. "Shane Larkin. That's the man who was angry and came to the office days before the planes hit the towers. He was a client Scott stole from."

I point to the sheet. "And these are the others?"

He nods. "I can only assume. What happened in the bank?"

I look down at my feet. "I lost her."

He chuckles. "You told me that already. You really think I'd be angry? I've done much worse. I won't throw rocks from my glass house." He shrugs. "You tried, and you were made. It's not the end of the world. I don't love you any less."

I look at him and can't help the tears that spring to my eyes. I lean over and kiss him, wrapping my arms around his neck. I don't deserve him.

After a few seconds, he pulls away. "Why was she there?"

I keep my arms around him, staring into his eyes. I don't care about Roxanne anymore. I don't care about anything but him. "I don't know. She was talking to a banker with blond hair."

"What was she talking to the banker about?"

"I wish I knew."

"Did they know each other?"

I'm tempted to tell him yes. It might show that I got something useful. "I don't know."

He looks away, and I wish I could climb into his mind and know his thoughts.

"We need a car," he says.

I release him and follow his gaze down the street. There's a yellow sign with a word that starts with *H* on it.

"I'll be right back. Keep an eye on the banker. If she comes out, call me."

He kisses me, then walks away.

He's gone twenty minutes. When I see him next, he's in a blue sedan. He pulls up in front of me, rolls down the window, and calls to me. I go to the passenger side and get in. It's a nice car. Roomy. It even has that new-car smell.

"What do you think?" he asks.

"I like it."

His hand is on the steering wheel. He looks so handsome. He checks his watch. "It's four forty-five. She's probably off at five."

He pulls the car away from the curb and enters a parking lot with a view of the bank.

"You should take me back to the pizza place," I say.

"Why?"

"What if Roxanne comes back? Wouldn't it be good to know?"

He looks at me, and I know he's considering it. I don't wait for an answer and lean over and kiss him, then get out of the car.

"Zsuzsa," he says.

"It's okay. I'll be fine. I'm going to walk back. I'll stay out of sight. Come and get me after you talk to her." I don't wait for a reply and walk away. I need to make up for before. I need to earn back his trust.

Chapter 27

Peter

Peter watches from the other side of the street as Stacey, the banker with blond hair, helps her kids exit her car. The kids are small, a boy maybe five years old and a girl of seven or eight. The girl is just like her mother. All girl. Her school bag is bright pink with sparkly jewels dangling from the zippers. She has long blond hair and stylish clothes. They enter the house, and Peter looks at his watch. He'll give them some time to settle in before he knocks.

When the ten minutes elapse, he exits the car and knocks on the door. He can hear them inside the house, and it's the little girl who answers. She looks up at him with curiosity.

"Hi, is your mother home?"

The girl turns and calls out to her mother that "some man" is at the door. The little boy is on the couch watching a TV show. Stacey comes around the corner with an exasperated look on her face. She's wearing an apron, and naturally, it's pink. The apron has an expression written on it, "If you think I'm sexy now, wait until you've tried my cooking." Her eyes crinkle as she looks at Peter. "Yes, can I help you?"

"Yes. My name is Peter Andrassy. I'm an investigator." Peter holds up a picture of Scott Lyon. "Do you know this man?"

She takes a step forward, looking at the picture. She stiffens and looks at him warily. "Is there a problem?"

Peter watches her closely. "Has he been in your bank?"

She ignores the question. "Is he okay?"

"When was the last time you saw him?"

"A few days ago. What's wrong?"

Peter narrows his eyes. "You saw *this man* a few days ago. You're sure?"

She nods, rubbing her hands together. "Yes, Josh is a customer in the bank. He came in because he was interested in a commercial building we recently foreclosed on. I took him to the building and showed it to him. Did something happen? Is he okay?"

Peter holds the picture closer to her. "This man? You showed him property this week?"

She frowns. "Yes."

Peter points to the photo. "This man was presumed dead in the terrorist attacks that took place recently in New York. He was in the building when the plane hit the tower."

"That's impossible," she says, shaking her head. "He's from New York, but he was in Cleveland when the towers were hit."

"Mom!" the boy yells.

She turns. "What?!"

"It's over," he says, pointing to the TV.

"Kenzie," she yells over her shoulder. "Will you help your brother?" She turns back to Peter. "Come in," she says, waving her hand.

Peter steps inside, and she brushes by him, making sure the door is shut.

"Come into the kitchen with me," she says, leading him to the back of the house. "Sorry, I'm cooking dinner."

The little girl comes down the stairs, and Peter has to stop while she steps in front of him on her way to her brother. Peter enters the kitchen behind Stacey. She goes to the stove with her back to him as he stands by the counter.

"Like I said, Josh wasn't even in New York when the attacks happened."

Peter sits at the counter and looks around the room, surveying the photos on the wall. He notices one photo that looks recent. It's Stacey with her two kids. "Is he still in Des Moines?"

She shakes her head, her blond hair bouncing. "He had to go back to New York."

Peter nods. "Is there anything else you can tell me about him?"

Stacey turns away from the stove and bends over, pulling a pot from the cabinet below the countertop. She goes to the sink and begins filling it with water. She looks at Peter. "You said you're an investigator. Are you helping him?"

Peter hesitates. "I'm helping his wife."

Stacey's head is down, watching the water fill in the pot. She whips her eyes back to him. "Wife?" Anger flashes in her eyes.

Peter nods. "He's married. I guess he didn't mention that?"

She stares at him, and when she turns back to the sink, she sees the water overfilling the pot and pouring out the sides. She turns off the faucet and pours some of the water out, then takes the pot to the stove and turns on the heat to the burner.

"I didn't know he was married. He didn't tell me."

"Did you have a relationship with him?"

She turns away from the stove and opens the pantry door. She pulls a box of noodles from the shelf and places it on the counter, then looks at him. "I went on one date with him. That was all. He had to go back to New York. He said someone stole money from him. But he also didn't tell me about his wife. Now, I don't put a lot of stock in anything he told me. He needed money. I gave him some. He said he'd pay me back." She turns back to the stove and stirs the sauce in the pan.

"How much did you give him?"

"Five hundred dollars."

She checks the pot, but the water isn't boiling yet. She turns back to Peter and places both hands on the counter. "There's one other thing. He said someone stole money from him. He said he had a business he sold. He had three million dollars in his bank account. He was upset when he came into the bank and learned it was gone. I asked him about it, and he said he thinks a former employee stole the money from him. I could see the withdrawals from the account. They went to a business called Rosenberg's Bomb LLC."

Peter takes out his notepad and writes the name. He raises it to Stacey and she nods.

"There wasn't much information about the company online. I couldn't find who owns it. But the PO Box was in Brooklyn."

"There was a woman who came into your bank today," Peter says.

"The young brunette?"

"Yes."

"Is she the one who stole the money from him?"

"I don't know. Maybe. She was asking about Josh's account."

"What did she want to know?"

"She claimed to be Josh's sister. Said he sent her to check on his account."

"Check it how?"

Stacey shakes her head. "I didn't ask. I told her I couldn't give her any information. If I had a way to reach Josh, I would have called him to tell him."

"Mom?"

Stacey and Peter hadn't noticed her son enter the room. He stands holding his crotch.

"You need to go?" Stacey asks.

"I already did."

Peter can see a wet spot on the boy's jeans.

Stacey sighs. "Go up to the bathroom. I'll be right there."

Peter stands from the stool. "Thank you. I really appreciate your help. I'll get going. Can I leave you my number? If you think of anything else or if he comes back, will you call me?"

Stacey has already moved to leave the room. "You can write it on that sticky note. There's a pen in the drawer. Can you see yourself out?"

"Stacey," Peter calls.

She turns.

"You need to be careful around him. He's a dangerous man."

They look at each other, an understanding passing between
them.

Chapter 28

Scott

It's a risk, but one I have to take. After thirty-six hours of riding on buses and sleeping in transfer terminals, I'm finally back in Des Moines outside my apartment building. When I arrive, I walk around the block, looking for any evidence of police casing the building. I see none. I examine the structure, counting the squares until I find the window to my apartment. A light is on inside. I don't remember if it was on when I left. That leaves one of two possibilities. Either Roxanne did it, or the police have visited. If it's the police, and they're inside waiting for me, I'm screwed. But, based on what the cop had said back in Brooklyn, it's Roxanne they want. I don't think they know I'm alive. I've got to get to her before they do.

I climb the fence, enter the parking garage, and walk up the ramp to the fourth floor. I climb the stairs the rest of the way and enter the building. The lights in the hallway are faint, and I slowly push the door open, examining both sides. I see nothing unusual. It looks the same as the last time I was here.

I walk down the hall, stop outside the apartment, and listen. It's faint, but I can hear her softly humming. She always did that in our office suite. She's close to the door. Probably in the kitchen. I, ever so gently, put the key in the lock and push the door. I only open it enough to see. Her back is to me. She's over the sink, washing dishes.

I step inside the apartment and hold the door as I push it closed. She hasn't heard me. Headphones are over her ears. She has a Discman on the counter beside her. I tiptoe to the nearest drawer. Gently, I slide it open and withdraw a steak knife. I was hoping for more. It'll have to do. She still hasn't turned. She's wearing a pair of shorts and a T-shirt. Her feet are bare. Her silky, long, dark hair is pulled back by a velvet scrunchy.

I take a step toward her, and when I do, she turns. Her eyes go wide, and she drops a bowl. It crashes to the floor, shattering into pieces. I raise the knife as she screams. I grab her by the neck and push her against the sink. My face is pressed within an inch of hers. "Where is it?"

She responds, but it comes out as a gurgle. Her eyes are wide with fear.

"I want my money, Roxanne. You thought you could steal it from me?"

She tries to squirm away, but I'm far stronger than she is. She's struggling for breath. I release my hand and grab her from behind, holding the knife to her neck. She coughs, gasping. In her movement, she leans closer to the knife, and it pierces her skin. She yelps and pulls away. I hold her tight, pressing the knife just above her collarbone.

"I killed Larkin. You don't think I'd kill you, too?"

She stiffens. She's breathing hard, but no longer struggling against me.

"Where's my money, Roxanne?"

"What money?"

I whisper in her ear, "You think I'm playing games? You know exactly what money. Now tell me what I want to know or else..."

"Larkin's money?" she asks.

"Larkin's and the others. Three million dollars. Where is it?"

She shakes her head. "I went to the bank. I talked to the banker. She wouldn't tell me anything. I thought you were dead. Scott, it wasn't me. I swear."

I drop the knife and grab her arm. I twist it behind her and slam her body against the wall. She cries out in pain. "I'm not playing, Roxanne. I know you took it. Now where is it?"

She's crying now. Mumbling with her head pressed against the wall. "The police took it."

My heart sinks. "They took it from you?"

"No. They took it from you. From your account with Iowa State Bank."

I push her head against the wall with my forearm. "That's a lie. I know about the LLC. Rosenberg's Bomb. That's where the withdrawals went. The PO box is in Brooklyn. You should never had done that, Roxanne. You thought you could betray me like this?"

I lean down and pick up the knife. I'm blind with fury. Without thinking, I thrust it into her back, between her ribs. She jerks violently and turns. She looks into my eyes. Shock covers her face. I push her back against the wall, and she slumps to the ground. Her head drops to her chest and she twitches. I watch her for several seconds. Blood pools beneath her. I shake my head as I stand over her, my chest rising and falling. She made me do it. She lied to me.

I go to her suitcase and sift through it. My eyes struggle to focus. My hands are shaking. I don't know what I'm looking for. Why did she make me kill her? Why did she lie? If she would have just given me my money, I would have let her live. The audacity. I gave her a job. I took care of her, and she repays me by stealing my money? She lied right in my face.

The police don't have it. No way. If they did, they wouldn't have been at her apartment back in Brooklyn. She took it. She set up an LLC and stole the money. I need to find where she hid the money. There has to be some clue here.

I go through every piece of clothing in her bag. I scan the bathroom and under the bed. Nothing even remotely tells me where the money is. I walk back to the kitchen and see her purse on the table. I sit down and open it. There's a few hundred dollars, several credit cards, her ID, spare change, and lipstick. Nothing else. I glance over at her body. Her head is slumped on her chest. Blood covers the floor around her. Where did she put it?

I turn the purse over and shake it. A sheet of paper drops from an unseen pouch. I unfold it and smile at the note written in blue ink. I look at the counter and see a set of keys. I pick them up and find a mailbox key. I've got it. Just one more thing to do, then I can get my money.

Chapter 29

Peter

"Couldn't you have gotten a bigger car?" Zsuzsa says as she turns away from the window and toward Peter. Her eyes are closed, and her hair is covering half of her face. She's been asleep for a couple of hours. She took the first shift of watching the apartment building while Peter slept. Now it's his turn. Although the sun hasn't yet appeared above the buildings, the sky has transformed from black to soft blue. He watches her and thinks she's gone back to sleep when she says, "Aren't you going to answer me?"

"Are you talking to me?"

"You, Peter Andrassy."

"Yesterday you said you liked it."

She opens an eye, then closes it. "I wasn't trying to sleep in it then."

He chuckles as a dairy truck passes. He's not sure what day of the week it is. Judging by the light traffic, he'd guess Saturday.

"How many of these have you done?"

"What, stakeouts?"

"Yeah, staying up all night in a car watching for someone." Her eyes are still closed, but she's turned from her side to her back. She pulls his sweater up to her chin, arms tucked below it.

"Too many to count."

"In TV shows and movies, they make the life of the detective seem glamorous. I wonder if any of those writers have ever actually been one?" Zsuzsa says.

Peter laughs. "What, this doesn't seem glamorous to you?"

She turns her head to him and opens her eyes. "Not in the slightest."

"You once told me you wanted to be a detective."

"Still do."

"Even with this?"

"Can't you be a detective without the stakeouts?"

"Not in my experience."

"You're doing it wrong then," she says, smiling. She pulls down her top to reveal cleavage. "I'll be the sexy detective who uses her femininity to dazzle the perps. Leave the stakeouts to the old guys."

Peter frowns. "You calling me old?"

"If the shoe fits, Andrassy."

They grin at each other and then jump when Peter's phone rings.

"You just got that yesterday. Who has your number?" Zsuzsa asks.

Peter frowns. "I've only given it to one person besides you." He looks at the incoming number listed. It's a New York area code. "Hello?"

"Peter?"

"Kramer?"

"Yeah. Where are you?"

"Des Moines, Iowa."

"Can you come to the police station?"

"In Manhattan?"

"No. Here in Des Moines."

"You're in Des Moines?"

"Yeah."

"Okay. Where's the police station?"

"I don't know. Hold on." Peter can hear him cover the phone. "On First Street."

"Where's that?"

Kramer covers the phone again.

Peter looks over at Zsuzsa, "Kramer's in Des Moines. Something must have happened to Stacey, the banker."

Kramer returns to the line and tells him how to get to the station.

Before they hang up, Peter asks, "How'd you get this number? Is Stacey with you?"

"I'll tell you when you get here."

Fifteen minutes later, Peter parks the car at the police station, and he and Zsuzsa walk through the front doors. Kramer stands in the lobby with another cop Peter doesn't recognize. Kramer looks at Zsuzsa with a questioning look but says nothing and holds out his hand to Peter. "Thanks for coming, Peter." He extends his hand to Zsuzsa. "Eric Kramer."

"Zsuzsa," she says, taking his hand.

Kramer looks to Peter.

"She's my wife," Peter says. "She's from Hungary. She doesn't speak much English."

Kramer raises an eyebrow, unabashedly looking her up and down. "I gotta get over to Hungary." He motions to the other man standing with him. "This is Detective Winters. He's head of the investigation here in Des Moines."

Winters is a tall, lean man in his early fifties. He and Peter shake hands, and he nods to Zsuzsa.

"What investigation?" Peter asks.

"Come on," Kramer says.

Winters opens the door into the bowels of the building. They follow the two detectives past a row of cubicles and meeting rooms. They stop at a conference room midway down the hall. Zsuzsa and Peter sit on one side. Winters and Kramer, the other.

"Do you want some coffee?" Winters asks.

"Do you have tea?"

Winters shrugs. "Probably."

"Coffee's fine."

"What about your wife?"

"Maybe some coffee and water."

When Winters is out of the room, Peter asks Kramer, "What's going on?"

"We'll explain. Just wait."

Two minutes later, Winters returns with two cups of coffee but no water. When he sits again, he asks, "How long have you been in Des Moines?"

"Just got here yesterday."

"What time?"

"Around noon. Why? Did something happen to Stacey?"

Winters narrows his eyes. "Stacey Heathcliff?"

Peter shakes his head. "I don't know her last name."

"Why did you come to Des Moines?"

Peter looks at Kramer. "Really? We're going to play this game?"

Kramer smirks. "What game?"

Peter turns back to Winters. "I was a cop with the NYPD for twenty years. Don't treat me like I'm an idiot. Now what happened to Stacey?"

"How do you know her?"

"I talked to her yesterday. I left my number at her house. She's the only person who had it. Now what happened to her?"

"Someone killed her," Kramer says.

"When?"

"Around one last night. Butcher knife stabbed into her heart while she slept."

"Who?"

"We were hoping you could tell us," Winters says.

"You found my number at her home."

It's not a question, but both detectives nod.

Peter looks at Zsuzsa and wonders how much of the conversation she's following. "I think it's Scott Lyon."

Kramer laughs. "Lyon's dead. Where's his assistant, Roxanne Stanley? That's why you're here, isn't it? You followed her?"

"She talked to Stacey yesterday in the bank. Zsuzsa stayed watching Roxanne in her apartment while I followed Stacey to her house. I asked her what she knew."

Kramer leans forward. "What did she know?"

"That Scott Lyon is alive."

Both detectives rear back in surprise.

"How?" Kramer asks.

"Because he came into the bank several days ago. I don't know for sure, but I think she slept with him. She gave him money."

"Money? Why? He's got three million dollars."

Peter shakes his head. "Not anymore. Someone stole it from him."

"Stanley," Winters says.

"Maybe," Peter says.

"Where's Roxanne Stanley?"

"She was staying in Scott's apartment on Locust Street. She saw Zsuzsa tailing her yesterday and ran. We don't know where she went."

Kramer and Watts look at each other and then stand. Kramer points at Peter. "You better go back to New York before you get another woman killed. Go protect your client. She's no longer safe."

Part II

Chapter 30

Cindy

Six weeks before the attacks

"Scott?" My husband doesn't respond, leaving the newspaper up with his face covered. We sit at our kitchen table. I'm sipping coffee and watching him read the *Wall Street Journal*. He'll be leaving soon to catch the train to Manhattan. This is my only chance to talk to him all day. "Scott?" I say more forcefully.

The newspaper lowers, and he looks at me.

"Are you coming to Vanessa's performance tonight?"

Vanessa, our seven-year-old daughter, just started dance three months ago. Tonight, she has a performance. It's a simple affair, something to show the parents their monthly fee isn't being squandered. Vanessa is very excited. She hasn't been able to talk about anything else in days. She loves attention, not unlike her father.

His newspaper raises, again covering his face. "What time?"

I reach over and push the paper back down. "Seven."

He gives me an exasperated look. "What could they have learned by now? Doesn't it seem too early for a recital?"

"It'll be cute. She's really looking forward to it. It'll mean so much to her if you're there."

He looks at his watch and stands. "Do I have to?"

"Yes."

He picks up his briefcase in one hand and his gym bag in the other. "I've got a late closing today. I can't promise I'll make it."

I put my cup down and stand. "Please try," I say, looking up at him.

He leans forward, gives me a peck on the lips, and walks out the door. I watch as he climbs into his truck and pulls out of our driveway. He'll drive the half mile to the train station and ride the train to work. He's a model of consistency. Every day feels like the same. Scott never takes time off. We never go on vacation. He leaves the house every morning by eight and returns late, sometimes after ten p.m.

When I can no longer see his truck, I turn and look at the clock on the wall. I've got to get the kids up. I've arranged a playdate for them. I've got a lunch appointment in the city. "Vanessa, Billy," I call, walking up the stairs, "time to get up."

Three hours later, I exit the subway station and walk the five minutes to the arranged meeting location in Brooklyn. When Trent suggested it, I was surprised. Every time we've met, it's been in the city, but always Manhattan. Why would he want me to come to Brooklyn? When I questioned him, he would only say, "You'll understand when you get here." That was a week ago. Now our arranged meeting time is here. I see the sign to the sandwich shop, cross the street, and enter the building.

I see him immediately. He's seated on a barstool at a counter-height table facing the window. He turns and nods at me as I walk in. I wave but don't approach. I've been preparing myself for this meeting, but now that it's here, I don't want to know. I don't want to hear what he's going to tell me. I stall, walking up to the counter at the front. I stare at the menu above.

"What can I get you?" a young man says from behind the counter. He's handsome with wavy, dark hair. He's wearing a white T-shirt and an apron. His rich caramel skin contrasts nicely with his attire.

I cross my arms. "How about some soup? What do you recommend?"

"Meat or vegetable?"

"Vegetable."

He leans forward so he can see the board above. There are only three options. Wouldn't he know that? He must be new.

"Lentil," he says.

"Okay."

"Cup or bowl?"

"Cup."

I open my purse when he rings me up. I give him a five and tell him to keep the change. He says he'll bring the soup to me, and I turn to walk away. I look at Trent, stop, and turn back. I ask the guy for water, and he hands me a Styrofoam cup. I take my time filling it before getting a napkin and a plastic spoon. At last, I approach Trent with a pounding heart. He's watching me, which does nothing to calm my unease. I see a file on the table.

"Wouldn't we be more comfortable in a booth?" I ask before putting down my cup.

He shakes his head, rising from the stool. He's a big man with a bald head and thick, graying eyebrows. "There's something I want you to see," he says, motioning to the window.

I sit beside him, and the young man brings my soup. He places it on the table, and I thank him, then turn back to Trent.

"Well...what do you have for me?"

He doesn't answer. Instead, he watches me, and my anxiety only increases, if that's possible. Finally, he moves one of his giant paws to the file before him, but he doesn't open it. He rests his hand on the outside. "I've followed Scott for a month now, like you asked. I'm afraid it isn't good news."

I reach out and grip my cup of soup. The warmth of the cup is welcome. It's a hot day, the hottest of the year, but my extremities are ice cold.

He opens the manilla folder and slides it before me. I look down and see a photo of my husband kissing another woman. I know immediately who it is. It's Roxanne, his assistant. She's worked for him for over two years now. "How long?" I ask.

He shakes his head. "I'm not sure. It took several days before I knew. They hide it reasonably well. The picture notwithstanding."

Tears spring to my eyes, and I brush them away. I look at the photo more closely. I recognize the street. It's dark in the photo, and it's a bright day today, but it's the same road I just walked down. The one right outside this window. In the photo, Roxanne stands on the steps leading to the building, and Scott stands below her. She's leaning down to him.

"That's her apartment building," he says.

I look up as he points across the street.

"How often?"

He watches me before answering. "Two or three times a week."

I return the picture in the file and slide it back to him. I take a deep breath and set my shoulders. "Thank you. It's not what I hoped, but it's what I feared. Thank you for telling me. I know this can't be easy for you."

He examines me, then looks down at the file before sliding it back. "There's something else you need to know." He sighs and reopens the file. He flips to the next page.

I lean over and examine the paper.

"You remember the Chicago trip he took a few weeks back?"

I nod, wondering if he's going to tell me she went with him.

"He didn't go to Chicago."

I look away from the paper and watch him. He points to the page, and I follow his finger. "He went to Des Moines, Iowa."

"Iowa?"

He nods.

My mind runs wild. Does he have another family there? What else has he lied about?

"Why?"

He bites his lip. "This is a bit strange. He only stayed for a couple of days. He rented an apartment and opened a bank account."

I stare at him, then look back down at the paper. It's a copy of the lease agreement. The page behind it is a bank statement. Trent slides a key across the table. I pick it up and examine it. It's the key to Scott's office. The one I made for Trent. It seemed stupid at the time. Would my husband actually store evidence of his betrayal in his own office?

"I don't understand. What was he planning with this? Do you know why he got a bank account and rented an apartment?"

Trent shakes his head. "I'm not sure, but look at the name on the lease and the account."

I inspect it and see the name of my husband's dead cousin. Joshua Staples. I look the sheet over for several seconds, then focus on Trent. "Can I trust you to be discreet about this?"

"I told you when you hired me, nobody will know. Any information I uncover is strictly between you and me." He takes an envelope from his pocket and hands it to me. "This is my last bill. It's not much. A few incidental charges for copies and stuff like that. Your initial retainer deposit covered most of it."

I open the envelope, see the figure, then reach into my bag. I withdraw just enough cash and hand it to him.

"Good luck. You can keep the file."

He stands and leaves the restaurant. I watch him walk away, then look back down at the folder. When my eyes come back up, I see a couple walking across the street. Although their backs are to me, I recognize the shirt and pants the man wears. I know them, because I bought them. I'm the one who shopped for them and wrapped them in gift boxes and put them under the tree. I'm the one who smiled and kissed him after he opened them with our children present. They belong to me.

The couple enters the building, and I think about the clothes. Seconds from now, they'll be lying in a heap at the foot of a bed, ripped from his body. Witness to the betrayal of the man who once told me, "I do."

Chapter 31

Cindy

I arrive twenty minutes before our assigned reservation. I've never been to this restaurant. It was recommended to me by another mom at Vanessa's dance practice. It's French, called Boucherie Union Station. The host welcomes me and graciously shows me to a table. I catch a glimpse of myself in the mirror as I follow him. My new dress is sexy. Different from what I'd typically wear, but tonight is a special night. Black isn't a color I wear often. The saleswoman in the shop said it accentuated my figure. She convinced me to wear it. I only hope my husband agrees.

When we reach the table, the host holds a chair for me, then hands me a menu and wine list. "I understand we're celebrating an anniversary tonight," he says, filling my glass with water.

"Yes, twelve years. My husband should be here soon."

"Congratulations. He's a lucky man. I'll be sure he finds you when he arrives. Your server should be with you shortly."

I thank him, and he walks away. I look around the restaurant. Most of the tables are occupied by couples. Some younger, some older. The table closest to me catches my eye, and I watch the couple seated there. The man is probably in his late forties. He's handsome, wearing a suit and a tie. He has a thick head of graying hair. He has the look of money. He probably works on Wall Street. His date is young, at least fifteen years his junior. She's toned and fit. She wears a sexy, clinging white dress with heels. Her jewelry looks expensive.

My server comes to the table and introduces herself. She wears a crisp white shirt and black apron. Her hair is pulled back in a ponytail. She asks me if I'd like anything to drink. I order a bottle of champagne, and she promises to return. My eyes go back to the couple. Neither wears a ring. The woman is talking, and the man stares at her, smiling. I wonder about them. How did they meet? Do they know each other well? Was he married before? Does he have kids? She doesn't. It's obvious. She's not wearing a bikini, but that dress is so tight she might as well be. Her body hasn't grown another inside it.

I look down at my dress as a wave of self-doubt spreads. The saleswoman said I looked sexy, but was she just being kind? Looking for a sale? My eyes go back to the woman just a few feet away. My body looks good for a mom. This woman just looks good. Period. She's almost ten years younger and two babies fewer.

My server returns with the champagne. I look at the clock on the wall. Scott's always late. The server asks if I'd like to wait for him, but I shake my head. Who knows when he might arrive. She opens the bottle and pours me a glass. I thank her and she leaves, promising to check back soon. I take a sip from my glass and hold it in my hand. I look at the other tables. Several of the couples are just like the one beside me. An older man with a younger woman. The men appear rich and successful. The women young and vibrant. Is that just the way it is? Is this life?

Men are superficial, everyone knows that. They may claim to "read" *Playboy* for the articles, but we all know better. They want beautiful, young women with perfect bodies. And it doesn't even seem to matter how old the man is. But what about the women? These girls aren't with boys their age. They're with men who could be their fathers. Isn't that just as superficial? They're attracted to wealth and power. Is that what's happening with Scott? Does Roxanne see him as rich and successful? Maybe she's really to blame. Maybe she seduced him. She knows he's married. She's chosen to sleep with him. Doesn't that say a lot about her?

I look up and see Scott coming toward me. He follows the host who seated me earlier. I smile at him and give a small wave. He looks at me, and although he smiles, there's nothing behind it. It's weak. I don't see joy. How long has it been since I saw happiness in his eyes when he saw me? Tonight is an obligation. *I'm* an obligation.

While he sits down, I straighten my dress and brush my hair. He accepts the host's menu and opens it without a glance in my direction. "Sorry I'm late," he says, examining the menu.

"Happy anniversary," I tell him.

"You too," he says without looking.

"I ordered champagne to celebrate."

He looks at me, then at the stainless-steel ice bucket holding the bottle. Our server approaches, welcoming him. She points out the champagne and offers to pour him a glass. He barely looks at her, telling her he wants a beer instead. She looks at me, and I shrug. She leaves, and he continues to review the menu.

"I got my hair done," I say.

"Oh?" he says without looking up.

"What do you think?"

He looks away from the menu. It's a passing glance. "Looks good." He puts down the menu and unrolls his silverware, then places the napkin on his lap.

"How was work today?"

He shrugs. He won't look me in the eye.

Our server returns and asks if we've decided. We order, and she leaves.

I decide to try a different tactic. "Can you believe it's been twelve years?"

He frowns. "Since what?"

"Since we got married."

"Oh." He nods absently. "Long time."

"Remember our honeymoon on the banks of Lake Erie? What was that restaurant we liked so much? Wharf something?"

"Smugglers," he says.

"Yes." I pick up my champagne glass. "We should go back there."

"Yeah, maybe."

"Would you want to? I could set it up. How about Labor Day weekend?"

"What about the kids?"

"Right... Maybe I could arrange for someone to stay with them. Should we? We need some time just for us."

He looks at me, then picks up his beer and drinks from it, his Adam's apple bobbing up and down. He doesn't match my enthusiasm, and I can feel my throat growing tight.

"What do you think?"

He puts down his beer and looks at me. "What do you want me to say?"

"What do you mean?"

He shakes his head and looks away.

"Scott, what?"

He's expressionless when he says, "That was a different time."

I feel as if I'm being choked. "What do you mean?"

He looks at his glass of beer, foam on the top. "It's not the same anymore. You know it and I know it."

I want to cry, but I fight to control my emotions. "I still feel the same," I whisper. "You don't?"

He gives me a tired look. "Let's not do this. Let's just enjoy our meal."

Our server returns with our food. For several minutes, we eat, saying nothing. Finally, I can't take it anymore. "Do you still love me?" I ask, staring at him. He's cutting his meat and stops. "Do you?"

He takes a deep breath and lets it out. "It's not that simple."

It's like a punch to the gut. I want to double over in agony. But I don't. I keep my back erect and my posture straight. "That's not an answer."

"Now's not the time," he says, looking away from me.

"Scott, tell me."

He sighs and puts down his fork. "Life was just different then. *We* were different. I love that you. The then you."

I feel sick. My cheeks are hot, and a wave of nausea overcomes me.

He shrugs. "It's just the situation. We're parents now. You're a mom. We aren't the same people we were before. It's life right now." He reaches across the table and grips my hand. "It's not you. It's the way life is. When we were younger, we had fun. We were spontaneous. Now...we're parents."

What am I supposed to say to that? I stare at him, openmouthed. He goes on eating and we finish our meal. I don't touch my plate. After paying, we ride the train in silence. We separate at the station and drive our own cars home. When I pull into the drive, I let out a few tears, then pull myself together. Inside the house, we go our own ways. I take care of the kids while Scott watches TV. When he comes to bed, he initiates sex. I'm surprised. It's been weeks since we were intimate. As we lay together, I analyze him. He's distant. I wonder if he's imagining her while making love to me.

After he finishes and falls asleep, I lie in bed looking up at the ceiling. I think back to what he said. Is it true? Have I become boring? Predictable? Is that why he's unhappy? True, I might not be as young as Roxanne, but I'm still attractive. I catch men noticing me. My husband is wrong about this. I'm not boring. I can be unpredictable. I'm going to show him.

Chapter 32

Cindy

I exit the subway at Cortlandt Street and look for a pay phone. It's five fifteen p.m., and I need to know if Scott is still in his office. This morning, when he left, he claimed to have another late-night closing. He didn't say it; he didn't have to. The deal he'll be closing has nothing to do with real estate.

He said I shouldn't expect him for dinner. He'd pick something up on his way home. He expected to be home around nine. It'll be closer to ten. He's always later when he's with her. I imagine her begging him to stay as he prepares to leave. It makes me sick. But tonight, it's a good thing. I have plenty of time. The only reason I'm here this early is I remember him mentioning the lobby closes at six. After that, you can only reach the office floors with a key card. I don't have a key card. That isn't easily duplicatable. Weeks ago, I stole his office key from his key ring. It was back before the weekend was out, and he was none the wiser. Getting into his office will be easy. It's all about timing. He needs to be gone before the building closes.

I reach a pay phone across the street and dial his office number. It rings and rings before the answering machine picks up. I thought about this scenario while planning my night. I debated whether I should leave a message and concluded I should. If he is truly still in the office, he might hear it and call me back. In the message, I tell him I need to speak with him urgently. I make myself sound panicked. I give him the phone number of the prepaid cell phone I have in my purse. It's a gamble, but I don't think he's going to call, and even if he does, I'll tell him I'm somewhere with the kids. He won't know it's a mobile number. If he doesn't call, I'll erase the message from the machine while I'm in the office.

I wait five minutes without a response, then decide to go to the building. His office is in the south tower, Tower Two. A man is exiting as I approach, and he holds the door for me. On Saturday, when I was out, I bought a wig and a skirt. I hid them in the back of my car and put them on at the train station once I reached Manhattan. I selected the wig because of its similarity to Roxanne's hair. It's long and dark. The skirt is also something she might wear. It's much shorter than I prefer. The last touch is a pair of sunglasses. I saw her wearing an identical pair a year or so ago. I don't look exactly like her, but close enough. I cross the lobby and call for the elevator. I keep my head down, knowing the only thing that can ruin this is seeing my husband. Although, even if he saw me, he's too stupid to notice. It's more likely he'd look because he sees a woman and wants to check her out. Once he saw it was me, his interest would vanish.

I enter the elevator and exit on the 104th floor. It's one level below Scott's. I didn't want the doors to open and see him standing in front of me. I cross the hall, looking for the stairwell. I find it and walk up one flight. When I enter his level, I'm turned around. I don't visit the office often, and when I do, it's always in the elevator. The elevators, stairs, and restrooms are on the inside of the level, while office suites are on the outside. It's quiet. The only sound is the rhythmic humming of the elevators going up and down.

I see the door to Sound Security Title and approach. It's solid wood, and I can't see beyond it. There's no way for me to know if Scott and Roxanne are still inside. I grip the door handle and turn it softly. It rotates in my hand, and I know they're still inside. I release the handle and walk to the other end of the hall. I pick a spot out of sight but with visibility to the door. I pull a book from my handbag and lean against the wall. My eyes scan the words on the page, but my mind isn't comprehending what I see.

After several minutes, an office-suite door opens behind me. I turn and look. A man exits. I turn back to my book and can hear his footsteps growing closer. The floor bounces as he approaches. I glance at him from the corner of my eye. He's looking at my legs. He looks up at me and smiles but thankfully says nothing and continues to the elevator. Five more minutes pass, and the door to Sound Security opens. Scott steps out, followed by Roxanne. He whispers something to her, and she laughs, pushing him. He locks the door without looking in my direction. She calls the elevator, and I take a couple of steps back so I'm no longer visible.

Seconds later, the elevator dings, and their laughter vanishes. I'm eager to get inside the office but decide it's more prudent to wait. After five minutes, I'm sure they aren't coming back and approach the door, inserting the key. It sticks in the lock and won't turn. I panic as I work it back and forth. Finally, it turns, and the door opens. I close and lock it behind me. I look at my watch. It's quarter to six. I have two hours before I need to get back to the subway, ride the train, then pick up the kids and get them to bed before Scott gets home.

I go to his office first. I search through his desk without knowing what I'm looking for. I find a deposit slip and check from his Iowa State Bank account and put them in my purse. I wake his computer and see he didn't even bother to log out. I locate a WordPerfect document that has all of his passwords. I print out the page and put that in my purse. He has a QuickBooks file, and I open it. It has all the accounting for Sound Security Title. I took an accounting course in college, but I haven't used it and don't really know what I'm looking for. I notice there's no bank account for Iowa State Bank in the file. He does his business banking with Chase.

He has an account labeled "Escrow." It has a large balance with over three million dollars, according to the ledger. That's a lot of money. Are these the deposits he talks about receiving from clients before sending them to a bank or lender? I check the detail and find deposits with corresponding withdrawals every few days. The money never stays in the account long, always coming to a zero balance. That changed several weeks ago. More than one deposit hasn't left the account. Those deposits are for big dollars. Maybe his accounting isn't up to date? Maybe there's an error?

I check the WordPerfect document with the passwords and navigate to the Iowa State Bank website. I find the login page and use the credentials. The homepage lists his account balance. There's a checking account with one dollar and savings with twenty-five. I look at the history and can't see anything other than initial deposits. Why does he have these accounts?

I log out and search around the office. I find a filing cabinet in the room with the computer server. I pull the files for each of the clients he listed with large deposits in the QuickBooks file. Each of those transactions was several weeks ago. I find copies of the wire transfers entering the escrow account, but there are also corresponding withdrawal transfers out. According to the files, these amounts have been paid.

I go back to Scott's computer and log into his bank with Chase. I navigate to the escrow account, and the balance matches the balance in QuickBooks. The wire transfers in the files are fake. He's stealing the money. I check his browser history and find he did a search several weeks ago about escrow funds and obligations. He also searched for timing. He wanted to know how long he would have before he'd be investigated.

I sit back in his chair and look at the screen, then at the files. Why did he make these fake wire-transfer receipts? Was it for the client's benefit? Maybe. But when would they ever look through the file? These files are internal. They're only for him and Roxanne. Roxanne... He made them for her. He doesn't want her to know he's stealing the money. I close QuickBooks and the WordPerfect document. I put everything back just as I found it. He'll never know I was in his office. Next, I go to Roxanne's desk. I can't get into her computer; she shut hers down. I look through her desk and files.

I pull my digital camera from my purse and take several photos. I note her address and whatever personal information she has. I find a document that has her social security number, date of birth, and parents' names.

When I've searched everything, I make sure I've put everything just as I found it. I do a quick search of the rest of the office, then walk to the door and stop. How could I forget? I go to the answering machine on Roxanne's desk and play the message I left. I delete it, scan the room one more time, then leave, locking the door behind me. As I ride the elevator down to the ground floor, I look at my watch. I won't be home by nine, but it shouldn't matter. As long as the kids are asleep before Scott returns, I'll be just fine. He won't see them in the morning, and by tomorrow night, they won't remember me being gone. My husband will never know what I've been up to.

Chapter 33

Cindy

"Mom?"

I turn away from the steering wheel and look back after pulling up to the curb and cutting the engine. Vanessa and Billy sit behind me in their booster seats. My daughter looks at me while my son holds his Giants football, spinning it in his hand.

"Yes, honey?"

"Where are you going today?"

"Mommy has to run a couple of errands."

"Why can't we come with you?"

I frown. "I thought you enjoyed playing at Jane's?"

"I do. But I miss you. You're always busy."

She doesn't know how much her comment means to me.

"I know. But these errands are important. Our family needs them. I'll only be gone a couple of hours. Tell you what, after we get home, I promise we'll make some sugar cookies."

Billy looks away from his football. "With frosting?"

I chuckle. "I guess so."

My kids look at each other and scream with delight.

"Now, come on. Let's get into Lori's house so I can do my errands."

They unhook their seat belts and open their car doors. I come around the back, making sure they don't run into the road. Lori's a friend I've made in the neighborhood. She has a boy and a girl who are very close in age to mine. When we open the gate, we see Lori sitting on the steps leading to her front door.

She smiles at me, then at the kids. When she speaks, it's directed at them. "Jane and Mark are in the backyard. You can go through the house."

My children hug me, then run past her and up the stairs. Seconds later, they're gone. I approach Lori but stop at the bottom of the stairs. "Thank you. I'm sorry to do this to you again. I won't be more than a couple of hours."

Lori waves a hand. "Take your time. We all know doctor's appointment times aren't for them. They make us wait in the lobby without a thought." I turn to leave when she stands and comes closer. She gives me a concerned look. "Isn't Scott going with you?"

I shake my head. "He couldn't get away from work."

She puts a hand on my shoulder. "I could ask Rhonda from next door to watch the kids. I could come with you."

"No, that's okay. It's a comfort to know the kids are with you."

She gives me a sympathetic smile, and I reach for her. "I'm praying for you," she says, and I return to the car.

I hate lying to her, but what choice do I have? I can't tell her the truth. I can't tell her why I've needed her to watch my kids several times over the last week. She wouldn't understand.

I pull away from her house and drive the two miles to our public library. I enter and head to the back. We have a computer at home, but today, I don't want any history of my online actions. And we have a dial-up connection. If anyone calls the house, I get kicked off, and it takes several minutes to log back in. Not to mention how slow the pages load. I regularly check the Iowa State Bank accounts but otherwise, spend little time on the computer at home. If the police ever search our house, today's activity can't be found.

As usual, the computers are mostly filled. There are six in the computer lab, and two are empty. I sit down at one and go to the website for Legal Zoom. The last time I was in the library, I researched company structures. I determined to set up a single-member LLC, but I wouldn't be the owner. Roxanne Stanley would be. I create a username and password, use a Visa gift card to purchase the product, then go about setting up the LLC.

When I've answered all the questions, I hover over the remaining field. What do I name the company? I open the search engine in another window and type, "Women in history betrayed by their husband." I get a long list of options, including Catherine the Great. But it's the woman halfway down the page who intrigues me. There's a photo. She sits beside a chain-link fence. A man, who I presume to be her husband, sits beside her on the other side. Her look is haunting, almost soulless. I click on her link and read about her. Her name is Ethel Rosenberg. She was executed, along with her husband, in 1953 for espionage against the United States. What stands out most to me is her proclaimed innocence. To her death, she insisted she knew nothing about the espionage. Her husband was the spy, not her. He sold government secrets, including information about the nuclear bomb, to the Soviet Union. She was guilty by association. Even her execution was sad. She didn't immediately die via the electric chair. She suffered greatly before finally succumbing.

Her story resonates with me. I flip back to the Legal Zoom document and name my LLC Rosenberg's Bomb. The name doesn't refer to his espionage. It refers to the bombshell when she had learned of his betrayal. The address I use is a PO box at the post office near Roxanne's apartment. It's a box I established several days ago.

I complete the articles of organization, have them emailed to a dummy yahoo account I set up, and prepare to leave when I think of something else. I search for ways to hide money and go down a rabbit hole. When I look at my watch, two hours later, I realize I'm late. I rush out of the library to my car. As I drive to Lori's, I know exactly what I'm going to do next. I'm going to steal that money and hide it.

Chapter 34

Cindy

I wake to see the sun streaming through the blinds. Without raising my head from the pillow, I look out the corner of my eye and see Scott beside me, his eyes closed. Moving slowly, I crawl out of bed and grab my robe from the end post. I slide on my slippers and tiptoe to the door, opening and closing it gently. I hear the TV in the main room, down the stairs. Since Vanessa was old enough to climb out of bed on her own, we told her and Billy to let us sleep in on weekends. They don't always follow instructions, but since Vanessa learned how to work the television, it's become more frequent.

I descend the stairs, and my children hear me coming. They turn and look, but quickly go back to the cartoons on the screen. The show is called *The Fairly Odd Parents* and features a ten-year-old boy named Timmy who has two fairy godparents. I've watched it with them occasionally, and apart from the annoying voices, I've found myself entertained. I lean across the couch and kiss Billy on the head and whisper, "Good morning."

He mumbles a greeting without taking his eyes from the screen.

I do the same to Vanessa, and she grabs my hand. "Sit down, Mommy. Watch with us."

"Don't you want breakfast? I was thinking French toast."

Her eyes sparkle when she looks up at me. "Really?"

"Really," I say. I know it's her favorite, and I've been putting her off all week.

"Can we have strawberries?" she asks.

"If we have any," I say, winking at her.

I enter the kitchen and cross the room to the desk in the corner. I turn on the computer, sign in to America Online, and wait as the modem connects to the internet through our phone line. I go to the fridge and get out the eggs, milk, strawberries, and butter before getting the bread from the pantry. I hear the voice say, "You've got mail," and go back to the computer. I'm tempted to check my email but open Internet Explorer and navigate to Iowa State Bank. I log in and gasp at the figure in the account. Scott has transferred the money. I've checked the account for weeks and seen no activity. Yesterday, the money was transferred. He's going to run.

I hear movement at the top of the stairs and close the browser. I log off the internet and turn off the monitor, knowing I don't have time to shut down the computer. I rush back to the kitchen counter and get out two frying pans and the bacon. I get a bowl and prepare to crack eggs when Scott comes around the corner.

"Do you have any coffee?" he asks, yawning while sitting down. He's wearing a T-shirt and boxer shorts. His hair is pressed on one side of his head.

"I'll get some going," I tell him and switch tasks.

He puts his head in his hands and yawns again.

"You were late last night. Is everything okay?"

He looks at me, and for a split second, I see his eyes darken. As quick as it comes, it's gone. He shakes his head. "I have this client, Shane Larkin. His mortgage company screwed up, and they aren't reflecting his mortgage payoff. He came to my office in a huff late yesterday."

I recognize that name. That's one client he's stolen money from.

"Can you fix it?"

"Sure," he says, resting his face on his hand. "But it means I'm going to be spending hours on the phone with them on Monday. He's supposed to come back on Tuesday morning to make sure it's all cleared up." He leans his head forward and rests his forehead on his arm. "The thing is, Monday is a really busy day already. It means I'm going to have to work most of the weekend in order to call Larkin's mortgage company on Monday."

I've finished with the coffeemaker, and I'm back to the stove. I place bacon on the frying pan and turn on the heat.

"Really? I was hoping we could spend time as a family. Maybe we could go to the park."

He shrugs. "Sorry. Today's going to be a workday for me."

I continue making breakfast, pour him a cup of coffee, then call the kids. We all sit down at the table, and I wonder if this will be the last time. What's he planning?

Scott doesn't eat much, but he stays at the table. He thinks French toast isn't "healthy." Aside from his coffee, he has the bacon and asks me to fry him three eggs. I do, and after the kids have left the table, I sit down across from him.

"Do you ever think about your parents?" I ask.

He's leaned over his plate, eggs on his fork. He looks at me, then shovels them in his mouth. "My parents?"

"Yeah. Do you ever wonder what might have been? Do you miss them?"

He frowns. "What are you talking about?"

I pick up the saltshaker and roll it around in my fingers. "I just think about our kids. How lucky they are to have both parents. It makes such a difference."

He sets down his fork and looks at me. I'm expecting anger. Whenever I bring up his parents, he tells me he doesn't want to talk about it. Today, he's calm.

"I had my parents at their age."

"But did you really? Your father was..."

"What, abusive?"

"Yeah."

He nods and picks up his coffee cup. He looks out the window. "You know, it's not the abuse that makes me hate my father."

"No?"

He shakes his head. "It's that he gave up."

"Gave up? What do you mean?"

His eyes focus and he looks at me. "Nothing."

"No, tell me."

He swallows. "After killing my mother, he didn't run. He didn't escape. Instead, he took his own life. He left me without parents. He gave up." He shakes his head. "That's what I can't forgive. He was a quitter. A coward."

"But if he had run away, wouldn't that be quitting?"

He frowns. "Not to me. If I were him, I would have disappeared. I wouldn't have let myself be found. I would have started again."

Our eyes lock, and I hesitate before saying, "But you're not him. You don't need to run away. I'd always help you."

He looks away, back to the window. "Some things you can't help with. I wish you could. But you can't."

He stands from the table and goes back upstairs. I sit stunned and realize what I need to do. I need to prevent him. Show him he's nothing without me.

We don't see him much the rest of the day. I take the kids to the park and spend time with them. He works in his office at home. When we go to bed, I wait for him to fall asleep, then tiptoe down to the computer in the kitchen. I log on, making sure the speakers are turned off. It takes several minutes, but I transfer the money out of his bank account. I move it to a bank account with Washington Mutual. One that's owned by Rosenberg's Bomb with a principal named Roxanne Stanley. Technically, she'll own the money. She could take it and be gone if she knew about it. But it won't be in there long. Tomorrow, once the transaction clears, I'll move the money again, and this time, nobody will find it.

Chapter 35

Cindy

"Why are you leaving so early?" I ask Scott as he exits the bathroom and drops his towel, putting on his underwear. It's not seven a.m., and he's already getting dressed, preparing to leave. He's an hour earlier than normal.

He acts as if he never heard me. Seconds pass before he responds. "I told you," he says with his back to me, pulling on his undershirt, "I've got a client coming into the office this morning, and I have to have everything ready."

Yesterday, I dropped an anonymous note at Shane Larkin's house, denouncing my husband as a liar. It's all part of the plan to help Scott realize how much he needs me. This morning, I'm going to take the next step. It's time I confront him. I was already awake when his alarm went off as I considered what I might say.

"Scott?"

He's standing in front of the closet, picking out his outfit. He doesn't respond.

"Scott," I say again.

Again, he doesn't respond, pulling down a shirt and pants. I get up from a lying position and sit on my knees in the bed. "Scott, I want you to look at me."

He puts down the pants and holds the shirt in front of himself. He scowls. "What is it?"

"I have a question for you."

He rolls his eyes and looks away from me. He takes the shirt from the hanger.

"I don't have time for this."

"What would you do if you were me?"

He pauses. "What are you talking about?"

"Have you ever thought about me? Have you wondered how I might feel? Do you care?"

I have his full attention now.

"Thought about you when?"

"When you were screwing her. When you made the choice to have sex with her. Did you ever think of me? Did you care?"

He's still. His eyes locked on mine.

"I don't know what you're talking about," he says and turns away from me. He pulls on his pants and begins buttoning his shirt.

"There's no point in denying it, Scott. I know about you and Roxanne. I know you've been sleeping with her for months. I just have one question for you. Do you love her?"

He's finished buttoning his shirt and pulls a belt from the closet. "Do you?"

He finishes cinching the belt and looks at me. "No."

I knew the answer before he said it. He wouldn't be keeping his theft a secret from her if he did. He sits down on the edge of the bed and begins pulling on his socks.

"There's something you need to know," I say. "I forgive you. I'm not happy about it, but I forgive you. I love you. I've always loved you, and that will never change, no matter what."

He stops pulling on his socks and turns. I meet his gaze.

"I don't care what you've done. I committed to you when I said, 'I do.' No matter what, I'm with you."

He finishes with his socks and shoes, then stands and turns to me. My eyes are swimming as I look at him. He puts one knee on the bed and leans forward and kisses me like he hasn't kissed me in years. It's long and passionate. When he pulls back, he holds my face in his hands.

"I love you too," he says, walking out the door.

I stay in bed for an hour thinking about him and our relationship. I consider my next steps and wonder what his might be when I hear Vanessa. She's up. The kids have to be at school in an hour. I get out of bed, prepare breakfast, and get them ready. Today is my turn to drive carpool, and I don't bother changing out of my pajamas. At least I put on my robe.

When we reach Lori's house, her kids aren't out front waiting. That's not like them. Lori's always on time. We wait a couple minutes, then I honk. They still don't come out. Angry, I put the car in park and tell Vanessa and Billy I'm going to get them. I walk up the steps and ring the doorbell. After several seconds, Lori answers the door. I'm about to vent, but the look on her face stops me.

"Are you seeing this?" she asks.

"What?"

"Come in."

She pulls me inside, and I see the TV is on in her front room. She's watching the *Today Show* with Matt Lauer and Katie Couric. The image on the screen is of the World Trade Center. One tower has a large hole in the side, with black smoke billowing out.

"What happened?" I ask.

"A plane hit the tower. They think it was an accident."

I cover my mouth.

"What tower does Scott work in?"

I look sharply at her as a jolt of fear pierces me. "The south tower."

She puts a hand on my shoulder, expelling her breath. "Oh, thank heaven. It was the north tower."

I take several deep breaths, my head spinning. I sit down on the couch with my eyes on the screen.

"Do you think the kids should go to school?"

I look up. "The kids," I say, jumping to my feet.

I run out to the car, shut off the engine, and help them out of their seats. I bring them inside, and Lori's son and daughter are there at the entrance. "Why don't you all go play outside for a little while," I tell them.

Lori agrees, and we shepherd them out the back door before returning to the TV. Katie Couric is asking a correspondent on the site about emergency vehicles when the correspondent lets out a scream and says, "Another one just hit." The screen was showing recorded footage and flips to live when a huge fireball blows out from the south building.

Lori screams beside me, and I cover my mouth.

On the broadcast, Matt Lauer says a plane was circling the building. They argue about if a plane hit the other tower, but we can see on the screen it's the south tower. They get another correspondent on the phone, and she confirms it was a large plane that flew into the south tower. They show a recorded video of the plane crash, and a huge fireball erupts from the building after impact. This strike is lower on the building than the first.

One correspondent speculates about air-traffic-control malfunction when I turn away from the screen and look at Lori.

"That's Scott's tower," I say.

She puts an arm around me, and we watch the broadcast on the edge of the couch. They repeat recorded footage from another angle. A large jet flies into the building at full speed.

"What floor is Scott's?" Lori asks.

"Uh..." I can't think. "One hundred and fifth."

We stare at the screen.

"How many floors are in the building?"

I shake my head. "I don't know."

Like me, she's trying to determine what floors are on fire when Matt Laurer says, "And now you have to move from talk about a possible accident to talk about something deliberate."

Chapter 36

Cindy

I stand in Manhattan across the street from the towers. A police officer is on the road before me, directing traffic. I try to cross, but he won't let me. He tells me to stay back.

"I need to go into the building," I tell him.

"No. You aren't allowed," he says. He looks like Chris Farley from *Saturday Night Live*. He's wearing a police uniform, but instead of pants, he wears shorts.

I look beyond him and see Scott. He's walking across the plaza. With each step, his pace slows. It's as if he's walking in wet cement. Each movement is harder than the last. He looks across the street and sees I'm waving to him, calling out "Scott! Scott! I'm here."

He reaches out a hand and calls to me, but he can no longer move. I try to cross the street, but the police officer stops me. He grabs me by the waist and pulls me back.

"Let go of me," I cry. "My husband needs me."

He only shakes his head and tightens his grip.

I turn back to the plaza and see Scott is sinking. The wet cement has turned to quicksand.

"Cindy," Scott cries. "Help me."

I reach for him but can't move.

Terror fills his eyes, and before long, he sinks beneath the sand.

I open my eyes and gasp for breath. Shadows creep along the walls in our living room. I'm breathing heavily, and tears roll down my cheeks. I raise my wrist and squint to make out the hands on my watch. It's half past seven, and the sun is setting. I should turn on the lights, but I don't want to get up. I don't want to move. I'm exhausted. I've been asleep for a couple hours, but my body feels a fatigue I've never experienced before.

I'm on the couch, having collapsed here after arriving back home. I stayed at Lori's for most of the day. Our eyes remained glued to the news coverage that swirled around the attacks on the towers, the Pentagon, and the plane crash in Pennsylvania. For two hours after the tower attacks, I tried calling Scott's office. I used Lori's landline, but none of the calls went through. After the tower collapsed, I knew there was little point in trying. The news reported that thousands were still missing, and survivors were still being found in the wreckage. Initially, I had hopes that Scott escaped, but when the towers collapsed, and the hours went by, my faith waned.

At first, Lori was in the same boat as me. Aaron, her husband, didn't work in the towers, but he did work in Manhattan. She tried to call him many times, but the calls wouldn't go through. Eventually, though, he called back. He said he was trying to leave the city, but it was a madhouse, and he didn't know how long he would be.

After hearing them talk, I decided the best place I could be was home. If Scott was still alive, home was where I'd hear from him first.

Lori kept the kids, and I drove myself home. When I walked into the house, I called out for Scott, hoping by some miracle he was already there. Silence greeted me, and I went to the answering machine. The red light blinked, showing I had unheard messages. Two were from neighbors. Friends who knew Scott worked in the towers. The other message was from my father. It was strange hearing his voice. I haven't talked to him in years and didn't think he had our number. His message was brief. He expressed concern and asked for me to call. I wrote notes, intending to call each, but not picking up the phone. I checked the caller-ID box, but it told me nothing more than I already knew from the answering machine.

I collapsed on the couch here in the living room, unwilling to turn on the TV. I couldn't take any more footage of the attacks. Eventually, I succumbed to my exhaustion and drifted off. I slept for two hours, and now I'm awake.

I force myself to stand and turn on the porch light. Seconds later, the telephone rings. I go to it, hoping to hear Scott.

"Hello?" I say.

"Cindy? Have you heard anything?"

My spirit deflates. "No, not yet."

She's silent on the other end. "Well, that doesn't necessarily mean anything. He could still be trying to get home."

I nod but know every passing minute reduces the likelihood he'll ever walk through the door again.

"Is Aaron home?"

"He just got here a few minutes ago."

"Should I come get the kids?"

"Do you want to? They're fine here. We can keep them tonight."

I sigh. That does seem easier. "Have they been asking questions?"

"I think they know something's going on, but they don't know what." She drops her voice. "They haven't asked about Scott."

I know I'm going to have to tell them, but I don't think I can do it today. "Would it be okay if I come get them in the morning?"

"Of course. Honey, do you need anything? Can I do anything for you?"

"No. I'm going to try to get some sleep. If Scott calls or comes in, I'll call you."

"Please do."

We say goodbye and I hang up. I pour myself a drink and sit at the kitchen table, allowing myself time to think. I knew this was a possibility today. Not the attacks, obviously. The idea that Scott could be gone. That he'd run away and leave us. I was prepared if that happened. I knew he'd come back. I left him no choice. I have the money. But this...I'm lost. I haven't worked since we had Vanessa. I don't know how I can provide for my children. We have a mortgage, car payments, bills. Am I going to have to sell the house?

I think of the money. It's necessary now. Before, I took it to bring my husband back. Now it's going to save us. I sigh and shake my head. Why did I deliver that note to Shane Larkin? Why did I tell him about Scott? At the time, I thought it was necessary. A way to force Scott to come back to me. When he realized he had lost the money and had Larkin breathing down his neck, he'd have no choice but to ask me for help. I'd be his savior. He'd see me for what I am. Now I see I've made the situation worse. Larkin will come after me.

A thought strikes me. Larkin was supposed to meet Scott this morning. He was going to be in the building, just like Scott. If Scott didn't make it, Larkin probably didn't either. Roxanne as well. All three of them are likely dead.

I roll my drink around in my hand. That's a key detail. Roxanne was always going to be my scapegoat, but now it will be even easier. It's always simplest to frame someone who can't defend themselves. I've learned that before. Long ago. Now I've got to strengthen my case against her.

Chapter 37

Cindy

The next morning, I still haven't heard from Scott. He never came home. There's little chance he's alive. I can only think of one last-ditch possibility. I take the prepaid cell phone from my purse, power it on, and dial the number. After several rings, Trent answers.

"Hello, Cindy. Was he in it?"

"I think so. I haven't heard from him since yesterday morning."

Trent pauses. "He could still make it. They're still pulling survivors."

It's what he feels he needs to say. He doesn't believe it any more than I do.

"Listen, I'd like to hire you again."

"Cindy, I can't do anything about finding him in the towers."

"I'm not talking about the towers. I'm talking about Des Moines."

That stumps him. "You think he could have gone there?"

"Why not? He was planning something."

"Yeah, but...hmm."

"So, are you available?"

"I can be."

"I'll pay you for travel plus time and a half if you can leave today."

"Afraid if you don't find him now, you might never?"

Each time I've talked to him, he's impressed me. He sees beyond the words.

"I can leave within the hour. But I just want to warn you, this is probably a wild-goose chase. The most likely outcome is I go there, sit outside the apartment for days, then come home. You need to be prepared for that."

"Believe me, I already am."

I end the call and raise my arm, realizing I never showered yesterday. I'm still wearing the same pajamas I wore at Lori's. I go to the master bedroom and undress in the bathroom. I turn on the water, letting it run down my body. I put my face into the hot water and think about Trent's last statement: "You need to be prepared for that."

I told him I was, but am I? An image comes to mind. The last moment I saw Scott. He had leaned over the bed and kissed me. He kissed me like he used to. I was more than a wife to him. He gave a piece of himself back to me in that kiss. Now, it's been ripped from me as if by some cruel joke. It was an awful tease.

I begin to cry. I sob as if my chest is being broken. I drop to my knees; the water pounding my head as I release the dam of emotions I've been holding. He was everything to me, and I wasn't lying when I told him I'd do anything for him. From the first time I laid eyes on him in that math class, my heart belonged to him. It was outside my control. I was his. Now he's gone, and all I have left is emptiness.

When the water grows cold, I turn it off and dry myself. I look in the mirror at my swollen eyes and red nose and remember what he said to me about his father. He hated his father because he'd given up. I stare into my gray eyes and make a promise to him and myself. I will not give up. I'm going to finish what I started. I'm going to prove to Scott I'm not boring.

I get dressed, apply my makeup, and style my hair. I go to the kitchen, brew some coffee, and prepare to leave to pick up the kids when the doorbell rings. My heart leaps, but reason quickly dashes any hopes. Scott wouldn't ring the doorbell. I exit the kitchen and see the silhouette of two men standing at the door. When I get closer, I see they're police officers. My mind races. Do they know? Are they here about the money? I fight the urge to run and go to the door. I prepare myself with several large breaths and open it. Both men wear city-police uniforms, complete with guns and radios.

"Mrs. Lyon?" the officer with sandy-brown hair asks.

"Yes."

"My name is Officer Christopher, and this is Officer Justice. Can we have a word with you, ma'am?"

"What about?"

"Can we come inside?" He looks out to the street. "It's a delicate matter."

I look at both and try to read something on their faces. "Look, officers, I was just on my way to pick up my kids. My husband worked in the towers. Now is not a good time."

I reach for the door when Christopher says, "It's about your husband. We won't take more than five minutes."

I scrutinize them, then motion for them to enter. I point them to the couch in the front room and sit on the piano bench opposite. A couch pillow lies on the floor, and I pick it up. I knocked it off when I got up yesterday.

"What's this about?" I ask, clutching the pillow.

Christopher looks at me and bites his lower lip. "You said your husband was in the towers in Manhattan."

"Yes, that's right."

"Have you seen him since yesterday?"

That's an odd question.

"No."

"You're sure?"

I scowl at him. He folds his hands in front of himself.

"We were supposed to come yesterday, but given everything that was going on... Are you aware your husband was under investigation for insurance fraud? He was sent several notices from the New York Title Commission but didn't respond to them."

I shake my head.

He waits for me to say something, but when he sees I won't, he goes on.

"A detective with the NYPD has been assigned to the case and asked us to come and deliver the news. But given the events of yesterday and your husband's disappearance...we're here today instead."

He stops and looks at the other officer. Justice looks at me and nods.

When I speak, my voice is hard. "My husband is missing, likely dead, and you choose today to tell me about an investigation? Do you see how insensitive this is?"

He holds up his hands. "I know how this must look, but you need to understand. We're only following orders. You'll be hearing from the Title Commission and Detective Kramer. Our job was to deliver the message to you directly."

I stand from the bench. "You've done that. Now I'd like you to leave."

Justice sighs, and they stand and walk to the door. When they're out on the porch, Christopher turns back. "I'm truly sorry. I really hope you find him."

"Thank you," I say, shutting the door in their faces.

Chapter 38

Cindy

I exit the train at Grand Central Station and look around. Yesterday, when it was confirmed Roxanne was still alive, I called her. She didn't answer, and I worried I might not hear from her, but within an hour, she called back. We arranged for a meeting here at a bakery in the station at ten. Now, it's ten minutes to, and I'm running behind.

I leave the platform, walk upstairs, and cross through the great hall. I've been here before. The sheer volume of commuters is mind-boggling, but today, there's a significantly reduced crowd. Many people haven't returned to work following the terrorist attacks, and security is heightened. The feel is different today. Normally, people keep to themselves, not looking at those they pass. Today, everyone makes eye contact. They smile and mumble greetings. Our city just experienced a horrific attack, yet never have we been more united.

I cross through the glass sliding doors and walk down the hall to the bakery. When I arrive, I see Roxanne sitting by herself at a table for two. She stands and waves and I go over. She's uncertain, but I don't hesitate walking directly to her and putting my arms around her. Her body trembles as she hugs me back and we sit.

A server greets us, and I ask for a latte while Roxanne requests a cappuccino. He leaves, and we look at each other.

"Thanks for meeting me," I say, crossing my legs.

"Of course. I'm so sorry."

She doesn't even know how sorry she's going to be.

"Thank you. I'm just so grateful you made it out."

She nods. "When I think of all those people..." She shakes her head. "I can't believe they're just gone."

"How did you make it out? Were you in the office that day?"

"I was, but Scott asked me to run a deposit to the bank. I was on my way there when it happened."

We sit in silence, lost in our thoughts. I reach across the table and take her hand.

"There's something I need to tell you. I think it's important. I want nothing between us."

Her eyes fill with concern, and she tries to pull back her hand, but I hold on.

"I know about you and Scott," I say, staring into her eyes.

She's holding her breath.

"He told me the day before the attacks."

Her eyes grow large, and her cheeks color.

"I won't lie and say I wasn't upset, but a tragedy like this gives you a new," I tilt my head, looking for the right word, "perspective. I'm not angry anymore. That's why I wanted to meet today. I wanted to clear the air."

The coffee arrives, and I release her hand. Her eyes are cast down as the server asks if he can get us anything else. I tell him no, and he leaves. She stirs her cappuccino, tears in her eyes.

"I don't know what to say," she says.

I pick up my cup but keep my eyes on her.

"I never meant for it to happen."

"Did you love him?" I ask, sipping the foam in my cup.

She looks away, and I already know the answer. Finally, she nods.

"We both did then. That's something we share, as strange as that might sound. I don't blame you. I understand."

I reach for her hand again; this time, she gives hers to me.

"So, what now for you?" I ask.

She shakes her head. "I don't know. I guess I've got to find another job. I've saved a little money, but it won't last long."

"I wish I could help."

She looks at me with concern. "You've got enough to worry about right now."

I shrug in agreement.

"What about for you? What happens now?"

I scoff. "On which part?"

"You weren't working, were you?"

I shake my head. "That's actually part of what I wanted to talk to you about."

She eyes me warily.

"What I'm about to tell you, I'd appreciate if we could keep between us. In fact, I'd prefer if nobody knew about our meeting."

She frowns but says, "Okay."

"Yesterday, I met with officials from the New York Title Commission and a detective from the NYPD."

Her eyes are grave and she swallows. After going through Scott's office, I was convinced Roxanne wasn't involved. Now, seeing how nervous she is, I'm not so sure.

"Did you know Scott was being investigated for fraud?"

She sips her coffee before answering. "No."

"They say he stole three million dollars. Did you know anything about that?"

She frowns and shakes her head. "No, not at all."

"Well, I guess he didn't pay some mortgages. They say he stole clients' money. It's become a big problem for me. I can't access any of the company's money. I can't even use my own accounts. Until the money's found, I'm powerless."

"Wow."

"Do you have any idea where the money could be?"

She shakes her head, but it's too quick. "No, not a clue."

I put a hand on the table. "If you do, I promise I won't tell anyone who told me. I just need to get that money back."

This time she's a better liar. She pauses and pretends to think. "I wish I could help. He never told me anything about that."

I nod, looking deflated.

"But if I think of anything, I'll let you know."

I pretend to feel a buzzing in my purse and reach for it. I pull out my prepaid mobile phone and talk into it. "Hello, this is Cindy." I hold up a finger, then cover the receiver and speak to her. "Do you mind getting me a pastry?" I hand her a five-dollar bill.

"Of course. What kind?"

"It doesn't matter. Any kind."

She gets up, and I talk back into the phone as if there's some emergency. She walks to the display counter as I reach forward and shuffle through her purse. I feel a key ring and lower the phone to use two hands. I slip the PO box key onto the ring. I keep my eyes on her, stuff a note at the bottom of the purse, and return it. Roxanne hasn't even turned. I put my phone away and sip at my latte until she returns. She has a croissant on a plate and places it on the table. I pick it up and take a bite. Nothing has ever tasted sweeter.

We stay for only another minute or two. When we separate, I watch her walk away, smiling to myself. She carries incriminating evidence, and she doesn't even know it.

Chapter 39

Cindy

I close the door and return to the front room to watch Peter and Zsuzsa walk down the path and off my property. I've got to be careful with them. I did my best not to show it, but Peter made me nervous. He asks questions in such a way that leaves you wondering if it's a ruse. Like he's a magician drawing your attention one way while examining your answer in another. I wish Gary hadn't called him into this. He complicates things. I've got to do more to mislead him.

I look at the clock. I've got several hours before the kids will be home. I go into the kitchen and find my purse. I search for the secret phone and locate Detective Kramer's business card, then stop. How stupid. I can't call him on this phone. That would have been a monumental mistake. I power it off and sit down on a stool beside the counter. I take several deep breaths. I need to be slow and deliberate. I've got to think everything through.

After fifteen minutes, I'm convinced calling Kramer is the right decision and pull my cordless phone from the wall and dial his number. After several rings, he answers.

"Detective Kramer, this is Cindy Lyon."

He pauses before saying, "Hello, Mrs. Lyon. What can I do for you?"

"I've been thinking about our conversation from the other day, and I remembered something. Something Scott told me when he hired Roxanne. I thought you might be interested."

"Oh, what was that?"

"She's a criminal. She spent several days in jail."

"Are you sure about that?"

"It might not come up on her record. It was several years ago, and she had it, what do they call it, sponged?"

"Expunged."

"That's it."

"How did Scott know this?"

"She told him."

"She told her boss about her criminal background? Why?"

I shrug. "I don't know. I know Scott said he was impressed. He said he knew he could trust her because she admitted her past to him."

Kramer pauses. "Did she tell him what crime she'd committed?"

"Embezzlement. She stole from a former employer."

"Do you have any other details about the theft? Did she tell him anything else?"

"She said she worked for a doctor's office and stole about a thousand dollars. They caught it and put her in jail for a week or two, and she had to pay it back. She paid it back, and it was removed from her record after probation. I just thought you should know."

"That's very interesting. Maybe she stole the money, not Scott."

"I don't know. You'd know better. I thought it might be important for you to know."

"It is. I appreciate the call. We'll look into it. Is there anything else?"

"No."

"Okay. We'll be in touch again. I told you in the office, but I'll tell you again. Please notify me if you travel outside the state."

I wonder why he says this. "Sure, I will."

I end the call and take the cell phone from my purse and power it on. Almost immediately, it rings. I look at the display and recognize the number.

"Trent?"

"Cindy, are you sitting down?"

"What is it?"

"Scott's alive. He's here in Des Moines."

My heart rate triples, and electricity shoots through my body. I grip the phone excitedly. "You're sure? You've seen him?"

"There's no doubt. He's in the apartment now. I don't know how long he's been here. Do you remember what he was wearing when you last saw him?"

I put my fingers to my lips, thinking back to that morning. I tell him about the pants and button-down shirt.

"Sounds like he's still wearing the same clothes. He probably hasn't been here long."

My head is spinning.

"What do you want me to do?"

"Just keep your eyes on him. Don't lose him. I have to think."

I tell him I'll call him back and end the call. I go to the sink and pour myself a glass of water, but don't drink it, staring out the back window. After several minutes, I call him back.

"If he leaves the apartment, can you get in there?"

"I can probably figure out a way."

"Good. If he leaves, I want you to replace the furniture. Leave a note saying it's from the landlord. Say it was pre-planned. When you do it, scour the place. Remove anything that might prove he's still alive. If he leaves anything behind, take it."

"Okay. It's going to cost you. I can't do it alone."

"I don't care about the cost. Whatever it takes. Just don't tell anyone else."

"Will do."

We hang up, and I remain seated at the counter. I look at my watch and realize I'm late to get the kids. I rush out to the car and focus on what I've got to do. I pick up mine and Lori's kids, and when I drop hers off, I get out of the car too.

"Mom, what are you doing?" Vanessa asks.

"I have to talk to Lori for a minute, honey. I'll be right back."

"Can we come?"

I shake my head as I help Lori's kids from the car. "No. I'll be really fast."

"We can just play?"

Lori's daughter looks at me hopefully, but I still shake my head. "No. I promise, tomorrow you can spend all the time you want together."

I shut the door and wait on the porch as her kids go inside. After a minute, Lori comes out.

"Cindy? Is everything okay?"

I shake my head, and tears come to my eyes. "No. It's the test results."

She puts a hand on her chest and comes forward, embracing me.

"Lori, it's not good. I've told you a little about my family. I need to go see them. If I wait, I don't know if..." I put my hand over my mouth and fight for control. "I don't want the kids to know."

She rubs my back in a circular motion. "Of course. We'll watch them for you."

"I might be gone several days."

She nods. "Whatever you need."

"Thank you. I'll call you. I'll drop them off in the morning."

Chapter 40

Cindy

I turn onto Locust Street and drive past the apartment building, seeing the blue sedan parked across the street. It's dark, the only light coming from light posts. I drive past with little concern about being seen. My hair is tied under a baseball cap, and I wear a grungy T-shirt and oversized pants. I don't even recognize myself when I look in the mirror. I arrived by bus only a couple of hours ago and rented this car. It's a brown Saturn. About the most nondescript vehicle you can imagine. I keep my head forward as I pass the blue sedan. Zsuzsa's awake, staring out the window while Peter sleeps. She sees me, but I'm sure she doesn't recognize me. I continue for two blocks, then turn and go up Walnut Street and park behind the Toyota Corolla with New York plates. I get out and walk to the passenger door and get in.

Trent looks me up and down. "Boy, do you look different."

"Pretty good, huh?"

He nods. "You just missed him. He snuck in through the garage entrance less than five minutes ago."

I look up at the building. "Is she in there?"

He nods.

It's late, and only a few lights are visible in the windows.

"When did Roxanne arrive?"

"Earlier today. I hired a local guy to keep an eye on the apartment while I followed Scott. She's been in the building for a couple of hours."

"You followed Scott back to Brooklyn and then back here?"

He nods.

"Any chance he saw you?"

Trent shakes his head. "I stayed out of sight. I had an advantage. I had a pretty good idea where he was going." He smiles. "It got somewhat dicey there for a minute when the cops showed up at her apartment while he was inside. I'm still not sure how he escaped that one."

I nod.

"He must really have it bad for Roxanne, chasing her back and forth."

I glare at him.

"I'm just saying..."

Trent doesn't know the real reason Scott went to Brooklyn or why he's back here. It's not out of love for Roxanne. At least, it better not be.

"How did he afford the travel back and forth?"

"The banker woman."

"The one you told me about on the phone?"

"Yes."

"She gave him money?"

Trent nods. "They met on the street and went to a little restaurant near her bank. When they walked back, she went in and came back out with an envelope. I think it's safe to assume money was in it."

"Tell me about her."

"What do you want to know?"

"Anything and everything."

He looks away from me and takes a sip from his soda can. "Decent-looking woman. Two kids, about your kids' ages. Lives on Hickory Drive in a house with a brown door and dead grass. She took him to see a commercial building. Later that night, he went to see her at her place."

"Did he sleep with her?"

He looks back at me. "Cindy."

"I want to know. Did he?"

He nods. "I think so. He stayed there all night. She left in the morning to get her kids. He was gone a few minutes later."

I'm seething. "That was the day she gave him the money?"

He nods. "He hasn't seen her since. Course, he just got back." Trent leans back and yawns. "Are you going to stick around for a while? I haven't slept in about twenty-four hours. The Red Bulls are losing their impact."

I examine the building. My entire plan rests on this moment. If Scott comes out, I know I have him. I know exactly where he'll go. But if he doesn't...I've got a big problem.

"Have you noticed any police? What about the Detective Kramer?"

His eyes are shut, and he shakes his head. "Nobody except the two in the car on Locust."

Movement ahead catches my eye. A shadow climbs the fence outside the building. It's dark and hard to make out, but I'd recognize his figure anywhere.

I smile and look over at Trent. "Your work is done, my friend." I put an envelope of cash on his lap. "There's more than we agreed. That should cover your expenses and the other guy you hired. I'll take it from here. Go back to New York, forget all about this, and thank you."

He mumbles something unintelligible, and I get out of the car to return to mine. I start it and follow Scott for a couple of blocks. At an intersection, he goes right, and I go left. There's one more thing I need to do. Two more days, then Scott will know just how much he needs me.

Part III

Chapter 41

Peter

Peter makes a U-turn on Locust Street and pulls the rental car to the side of the road opposite the apartment building. From here, he and Zsuzsa have a clear view of the front doors. They arrive just in time to see Kramer and Winters enter with two uniformed officers. Another stands at the front of the building, looking like a security guard. Two police cars are parked in front. If Scott's inside, he knows they're coming.

Peter and Zsuzsa keep their eyes on the building and wait. After four minutes, another emergency vehicle pulls up, and several technicians get out.

Peter looks at Zsuzsa and says, "That's odd."

"What?"

"Those guys are sent out when a crime scene is blocked off."

"Meaning what? Did they shoot Scott?"

Peter shrugs and looks at the front of the building. Another vehicle pulls up. This time it's the coroner.

"I'm going to go see if I can get in. Wait here."

Before Zsuzsa can reply, he's out of the car and crossing the street. Rather than try with the officer impersonating a bouncer, he circles the building and enters through the parking garage. He climbs the ramp to the third floor and looks into the door's window. The elevators are closed, and they're directing all traffic to the stairwell. He enters the building and walks up the stairs to Scott's apartment. When he reaches the hallway, he looks out and sees a forensic team, along with Winters and Kramer. He steps into the hall and approaches the detectives.

Kramer sees him first. "What are you doing here?"

"What happened?"

"The," he stumbles, looking for the right word, "the fletcher killed her."

"Who? Roxanne?"

Winters nods.

Peter reaches into his pocket and withdraws a paper. He hands it to Kramer.

"What's this?"

"Something I found in the apartment yesterday."

Winters leans over Kramer to get a look at the writing. "Scott wrote this?"

Peter nods. "I believe so. I found it in the trash can."

"What is it?" Winters asks.

Kramer looks at him, then back down at the sheet. "It's a list of his clients. The ones he stole the money from." Kramer raises his head to Peter.

"If I had to bet, I'd guess he thinks one of them had something to do with the money disappearing," Peter says.

"You think he'll go after them?" Kramer asks.

"I think it's better to be safe than sorry."

Kramer nods. "I'll arrange protection for them. Well...two of them."

Peter frowns.

Kramer points to the name at the top of the list. "Larkin's dead. He hasn't been seen since the morning of the attacks. He was meeting Lyon that morning."

The three men exchange a look.

"How did he do it?" Peter asks.

"Kill Roxanne?" Kramer says.

"Yeah."

"With a kitchen knife. Something from the drawer. I don't know what went down, but I don't think he was planning it."

"What changed?" Peter asks.

All three men look down at their shoes.

Peter turns to Winters. "Stacey had kids."

Winters nods.

"She's from Houston. Her husband left her. Make sure those kids are taken care of. See that they go to a good home."

"I will."

The three men fall silent again.

After a moment, Peter says to Kramer, "Call me on the number you have for me if you need me."

"Where are you going?"

"Back to New York. You told me to go protect my client. I'm following your advice."

Chapter 42

Zsuzsa

"What state are we in now?" I ask Peter without looking at him. I'm watching the lush natural landscape pass outside my window. When there's a street sign, they all look the same. Sometimes I can make out the words, but I wouldn't feel confident pronouncing most.

"Still Iowa," he says.

"Are you serious?" I ask, turning toward him.

He looks at me and grins.

"But we've been driving for hours."

He shrugs. "Only a couple. It's a big country."

I shake my head and look back out the window. "You could drive halfway across Hungary in a few hours."

He smiles. "Yes. America is a big country."

"You said that already."

"I did?" he asks sarcastically.

"You did."

He chuckles. "Well, we've been married about two weeks. Isn't it about time you stop listening to me?"

I lean toward him. "Hmm? Did you say something?"

He looks back to the road. "I was starting to worry about your hearing."

"*My* hearing? You're the old one. Not me."

He looks at me with mock pain. "Hey."

I shrug and look away. "What? It's true. Should I remind you that you're already retired?"

He scoffs. "I retired at fifty-two."

"And your point is? You still retired."

He turns on his blinker and exits the highway. I look at the sign and see the letters, but I'm not sure how it's pronounced. Davenport.

"Why are you getting off? Are we out of gas?"

He doesn't answer.

I exaggerate the volume of my voice. "Sir, why are we getting off here?"

He looks at me and rolls his eyes. He comes to a stop at the light and turns right.

"Peter, tell me. What are we doing?"

He pulls into a Kmart parking lot and finds a spot. When he shuts off the car, he looks at me. "You ready?"

"Ready for what?"

"To go in."

"Why?"

"Have you ever seen the movie *Rain Man*?"

"What?" I look at him like he's lost his mind.

"The movie *Rain Man*. With Tom Cruise and Dustin Hoffman."

"Peter, what are you talking about?"

He takes my hand and kisses it. "Just answer the question."

"No, I've never seen the movie."

"We've got to watch it. Hopefully, it's translated into Hungarian. Anyway, Dustin Hoffman plays Raymond, a man with high-functioning Asperger's. Tom Cruise, Charley, his little brother, has little patience, but because their father died and left all his money to Raymond, Charley takes Raymond from the care center and decides to be his guardian. Charley wants to fly home, but Raymond won't have it because he's afraid to fly. They end up driving the entire country, and Raymond will only buy his underwear from Kmart. Tom Cruise is irritated and tells him Kmart sucks. By the end of the movie, Raymond is repeating Kmart sucks."

"Spoiler alert," I say.

He chuckles. "Sorry."

I look at the store. There aren't many cars in the parking lot, and it looks like it might not be open. "So, what are you saying? You want me to buy underwear here?"

He smiles. "You haven't lived until you've worn Kmart underwear. I'll even let you pick out a new sweater."

I smile, and I must admit, after hearing the story, I'm more interested in going inside. We get out of the car and walk into the store. It's the opposite of my vision of an American department store. It's empty, and some lights are burned out. I see only a handful of workers, and the shelves are a mess. We find the clothing section and pick through the meager selection. I pick a blouse and jeans that might fit, but I'm not going into the changing room alone. Peter picks a pair of jeans, T-shirt, and underwear.

"Really? Underwear?"

"He shrugs. Raymond was right."

I hold up a finger and return to the ladies' section. I find a set that looks far more comfortable than attractive, and as I walk past him, I hold them up. "I bet you can't wait to see me in these."

I walk toward the cashier, but Peter calls out to me and points in another direction. He walks toward the sporting-goods section, and I hurry to catch up. There's hunting and fishing equipment, along with camping gear. That's not what he's after.

He walks up to the guy behind the counter and points to a hand-gun. "Can I look at that Glock?"

The man behind the counter unlocks the display case and hands it to Peter.

"What are you doing?" I ask in a low tone. I've found people look at us funny when we speak Hungarian.

He fiddles with the gun and says, "Buying a gun."

"Why?"

"Because you need protection."

I frown at him.

Peter tells the guy behind the counter that he wants to buy it, along with ammunition. The man asks for his ID, and Peter takes out his wallet and hands it over. The worker walks to the back and calls someone on the phone.

"Who's he calling?" I ask.

"The FBI."

"Why?"

"To see if I have any warrants. If I do, I can't buy it. If I don't, I walk out of here with the gun."

"Just like that?"

"Just like that."

The guy puts the phone down and nods at Peter. He returns his ID, and Peter pays for the gun, the ammunition, and the clothing. We walk out and get in the car.

"Peter?"

"Yes?" he says as he starts the car and pulls out of the parking space.

"I've never shot a gun before. I don't know the first thing about it."

He winks. "About time you learn."

Peter gets back on the highway and drives for several minutes before pulling off on a remote exit. He drives down a dirt road about a mile, then stops and shuts off the car.

He looks around and nods in satisfaction. "Ready?"

"For what?"

"Take a guess," he says, getting out of the car.

I follow him to the back, and he opens the trunk and gets the gun out and loads it.

"I don't know about this," I say.

He gives me a serious look. "Zsuzsa, since you've known me, how many times has your life been in danger?"

I smile. "Too many."

He nods and walks fifteen paces. He holds a soda can in his hand, places it on top of a large rock, leans over, picks up some dirt, puts it in the can, then walks back to me.

"When I saw what Scott did to Roxanne, I knew this lesson was long overdue. I hope you'll never have to face him, but if you do, I want you prepared." He holds the gun out so I can see it. "We start with gun safety."

He instructs while I listen and ask questions. It's at least thirty minutes before I even shoot. He teaches me everything, including properly holding and loading the firearm, shooting stance, technique. He's patient with my questions and thorough. He's a wonderful teacher, and I feel surprisingly confident when I stand and aim at the soda can with both hands on the gun.

"Go ahead," he tells me.

With my arms extended, I put my finger on the trigger and pull. The gun goes off and bucks in my hand.

"Where did that go?" I ask, looking forward.

"Lower the weapon," he says. I do, and he comes forward. He leans into me, pointing. "There," he says, showing a spot at least five feet before the rock.

"I missed by that much?" I ask.

He shrugs.

"Can I go again?"

"Of course."

He steps back, and I raise the weapon and shoot. This time I hit the rock.

He chuckles. "Good. Try again."

I practice for several more minutes, hitting the can more than once.

"Okay," he says. "That's a good start. We've got to get back on the road. Scott's on a bus. He'll be slower. But we've got to continue to push the pace."

I give him the gun, and he stores it in the trunk. He looks around, then takes his shirt off.

"What are you doing?"

"Changing my clothes. We've been wearing the same clothes since New York. I'm afraid if I wait much longer, you might rethink marrying me."

"Well, I want to change too."

"I'm not stopping you."

"Right out here, in the open?"

"Who's going to see you? Besides, I promise not to stare too much."

"You might when you see these panties."

When we're back in the car and on the highway, I grab his free hand. "Thank you."

"For what?" He smiles. "Oh, I know, Dustin Hoffman was right, huh? Kmart does have nice underwear?"

I laugh. "No. I'm not a big fan of these granny panties. They are comfortable, though."

We smile at each other.

"No, thank you for teaching me."

He winks. "You're a natural. We'll stop again along the way and practice a bit more. For now, get some sleep."

"Why?"

"Because I'm exhausted, and we don't have time to stop at a hotel. We've got to keep going. You sleep first, then I'll take a turn."

"You're going to have me drive?"

"Unless there's another option while I'm sleeping."

I raise my fingers to my mouth. "It's been a long time since I drove a car."

"But you've driven before?"

"Yes."

"Good enough. Now take a nap. When you wake, we'll do a refresher."

Chapter 43

Peter

Peter sees the Akron city sign and exits the highway.

"Another shooting lesson?" Zsuzsa asks.

He looks at her and shakes his head. "Way too many people around here. Plus, you're getting pretty good."

After the first lesson, Peter drove for several hours while Zsuzsa slept. When she woke, he pulled off, and they ate in a diner. Afterward, he let her drive, and once they were both comfortable, he climbed in the back and went to sleep. He slept for several hours. From that point, they took turns driving. When they reached Ohio, they pulled off at a remote exit and practiced shooting again.

"What's here?"

He frowns. "Something has troubled me since we met with Cindy in her house."

"Just one thing?"

He grins. "Okay, several things. But one in particular. She said Scott's father killed his mother, then killed himself. She said Scott couldn't forgive his father for giving up."

"Yeah."

He shakes his head. "Something about that story isn't sitting right with me."

"What?"

He shrugs. "I'm not sure. After we met with Cindy and returned to Gary and Becky's house, I scoured the internet for stories about the incident. I also found the detective who investigated it."

"Oh?"

"Guess where he lives?"

"Here?"

"Bingo."

They drive through town and stop at a 7-Eleven. They get a few snacks and gasoline, and Peter finds the address of the retired detective in the phone book. He gets instructions for finding the house from the cashier, and they set out. He finds the house within ten minutes.

"It's probably going to be a lot of English again," he tells Zsuzsa.

She smiles. "I enjoy watching you work."

They get out of the car and approach the door. The home is well maintained, and the yard is immaculately cared for. He knocks on the door, and an old woman answers. She looks up at him, her white hair sparkling in the sunlight.

"Hello," she says in a friendly tone.

"Hello, does John Nagy live here?"

She looks at him closely, noticing his pronunciation of Nagy.

"You bet he does. He's out back tending to the roses."

"I don't mean to intrude, but I'd love to talk to him."

She looks at him, then at Zsuzsa, and smiles. "Wait here. I'll fetch him."

Peter nods, and she walks away.

"Nagy?" Zsuzsa asks.

After a minute, the woman returns with John. He's an elderly man with glasses and has a thin patch of hair. He approaches Peter, hand extended with a slight stoop.

"John Nagy."

"Peter Andrassy." Peter gestures to Zsuzsa. "This is my wife, Zsuzsa."

"Zsuzsa," he says. "Magyar?"

Zsuzsa rears back in surprise. "*Igen*."

John speaks to her in Hungarian. "Are you from Hungary?"

"I am." She looks at Peter. "You knew."

"I guessed," he says to her in Hungarian. "There's a lot of Hungarians here in Akron."

"There sure are," John says. All conversation is in Hungarian. "Come in." He turns to his wife and speaks to her in English. "Clara, would you mind getting our guests some lemonade? We'll be on the back porch enjoying some of the fresh air."

John walks to the back of the house and exits through the sliding door. Peter and Zsuzsa follow. They sit down at a patio table beneath a sunshade.

"How do we know each other?" John asks in flawless Hungarian.

"I was a detective with the NYPD for twenty years. My wife and I came from Hungary to the US for our honeymoon. We were driving through Akron and wanted to meet you."

He smiles. "Why would anyone want to do that? I appreciate it, though. I love practicing my native tongue."

"How long have you been in the States?" Zsuzsa asks.

"Long time. I came when I was a teenager. My parents had to flee Budapest during the revolution in fifty-six." He gazes at Peter. "Sounds like we've got a lot in common. I was a detective as well. I worked in Indiana and here in Ohio."

"I know," Peter says. "That's why we're here. We'd like to hear your thoughts on an investigation you were part of in Indiana."

Clara carries several Dixie cups and a pitcher of lemonade. She puts them on the table, and each person thanks her in English. John reaches for her as she passes back into the house, and they squeeze hands. John pours Peter and Zsuzsa a cup of lemonade, then leans back in his chair, cup in hand.

"Which investigation?"

"A murder-suicide in Muncie," Peter says.

John nods. "The Lyon case. What's your interest in that one?"

Peter and Zsuzsa tell him about Scott and the case they've been working. They report on the fraud, the disappearance, the reappearance, and the murders. John clearly becomes agitated the more he hears. His hand is visibly shaking when they finish.

"What do you know about me?" John asks.

"I know you're from Ohio. I know you were the lead detective on Scott's parents' case. I know soon after, you came back to Ohio, and I presume you've been here since. That's about it."

"I'm an old man. But what I'm about to tell you, I'd like to stay between us. I'm going to trust you because of the kinship we have. My wife doesn't even know."

He looks them each in the eye, making sure they have an understanding.

"The year was nineteen eighty-six. I was a policeman for maybe ten years at that point. Five years as a detective. It was the job I always wanted, but not the location. We left here to move to Muncie, so I could be a detective. It was a small town, and the crime was typically minor. I did a lot of petty-theft cases. Stuff that doesn't make headlines. It was, let's just say, not the most challenging work. I was a little bored and wanted something bigger. It makes little sense saying it, but it's true. You probably don't understand being a New York detective."

Peter shrugs.

"Anyway, I get this call late one night. It's something big, and I go to the residence. It's a mess. Scott, the kid, is sitting in the front room. He's in high school. No older than sixteen. Two officers surround him. He's staring at the floor. He doesn't even look at me when I enter. I walk past him to the kitchen. I immediately see a lot of blood. His mother lies on her back, face up. Her skin is gray. The blood has pooled beneath her, and I can see it's coming from a head wound. The officer with me points to the connecting room. We walk over and find the father on the couch. Again, blood is everywhere. It's splattered on the wall behind him. There's a bullet hole in the drywall. The gun rests on the floor at his feet."

John gulps his lemonade. "I examine the father and quickly identify he didn't pull the trigger. The angle of the shot is all wrong. It couldn't have been him. Someone shot him."

Zsuzsa gasps, and both men look at her. "Sorry."

John waves his hand. "No, that was my reaction as well. I was shocked. I was looking at two murders in the same house performed by two different people. I examined the father's hands and found traces of blood under his nails. Later, we confirmed the blood was his wife's. He killed her. I was sure of that. But I was also sure someone killed him afterward."

John comes forward in his chair, leaning across the table. "Well, we brought Scott down to the station, and I talked with him. He claimed to be upstairs in his room the whole time. He said he never heard the shot. He heard them screaming and yelling, but that happened frequently. The kid admitted to lying on his bed with the pillow over his ears. After things had quieted down, and he thought they were in bed, he went downstairs. That's when he found them. He went to the phone and dialed nine-one-one and waited for the police to arrive."

John stops and looks out over his meticulously maintained garden and shakes his head. "The kid had bruises all over him. It was clear his father had been abusing him for years. I went and searched his medical records and found he was treated for several broken bones. One as early as five years old. I knew what had happened. His father had finally gone too far with his mother and Scott shot him."

John turns back and looks at Peter. "Well, I just couldn't pin the murder on the kid. He had been through so much for so long, and I didn't have the heart to see him go to jail or even be dragged through legal proceedings. I knew what I had to do. I had to claim it was a murder-suicide. So, I did. Nobody asked questions, and Scott was placed with a foster family in a neighboring town."

John pauses and looks at his hands. "I always thought I did the right thing. But now, after hearing what you've told me..." He looks at Zsuzsa like the weight of the world is on his shoulders.

"Nobody questioned you?" Peter asks.

He shakes his head. "I think the captain knew what I was doing. I think he agreed with me. But we never talked about it."

"So why did you leave Muncie?"

"A detective position became available back here, and I applied. I wanted out of Muncie. It's such a small town. I drove by the Lyon home all the time. Every time I did, I saw the murder scene in my mind. I was reminded of Scott."

His eyes turn hard as he looks at Peter. "You've got to find him. You've got to stop him. I don't need any other bodies on my conscience."

Thirty minutes later, Peter and Zsuzsa are back on the highway headed toward Pennsylvania when Zsuzsa turns to Peter. "You've been quiet since leaving John's house."

Peter looks at her but says nothing.

"What are you thinking?"

"Just thinking about what he said."

"I want to ask you something."

"What?"

"Back in Des Moines, why did you tell Kramer about the note with the clients?"

"He's the police. I wanted to see those clients protected."

"Then why are we in such a rush to get back? Do you really think he's going to go after Cindy?"

Peter looks at her and shakes his head.

"Then why?"

"Because I think he's going to the PO box listed as the address for Rosenberg's Bomb, and if we don't get there first, we could lose him for good."

"You think the money's there?"

"Not necessarily. But I think it might lead us to where it is."

"And where's that?"

"I'm not sure yet."

"But you've got a guess."

He nods.

"And you're not going to tell me?"

He looks at her and says nothing.

She looks away from him out the window. "Fine, I won't tell you what I was thinking."

"What?"

"No. Too bad."

Peter smiles. "I already know what you were thinking. You were thinking that this honeymoon has been way more than you thought it would be."

She smiles. "Nice try."

"Fine. I was thinking we might have been trying to help someone who didn't need help the whole time."

Zsuzsa turns back to him. "Cindy?"

He nods.

"You think she took the money?"

He nods.

"Why?"

He changes his grip on the steering wheel. "I might be wrong, but I think she took the money to keep him from leaving her. All along, I thought she knew more than she was telling."

"So why did he kill Roxanne?"

"Maybe Cindy framed her."

Zsuzsa's mouth drops open.

"But that's just a guess. There's something more to their relationship I haven't put together yet."

"Like what?"

"I'm not sure. That's what's troubling me."

They fall silent, both lost in thought, when Zsuzsa says, "You know, I like you better when we aren't in New York."

Peter frowns. "Huh?"

"You told me what you were thinking. I'm telling you what I was thinking."

He chuckles. "Why don't you like me in New York?"

"I didn't say I didn't like you in New York. I said I like you better outside New York."

"Okay, why am I better outside New York?"

She takes his hand. "I know you brought me to New York because it was a dream of mine. But don't think I don't see the pain. We go by something, and I can see a memory flash in your eyes. You endured heartache in that city, I can only imagine. A piece of you was taken. You're reminded of your wife and daughter when we're there."

He looks at her, and tears form in his eyes. He's again impressed with how perceptive she is. He can't get much past her.

"You don't have to say anything. I already know. But let's finish this thing and go back home."

She leans over and kisses him.

"Deal."

Chapter 44

Scott

I exit the subway station at Borough Hall and walk along Cadman Plaza until I reach the post office. It's located on the bottom floor of a colonial-style building. The structure should be a city hall rather than an office complex. It even has a bell tower on the far side. As I approach, scanning my surroundings, a police car flips on its siren and zooms by. I startle, preparing to run, thinking maybe they're waiting for me.

I circle the building, staying on the opposite side of the street. I can't see any visible signs of police, and the many people walking along the sidewalk stride with purpose. They aren't waiting for me; they have a destination. My heart pounds as I approach the front doors and enter. There's a block of service windows in front of me, and to my left, another set of doors and a line of people waiting to be helped with their packages. To my right, just beyond the block of shuttered service windows, is a double door with one side open. I follow it and see two mail-drop boxes with the label *Self-Service* written in blue block letters. Beyond those, tucked away in a little corner, I see a large block of mailboxes.

I walk along the white-and-gray-checkered floor until I reach the boxes and look for the number written on the note in my hand. When I locate the box, I look behind me and see a man dropping a package into the self-service box. I wait for him to finish and leave, then withdraw the key from my pocket and stare at the box. I examine it, wondering if an alarm could be located somewhere within. I imagine inserting the key when a chorus of flashing lights and horns sound and police descend upon me.

I examine the box for any signs of a wire but don't see any. I take a deep breath and insert the key into the lock. Nothing happens, and I rotate it clockwise. The door opens. A white envelope lies on the metal shelf. I remove it, turning it over. The envelope is plain, with no postage stamp. It was placed in the box by a civilian. It didn't travel through the mail.

Before I open it, I check behind me one last time. I'm still alone. Nobody else is on this side of the post office. I open the envelope and find a sheet of folded paper. After unfolding it, I see the note is printed in large letters.

You told me at dinner things would never change

I told you that morning, my heart was still the same

I never believed your heart was out of range

Look for me under the elm tree where we watched the children play their game

I'll be waiting for you

The time and date are still unchanged

Roxanne

I look up from the note and stare at the row of mailboxes. This note wasn't written by Roxanne. It was written by Cindy. When we first moved to New York, we visited Central Park for the first time. It was a Friday in late September. It was midday. We sat beneath an elm tree and watched as a group of kids played tag. That's when Cindy told me she was pregnant with Vanessa. It was a cherished memory that Cindy often repeated. Any time we visited the park, she'd make me relive the moment.

Today is Friday, maybe even the same date as the memory. My mind spins with the implication. It was Cindy. Cindy did it all. She planned everything down to the smallest detail. She took the money. She convinced me it was Roxanne. She knew about Des Moines and the clients. She knew what I was doing.

I close the box and withdraw the key, staring at it. She planted it in Roxanne's purse. She planted the note directing me here. She was way ahead of me the whole time.

I think back to the last time I saw her. She told me she knew about Roxanne. She knew about all of it. She said she didn't care. She said she'd do anything for me. She stole the money to keep it safe. Maybe even after she thought I was dead in the towers. She did all of it for me. Just like eighteen years ago. She acted when I didn't ask her to.

I turn and see a tall, middle-aged man with a graying beard and large square shoulders staring at me. He's blocking my exit.

"Hello, Scott," he says.

Chapter 45

Peter

Peter and Zsuzsa reach New Jersey at six a.m. on Friday, completely exhausted. They've been driving for a day and a half, and other than a few pit stops to practice shooting and interview Detective Nagy, they've been pushing the pace.

"Do you think we'll make it in time?" Zsuzsa asks.

Peter shakes his head as they cross through the Holland Tunnel. "If we don't, I'm not sure what else we could have done."

They exit the tunnel and cross through Lower Manhattan on their way to the Brooklyn Bridge. Traffic is heavy, and they make slow progress. When they finally exit the bridge in Brooklyn, they turn right on Cadman Plaza East, then onto Brooklyn Bridge Boulevard, and continue until they reach the corner at Tilery Street.

Peter points to a building on the opposite side of the street. "That's it."

"The building with the tower?"

"It's on the ground floor."

He stops the car at a red light and examines the pedestrians on the sidewalk. As the light turns green, he spots Scott walking toward the front doors.

"That's him," Peter shouts.

"Where?"

"There," Peter points to the entrance.

He throws the gearshift into park and opens his door as cars behind him honk.

"Circle the block. I'm going after him. Call the police."

He jumps out of the car and slams the door. Zsuzsa's left open-mouthed in the passenger seat. Peter dodges traffic and enters the building several seconds behind Scott. He looks around, trying to get his bearings, not seeing Scott. First, he goes left, then reverses his path. Next, he goes right and sees self-service drop boxes. Confused, he rounds the corner and smiles, seeing the rows of mailboxes. Scott stands in front of one, his back to Peter. He's reading a sheet of paper with the box open. Peter takes out his cell phone and dials 9-1-1, just finishing as Scott closes the box and turns around.

"Hello, Scott," Peter says.

Scott looks at him. "Who are you?"

"My name is Peter Andrassy. Your wife hired me to find you."

He looks confused. "Find me?"

"She was angry you stole all that money and wanted to leave her behind. She's a vindictive woman."

Scott glares at him. "You're a liar."

Peter smiles. "I'm not."

Scott moves forward, withdrawing a knife from his pocket. "Move out of my way. I don't want to hurt you."

Peter looks at the knife. "Give up, Scott. There's no point. The police are already outside."

"You really are a liar. If that was the case, they'd be in here, not you."

Scott takes two paces toward him, but Peter doesn't back down. Scott slashes at him with his knife, and Peter takes a step back. Scott comes at him again, and Peter catches his arm, pushing it forward. Scott loses his balance and slams into the self-service mail drop. He screams in fury and spins around wildly, coming at Peter again. This time, he slashes Peter in the arm, just above the bicep. Peter falls back a step, and Scott comes forward, slashing down with the knife. Peter rolls just in time to miss the knife as it jabs into the checkered floor.

When Scott rises, he prepares to leap at Peter when a woman screams, "Stop!"

Scott turns in surprise to see a blond woman with long hair holding a gun pointed at his chest.

Chapter 46

Zsuzsa

Peter jumps out of the car and tells me to dial the police as I sit in the passenger seat in the middle of a busy intersection in Brooklyn. Cars honk all around me as I watch him dodge traffic and run into the building. I climb across the front seat to the driver's side and adjust the seat and mirrors. Cars are blasting their horns, and people are yelling at me. I put the car in drive and weave my way to the side of the road and up onto the sidewalk beside a park. We park on the sidewalks all the time in Europe, but apparently, it's frowned upon here. Several pedestrians gather around the car shouting at me.

I take the mobile phone from my pocket and stare at it. What's the emergency number in America? In Europe, it's 1-1-2. Is it the same here? I dial it and hit send. Nothing happens. I can't remember and walk to the back of the car as a woman follows me, shouting and pointing. I ignore her and open the trunk, searching for the gun. I make sure it's loaded, then swing around toward the building. People see the gun and scream, running away. I realize what I must look like, but don't have time to care. I run for the building and nearly get hit by a passing truck.

I enter and look around. I don't see them, but I can hear them. A crash sounds to my right, and I move around the wall and see both men. Peter rolls as Scott swings wildly with a knife. He jabs it into the ground and gets to his knee, moving toward Peter again.

"Stop!" I scream in English.

Scott turns and looks at me. I hold the gun as Peter taught me. I aim it at his chest. I can see Scott's debating what to do next, then turns toward me. He takes a step in my direction, and Peter pushes him in the back. Scott falls to the side, hitting the wall beside the self-service mailboxes, but doesn't go down.

"No," I scream, but he doesn't stop.

He rushes toward me. I react by pulling the trigger. The gun bucks in my hand, and Scott's eyes go wide. He stops three feet before me and drops the knife. He reaches for his shoulder and pulls away a bloody hand. Peter kicks the knife away and joins me, taking the gun. Scott falls back, blood pooling around the wound. His face has gone ashen.

Chapter 47

Peter

Peter takes the gun from Zsuzsa and turns back to Scott. He's on the floor now, his back against the wall. Blood covers his shirt.

"Help me," he says, reaching out a hand to them.

Peter steps forward, and a voice from behind commands, "Freeze." Peter keeps the gun low and turns his head. A police officer stands in the doorframe, a gun pointed at Peter. Peter drops the Glock and gets on his knees, clasping his hands together on the back of his head.

"This man has a warrant issued for his arrest," Peter says. "He's been shot. He needs immediate medical attention. My name is Peter Andrassy. Retired detective with the NYPD."

"Shut up," the officer yells, then speaks into his radio, calling for backup.

No one moves, and moments later, the office is flooded with emergency personnel. Peter is handcuffed and walked out of the building. As he passes Zsuzsa, he clamps his mouth shut. She nods, getting his message. The cop sees the interchange and motions to another officer.

"Bring her too," he says.

The officer grabs Zsuzsa and puts her in handcuffs. They place both Peter and Zsuzsa into the back of a police car. A black Chevy Impala pulls up next to the caution tape and Detective Kramer exits the vehicle. A mass of people are now congregating outside the tape. Kramer pushes through them and approaches the building and stands with other cops as they watch Scott be carted away on a stretcher. Kramer speaks with the other officers for several minutes, then turns and points toward Peter in the police car. He walks to the car and climbs into the front seat. He looks at Peter.

"You made good time. You drove all the way?"

"We did."

"What happened here?"

"I think you can figure it out."

"You shot him?"

"He had a knife." Peter shifts in the seat, raising his shoulder so his arm is more visible. His hands are still cuffed behind his back.

Kramer studies the slash in his arm. "You'll live. How'd you know?"

"I didn't," Peter says.

Kramer frowns.

"I guessed."

"What made you guess here?"

"I figured you were already watching the clients. It was either go check on his wife or come here. This was closer."

Kramer smirks. "Couldn't you have at least killed him?"

"How bad is it?"

"He'll live. He's going to be uncomfortable for a while, though."

"Speaking of uncomfortable..."

Kramer nods. "I'll take you and Zsuzsa over to my car. I'll give you a lift to Gary's."

"I've got a car."

"Oh? Where?"

Peter shrugs. "Good question." He asks Zsuzsa, and she looks over to the car parked on the sidewalk across the street. Kramer opens the back and helps Zsuzsa first, then Peter. He motions to Zsuzsa, and she walks beside him and Peter. A tow truck has arrived and is preparing to tow their car.

Peter looks at Kramer. "Can you help me out?"

"Yeah. Wait in my car." Kramer opens the back door, and Peter and Zsuzsa get in. Both are still handcuffed. Kramer walks across the street.

"Are you okay?" Zsuzsa asks.

"Fine. You?"

She smiles. "We're living out one of my fantasies."

"Oh?"

"I kinda always wanted to be handcuffed on my honeymoon."

Peter laughs. "I'm glad I could give you what you always wanted."

She winks at him. "I never thought it would be in the back of a police car. You're kinky. Next time, though, can we get the ones with velvet on the inside?"

Peter grins. "Your wish is my command."

Zsuzsa looks out the window and watches as Kramer talks to the tow truck driver. "I shot him."

Peter shakes his head. "No, you didn't. I did."

She looks at him.

"Got it?"

She nods.

Kramer returns and gets in the driver's seat. He looks back at them and realizes he never took off the cuffs. "Oh, sorry." He comes around and uncuffs them.

"How about one more favor?" Peter asks.

"What?"

"Can you get my gun back?"

"Planning to shoot someone else?"

"You never know."

Chapter 48

Cindy

"My legs are getting tired, Mommy."

I'm walking with my children, and Billy is looking up at me.

"How much more?"

"Not too much."

"I'm tired," he says, dragging his feet.

We rode the train into Manhattan and the subway to Central Park. Now we're walking along one of the many paved paths on the way to the elm tree.

"Don't you want to see Daddy?"

"Why is he here?" Vanessa asks. "We haven't seen him in a long time."

"That's true. But you get to see him today."

I look at her and note her hair color. With the sunshine, the color looks identical to Scott's. She also has his nose.

"Is that where you went away to, Mommy? Did you leave to go see Daddy?" she asks.

"I did."

My daughter frowns, and I notice Billy is keeping up better now. The conversation has distracted him from the walking. His hair color is a mix of mine and Scott's. He has my chin and gray eyes. If anyone saw the four of us together, there would be no question we would belong with each other.

"I thought you had to go see your dad?" Vanessa says.

"No, that's what I had to tell Lori because she wouldn't understand. But I was actually going to see your daddy."

She looks perplexed.

"Guess what?" I say, looking at Billy. "We made it."

He looks around the park. "Where?"

"Over there," I say, pointing to the bench under the elm tree.

"I don't see him," Vanessa says.

"We beat him. We got here first. Should we sit down?"

They nod, and we walk over to the bench. We sit down with my children on either side of me.

"You know what?"

"What?" they say in unison.

"This is a very special place for me and your daddy."

"Why?" Vanessa asks.

"Because this is where I told him we were going to have you," I say, pointing to her.

"When I was a baby?"

"Yep."

"What about me, Mommy?" Billy asks.

I put my arm around his shoulders. "You were very special, too. Your daddy took me to see a Broadway play right by Times Square. You know the place with all the lights?"

"Oh, yeah."

My children smile, and it's the happiest any of us have been in weeks. My excitement is palpable, and they sense it. We're going to be a complete family again. We sit, basking in the sunlight, enjoying the sights and sounds of the park.

After several seconds, Billy pulls at my sleeve. "Mommy, do you have some water?"

"I do."

I dig in my purse and get out a water bottle. I help him drink from it, then offer it to Vanessa. They both spill drops of water down the fronts of their shirts. I wipe them off with a tissue, and Vanessa points to the pond with ducks.

"Can we go watch the ducks until Daddy comes?"

I nod. "Help your brother."

Vanessa takes Billy by the hand, and they walk the twenty feet to the duck pond. I watch them for several minutes, then stand and look around. I check my watch. He's late. Was I wrong? Did he not find the note?

Thirty minutes pass, and my children are growing restless. They're hungry and tired and continually ask where Scott is. My irritation is growing, and I finally break down and pull the phone from my purse. I power it on and call my cousin. Rachel, her daughter, answers. I ask for her parents after introducing myself, and she tells me her father is gone, but her mother is home.

Becky comes on the phone. "Cindy?"

"Hi, Becky."

"How are you holding up?"

"I'm fine."

"Crazy news, huh? I can only imagine what you must be going through."

I frown. "What are you talking about?"

"Scott."

"What about him?"

"You didn't hear about what happened today?"

"No. Tell me."

"He's alive. Well, he's in the hospital now, but last I heard, he's alive. He didn't die in the towers."

My mind spins. "What? What happened? Where is he?"

"I heard it all from Peter. Scott went to hide out in Iowa. He escaped before the towers went down. For some reason, he came back, and Peter found him."

"Where? How?"

"I'm not sure. Peter found him at a post office in Brooklyn. He tried to kill him with a knife, and Peter shot him."

I sit down on the bench, my hands trembling.

Vanessa sees me and comes over. "Mommy?"

I push her away, tears running down my face. "Where's Scott?" I say into the phone.

My children stand around me with fear in their eyes.

"He's at Manhattan Hospital. The police have him. He got shot in the shoulder. He's going to live."

I raise my hand to cover my mouth.

"Gary went to talk to the detective. He should be home soon."

"Can you have him call me when he gets home?"

"Of course."

We hang up, and I bury my face in my hands. Eventually, I look up and see my children are also crying. They have fear in their eyes. I wipe my tears and stand.

"Come on," I say, gripping each by the hand. "Daddy's in the hospital. We need to go see him."

We walk out of the park, ride the subway to Manhattan Memorial, and enter the lobby. I walk to the information desk, and an elderly couple sits watching as I approach. Concern registers on the man's face as he looks at me.

"My husband is here. He's been shot. Can you tell me how I can find him?"

"Wait right here," the woman says.

The man dials someone on the phone, then looks at me. "What's his name?"

"Scott Lyon."

The man learns he's on the fourth floor, and the woman guides me to the elevators and joins me as we go up to his level. I still have Billy and Vanessa holding each of my hands. We reach the floor, and I see Detective Kramer in the hallway. He sees me and comes over.

"Mrs. Lyon, now is not a good time for you to visit."

"How is he?" I ask.

"He'll be fine. He took a shot to the shoulder. He's stable."

"Is he awake?"

"Yes."

"I want to see him."

He shakes his head.

"Detective, I thought he was dead. Killed in the towers. I'll go to the press if I have to. I demand to see my husband, now."

Kramer watches me, then finally nods. "Not the kids."

I stare at him and can see by the hardness of his eyes that this isn't negotiable. I turn to the kind elderly woman. "Would you mind watching them until I return?"

"Of course, deary."

Vanessa and Billy object, and it takes pleading before they eventually release me and allow me to go. We walk down the hall, go through a security door, then reach a room with two large male police officers stationed outside.

Kramer turns back to me. "Wait here."

He enters the room. I look through the window and can see between the blinds my husband lying in the bed. His leg and arm are cuffed to the bedframe. He's wearing a hospital gown, and his shoulder is heavily bandaged.

Kramer stands over him. Scott looks up at him, then turns and looks out the window toward me. I smile and raise my hand in greeting. He doesn't react. His face is stoic. He says something to Kramer, and Kramer comes back out. He shuts the door as I take a step toward it. He pulls me gently to the side several paces away from the door.

"I'm sorry. Scott doesn't want to see you."

The blood rushes from my face, and I feel as if I might throw up. "What?" I gasp.

Kramer frowns and shakes his head. "I'm sorry. Maybe today is just a bad day. Another day might be better. He says he has nothing to say to you."

I stare at him, not comprehending the words. "How could he not want to see me?" I shout. "After all, I've done for him? What he's put me through!"

I turn back to Scott and see the other officers are watching us. Kramer reaches for my arm, but I slap his hand away. I turn back to the room and take several steps forward, but the officers block my path. I push one of them, and he falls back a step but grabs my hands. The other comes around me.

"Scott!" I scream. "I'm your wife."

I'm lifted from the ground, and I kick and punch, trying to free myself. "Scott," I wail. I glimpse him through the blinds. He's turned away from me. He won't look in my direction. He doesn't want to see me.

Chapter 49

Peter

Peter sits beside Zsuzsa at Gary and Becky's dining table. Becky prepared a traditional American breakfast, complete with pancakes and syrup, bacon, hash browns, fried eggs, and orange juice. Rachel and Becky sit across from them, and Gary is stationed at the head of the table.

"It's been a while since I ate like this," Peter says, piling pancakes on his plate with bacon and eggs.

"What do they eat in Hungary?" Rachel asks.

Before Peter can answer, Zsuzsa says, "Good food." She says it in English.

The whole family looks at her in surprise.

Zsuzsa smiles. "I can talk a little bit."

They all laugh.

"Look at you, speaking English now," Becky says.

"Eh," Zsuzsa says, rotating her hand.

Gary laughs, and Peter holds the pancakes for Zsuzsa. She gives him a wary look. "Just try them. You put butter and maple syrup on them."

"That sounds more like dessert."

"That's American breakfast," Peter says, grinning.

Zsuzsa takes the smallest pancake and puts a dab of butter on it and a small amount of syrup. She bumps Peter with her elbow. "Translate for me."

"Okay." He looks over at Becky. "Zsuzsa has something she wants to say to you."

Becky holds a piece of bacon, and her eyebrows shoot up in surprise.

"Tell her I'd like to ask her to take me shopping again today. Tell her I'm sorry for the way I acted last time and would be pleased to go with her again if she'd have me."

Peter translates and Becky smiles. "Of course. I'd be happy to." She looks at Rachel. "Would she mind if Rachel came along? We were planning to do some shopping today."

Peter translates, and Zsuzsa smiles at Rachel. "That would make it even better."

"Great," Gary says. "I'm going golfing. Peter can come along."

Peter looks at him and shakes his head. "I don't golf."

"Oh, come on. You're fantastic," Gary says.

"I'm awful and you know it. You only want me to come so you can laugh at me."

Gary shrugs. "I guess some of the houses lining the course will be safer." He bursts out laughing at his own joke and Peter smiles.

"I'll stay here. I still haven't recovered from yesterday."

An hour later, Peter sits in Gary's office searching the internet as Zsuzsa comes in. She looks lovely with her hair done. She's wearing the outfit she bought with Becky the last time they went out.

"You'll be okay here alone?" she asks, leaning down to kiss him.

"I'll be fine. Have a great time. I've got to call the rental-car company anyway and have the car returned. I can only imagine how much this is going to cost us."

"When are we going to fly home?"

"Monday."

"Zsuzsa," Becky calls. "Are you ready?"

Becky and Rachel stand at the entrance to the home.

"Go," Peter tells her and winks.

She blows him a kiss and walks down the stairs.

Peter hears the front door open and close. When he's sure nobody is left in the house, he picks up the phone and dials John Nagy in Akron. After several rings, John answers.

"John, this is Peter Andrassy."

"Peter. How'd it go up there?"

"We caught him."

"I heard you shot him."

"I did. Got him in the shoulder. He's going to live. Thank you for your help."

"You're welcome."

"I have a question I have to ask you."

"What's that?"

"It's about Scott's parents."

Peter hears what sounds like the front door open.

"Yes?"

Peter waits to see if any of the girls have returned, but nobody comes up the stairs. He shrugs and looks at the image on his computer screen.

"Is it possible someone besides Scott killed Scott's father?"

"Why do you ask?"

"When we talked with you, you said Scott claimed to not hear the gunshot. Is it possible the gun that killed his father wasn't the gun that was left at his side?"

"Yes."

His response surprises Peter. "You knew? You said the gun at the scene was a Smith and Wesson three-fifty-seven."

"Right."

"You and I both know that gun has quite a kick. That wasn't the gun that killed him."

"Don't you remember what I told you? Scott claimed to not hear it, because he's the one who fired it."

"But what if he didn't?"

"Huh?"

"What if someone else shot his father? What if that person used a smaller gun? Maybe a Smith and Wesson Model Ten. Something like that?"

"I guess if that were true, that might make more sense. I never verified what gun the bullet came from, but I know it wasn't the three-fifty-seven. I just assumed Scott had a different gun he used, but we never found it. But if it wasn't Scott, who was it?"

A pistol's hammer cocks, and Peter looks at the doorframe of Gary's office. Cindy Lyon stands in front of him, holding a gun.

"Hang up the phone," she says.

Peter watches her, then lowers the receiver and places it back on the cradle. "Mrs. Lyon, good of you to come and see me."

She walks toward him, taking several steps, keeping her gun pointed at him. "I had a feeling you'd figure it out. I just hoped we'd be long gone before you did."

"I've had it figured out for a while. I called your father. You gave up everything for Scott."

She chuckles. "Is that what he told you? I grew up without a mother. He was always working. Scott was my family. Not him."

"So, you had the money all along?" Peter says.

She shakes her head. "No, only after the planes hit the towers, and I thought Scott was dead. I needed some way to provide for my family."

"By stealing already stolen money?"

"That's easy for you to sit in judgement over there. You didn't lose your husband and all income sources at the same time."

"I lost my wife two years ago. Or did you forget that?"

Cindy glares at him. "All I ever wanted was to be a wife and mother. I wanted a complete family. I never wanted my kids to have what I had."

Peter scoffs. "A loving father who cared for you? Don't you see your own hypocrisy? You killed Scott's father."

"I executed his father. His father beat him and his mother. I told you, Scott had bruises all over his body. His father would scream at him and beat him. I saved him once and almost saved him again, if not for you."

"Yeah, and in the process, look at how many people died. Roxanne. Stacey. Larkin. Think of the families you hurt. Stacey's kids lost their mother. Again, look at your own hypocrisy."

She shakes her head. "Roxanne deserved to die. So did Stacey. They slept with my husband. They tried to take what was mine. They tried to break apart my family. Larkin didn't need to die. He was just unlucky."

Peter shakes his head. "You're delusional."

"You've got a lot of nerve talking to me like that, considering I'm holding the gun."

"You won't shoot it."

She laughs. "You don't know how much I look forward to killing you."

"You won't shoot it because you love your kids. If you kill me, everyone will know you're behind it. Kramer will find you immediately. Your kids will be taken. Scott will rot in jail. You can't handle that."

"You're right. But once I kill you, I'll go get my kids and disappear. The money is hidden. We'll be out of Kramer's reach. Scott will come to his senses. He'll be out, eventually. Someday we'll be together again."

"Don't you get it? Scott doesn't love you. He doesn't want to be with you."

"Liar!"

"Becky and Zsuzsa will be home soon. You don't have enough time. Put the gun down."

"No. You turned Scott away from me. You have to die."

She aims her gun, and Peter turns his attention from her to the hallway behind her. It's enough of a distraction to give him a moment before she pulls the trigger. He leans to the side, away from her aim. The bullet hits him, and he falls below the desk. Cindy strides to the corner of the desk and leans over it. She sees Peter lying motionless on the floor. She aims the gun, but before she can pull the trigger, Peter extends his own gun and shoots. He catches her square in the chest. The bullet slams her backward, and her gun falls to the floor. Peter struggles to his knees and crawls to her, favoring his left side. He sees the bullet wound and knows he's killed her. He stands, slumps over to the phone on the desk, and dials 9-1-1.

Chapter 50

Zsuzsa

They wheel Peter into the hospital room, and I stand and go to him. He just came out of surgery and wears a sling on his left arm. His wisps of hair on top of his head are standing up, and his beard is disheveled, but his color looks good. I turn and watch as the doctor talks to Gary and Becky. I only understand bits and pieces of what he's saying, but based on the thumbs-up the doctor gives me, I know the surgery went well.

The doctor shakes Gary's hand, then Becky's, then comes over to me. I hold out my hand and say, "Thank you." Tears run down my cheeks, and he gives me a reassuring smile.

When Becky, Rachel, and I returned home from shopping, we found an ambulance and police cars blocking the street. That's when we saw them take Peter from the house on a stretcher. He was unconscious, and I feared the worst, but Becky learned he was stable and somehow, between gestures and words with few syllables, could express it to me. Becky told me where they were taking him and we followed. She called Gary, and he met us here.

The doctor leaves the room, and Becky joins me on the side of the bed. She takes my hand and puts an arm around me, saying, "It's good. He's okay."

I look at her and smile through my tears. Gary brings a chair over and has me sit in it while I reach out and take Peter's hand. His hand is warm. It's another positive sign. He groans and moves, and I stand and watch him.

"Peter? Peter? Can you hear me?"

I can tell how disoriented he is because he answers in English. His eyes are still closed.

"Yes."

"Can you open your eyes?"

After several seconds, he does. He looks at me and smiles, switching to Hungarian.

"How am I doing?"

I smile and lean over the rail of the bed to kiss him.

"The doctor said the surgery went well. You're going to be okay."

"I'm in the hospital?"

"Yes."

He looks over and sees Becky, Gary, and Rachel. Gary says something about Peter hating golf, then laughs. Becky rubs his leg over the blankets. They speak for a couple of minutes. I don't get all of it, but I can tell they're explaining to him what happened since he passed out.

Peter looks back at me. "Gary and Becky are going to leave for a while. They'll all be back later."

I turn to Becky, and she hugs me. Rachel comes forward and embraces me too, and Gary waves as they leave. Peter adjusts in the bed, and I can tell he's coming out of the effects of the drugs.

"Is Cindy dead?" Peter asks.

I nod. "Your shot killed her. I can't believe she came after you."

"That was the person she was. Anyone who ever impeded her relationship with Scott, she killed. *Fatal Attraction*. Too bad she didn't look more like Glenn Close, or maybe I would have seen it from the start."

I shake my head. "Is this another movie?"

He sighs. "So much culture I need to teach you, so little time. How was the shopping?"

"Good. I've got a few new outfits to show you."

He smiles. "I can't wait."

I sit down in the chair and hold his hand in both of mine. "I guess we aren't flying back to Hungary on Monday, huh?"

"Sorry. But there's one more thing we need to do before we go back."

"Oh?"

"We need to go back to Port Washington."

"To Cindy's house? Why?"

"For my peace of mind."

"Are you okay?"

He looks away from me. "Remember your question after we visited Cindy in her home?"

I shake my head.

"You asked if I ever killed anyone."

He turns back to me, and I can see sadness in his eyes.

"Peter, you can't blame yourself. It was her or you."

I watch him for several seconds. He doesn't say it, but I can see he's unconvinced.

"How did their relationship go so wrong?" I ask.

He frowns. "It was a relationship built on deceit. Cindy killed his father and never told him. He cheated on her. They weren't open and honest with each other."

I look away.

"What is it?" Peter asks.

"Nothing."

He's watching me. "They're not us, Zsuzsa."

"I know."

"What is it?"

I look into his eyes. "Sometimes I worry."

"About what?"

"This honeymoon has been nothing like I expected. Nothing has gone right, yet I wouldn't change a second of it."

He grins. "Even me getting shot?"

"Okay, I could do without that."

"So, what's troubling you?"

"Do you think Scott and Cindy were ever happy?"

"Yeah, probably." He looks at me closely, his green eyes studying me. "You think they were once like us? You see other couples that don't make it and worry we might be the same?"

I look down. "The thought has crossed my mind."

He squeezes my hand tighter. "Remember earlier, when you told me I had to tell you exactly what I was thinking?"

"Yes."

"You were right. Scott and Cindy were never open with each other. They never trusted each other. Let's promise each other, here and now, to never keep secrets. To always be open and honest, no matter how much we worry the other person won't like it."

I grin at him. "I'm going to be better at it than you."

He shrugs. "What else is new?"

Chapter 51

Peter

Peter shuffles out of his hospital room and enters the hallway. He pushes his IV cart as he walks. A nurse sits at the station outside his door. It's late, and the lights are turned low.

"What do you think you're doing?" she asks.

"I thought you wanted me up walking around?"

"Wouldn't it be better if you were sleeping right now?"

"I agree. Tell that to my brain."

"Having trouble, huh? I could give you something to help you sleep."

Peter shakes his head. "How about you let me just walk a bit?"

"Okay. But stay on this level."

"Fair enough."

Peter walks down the hall and goes around the corner. He reaches a room with a police officer sitting out front.

"You monitoring someone in there?"

The cop nods. "Peter?"

"Hi, Jimmy."

"What are you doing here?" Jimmy stands and takes two steps toward Peter. He puts a hand on his shoulder. "What happened?"

"I went and got myself shot."

"I thought you left the force and went to Europe."

"I did. I just came back to visit. Picked a heck of a time."

Jimmy shakes his head. "We lost a lot of good cops in those towers."

Both men stare at the floor.

"Who shot you?"

"I was helping a friend. Doing some PI work. I guess I need to get better at it. Pick better clients."

"Your client shot you?"

Peter nods.

"Sounds dangerous," Jimmy says, smiling.

"Who do you have in there?" Peter asks, pointing behind the door.

"Crazy story. This guy faked his death in the towers. He got shot by a PI in Brooklyn when he was found." He stops watching Peter's face. "You're the PI."

Peter shrugs. "Scott Lyon?"

"Yep."

"I'm the PI."

Peter looks through the window. He can't see much through the blinds. "Is he awake?"

"The TV's on."

"Can I talk to him?"

"Technically, no. But..." He looks Peter over. "If it's quick. I have to go in as well."

"I'd prefer you alongside."

Jimmy opens the door, and Peter follows him in. Scott lays in the hospital bed. He's gray, and his skin matches the sheets and pillows. He looks at Peter and recognizes him. His arm and leg are handcuffed to the bed.

"Hello again, Scott," Peter says.

Scott stares back at him. "What happened to you?"

"Your wife."

"Cindy shot you?"

"Yes."

He looks at Jimmy. "Too bad she's not a better shot."

"Thanks," Peter says.

Scott glares at him. "You're the one who put me here. You and your girlfriend."

Peter didn't come in to answer questions about himself. "Did you know?" Peter asks.

"Know what?"

"That Cindy shot your father."

He eyes Peter. "How'd you know that?"

Peter nods. "That's what I thought. When did you know?"

"We were already married. She said something a while back that made me wonder. I did some research and realized my father didn't kill himself. I figured it must have been her."

"Did you ever tell Cindy you knew?"

"No."

"Why not?"

"What did it change? It wouldn't bring him back. And it's not like I loved him."

Peter nods. "Did it change anything for you about Cindy?"

"You mean was I angry? Yeah, I was."

"Did that change your love for her?"

Scott looks up at the ceiling. "I haven't really thought about it, but maybe." His eyes refocus on Peter. "You killed her?"

Peter nods. "Was it you? Or did she kill Stacey?"

"Stacey?"

"The banker in Des Moines. Did you kill her?"

"She's dead?"

Peter watches him closely. The reaction is genuine.

"She came here, you know."

"Cindy? She came to see you?"

Scott nods.

"What did she say?"

"I wouldn't see her."

"Why not?"

Scott glares at Peter. "She never got it. She's the reason I stole the money."

Peter frowns. "What do you mean?"

"I couldn't stand to be married to her anymore. I hated her. When those planes hit the towers, I got what I wanted. I could disappear and never have Cindy find me. I stole the money planning to run, but always worrying Cindy would find me. When the planes hit the towers, I could fake my death. I thought it was a sign from God. It was my chance to disappear and leave her for good."

"Why did you hate her so much?"

"Have you ever been around someone who needs your constant attention? Plans your every movement? That was Cindy. She was obsessed with me, and I hated it."

Peter shakes his head. "Yeah, it must be awful having someone love you."

Scott glares at him, and Peter looks at Jimmy.

"Thanks."

Jimmy nods, and Peter shuffles back to the door. When he reaches the threshold, he stops and turns back to Scott. "I'd wish you luck. But after what you did to Larkin and Roxanne, you don't deserve it. Enjoy spending the rest of your life in prison."

Chapter 52

Peter

Peter pulls the car to the side of the road, and Zsuzsa reaches over and helps him put the car in park, then releases his seat belt.

"Thanks, babe," Peter says.

"What did you call me?"

"Babe."

She smiles. "I like it. Do it more often. You know, I kind of like this," she says.

"What? Me being a cripple?"

"You depending on me."

He winks at her. "Then come around and open my door."

After she opens the door and helps him out, his arm still in a sling, they walk up the steps to the front door. Zsuzsa knocks, and a woman answers. She's in her early thirties with light-brown hair and a button nose.

"Lori Robinson?" Peter asks.

She looks at him curiously.

"My name is Peter Andrassy. We spoke on the phone."

"Yes. Come in."

Peter lets Zsuzsa go first, then they follow Lori.

"The kids are in the back, playing. Would you mind sitting out on the deck?"

"Not at all."

She shows them to a square table with four chairs. She positions herself so her back is to the four kids playing on the trampoline in the backyard. Peter sits opposite her. Zsuzsa to the far side.

"Thank you for seeing us," Peter says.

"Of course. Actually, I'm happy you came. I have some questions for you." She pauses, as if thinking of something. "Can I get you anything to drink?"

"No, I'm fine," Peter says.

She looks to Zsuzsa, but she shakes her head.

"I still can't believe all this. I thought I knew them."

"The Lyons?" Peter asks.

"Yes. They were my neighbors for years. I was with Cindy when the planes hit the towers. This has rocked our entire community."

"Did Cindy seem surprised? I mean, did she believe Scott was inside when the planes struck?"

"Absolutely. At least, that's how it seemed to me. But, obviously, she was a good liar."

"You watched her kids a lot over the last several weeks. What excuse did she give you?"

Lori lets out a sarcastic chuckle. "She told me she was sick. I guess she was. Just not in the way she said."

"What did she say?"

"She said she had cancer. After we thought Scott was dead, she claimed she got news that her cancer was stage four. She asked me to watch the kids so she could go back home to see her family."

"Did she see them?"

"Not according to her father. She said she was going to see him."

"Do you know where she went?"

Lori shakes her head.

"How long was she gone?"

"Just a couple of days. When she came back, she told me she had decided to move back home. She was going to take the kids and go live with her family in Indiana. I asked her about her house, and she said she couldn't worry about it. That it didn't matter to her anymore. It was strange." She looks at Zsuzsa. "Isn't it odd for a woman to just abandon her house?"

Zsuzsa smiles. "I'm sorry. I don't speak English."

"Oh," Lori says and looks at Peter.

"She's from Hungary. We're headed back soon. We came here for our honeymoon."

"But you're from here?"

"Well, technically I'm from Hungary too. I came and lived in New York for thirty years. As I told you on the phone, I was NYPD and retired a couple of years ago."

"And you're the one who shot Cindy?"

"Yes. But she shot me first." He motions to his shoulder.

A little girl climbs the steps up to the deck and approaches Lori. Peter sees her resemblance to her mother. She has the same eyes and nose.

"Lori," she says. "Carl isn't being nice to Billy."

Lori turns to her. "What's he doing, Vanessa?"

"He's not letting him play with the football."

"Will you tell him I said that he has to share with Billy or I'll take it away?"

"But he won't."

"Just tell him. I'm almost done here."

She pouts but goes back down the stairs.

Lori turns back to Peter. "She's very protective of her brother. I'm so glad they have each other."

"What will happen to them?" Peter asks.

"I'm going to keep them. Scott doesn't have any family, and Cindy only had her father and brother. Her mom died years ago. Her father can't raise them, and her brother doesn't know them. They asked if I'd be willing, and I couldn't say no. They've been through so much. I want to take care of them."

"Thank you," he says. "What do they know about their parents?"

"Nothing yet. Cindy told them Scott was alive. They know about the towers, everyone does. I'm not sure how to handle it. Right now, they think their parents are gone for work. I'm going to have to tell them soon. I just don't know how."

Peter nods. "Good luck. If I can offer some advice, tell them their mother loved them and only wanted the best for them."

An understanding passes between them. They all stand, and Lori walks them to the front door.

"I'm so grateful to you. We appreciate your time today. Thank you for taking care of the kids," Peter tells her.

She and Zsuzsa nod to each other, and Peter and Zsuzsa go back to the car. Zsuzsa helps him in.

Once they're both seated, Zsuzsa looks at him. "Is she going to keep them?"

Peter nods.

"That's why you wanted to come. You wanted to make sure the kids were going to be okay."

Peter says nothing.

"You love kids."

"I do. I also shot both of their parents. I feel responsible."

"No, you shot one of their parents. I shot the other."

He gives her a knowing nod.

"You and Karen had a daughter."

"Yes."

"How old was she when she passed?"

He looks away from her and stares at the steering wheel. "She was four."

"How would you feel about being a parent again?"

Peter turns and looks at her. Tears well up in his eyes. "Why are you asking me that?"

Zsuzsa reaches out and takes his good hand. She places it on her belly. "Because you're going to be a father again."

Epilogue

To read an exclusive interview with D.J. Maughan, scan the QR code below. D.J. discusses aspects of the book like why he wrote 9-1-1, what inspired him, what happened to Scott, and what's next in D.J.'s writing career.

https://dl.bookfunnel.com/fhehh0ehdw

Also by D.J. Maughan

D.J. Maughan novels by date of publication

Vanished From Budapest – published December 9, 2022. Peter Andrassy novel one. Psychological thriller. Standalone.

The Villains Mask – published March 15, 2023. Prequel to Vanished from Budapest. Short story. Standalone.

Pursuit of Demons – published March 17, 2023. Peter Andrassy novel two. Book one of the Vanished series.

Revealing the Shadows – published July 23, 2023. Peter Andrassy novel three. Book two of the Vanished series.

Chasing the Wicked – published November 22, 2023. Peter Andrassy novel four. Book three of the Vanished series.

One Desperate Life – published April 26, 2024. Standalone gripping thriller.

Idaho Fall – published October 1, 2024. Hank and Joyce novel one. Standalone twisty whodunit.

9-1-1 – published March 27, 2025. Peter Andrassy novel five. Crime thriller.

The First Five Peter Andrassy Thrillers box set – published October 12, 2024. Available in eBook on Amazon.

Hank and Joyce novel two. Expected Fall of 2025.

About D.J. Maughan

D.J. Maughan is an avid reader, event manager, father, husband, public speaker, and award-winning author. No surprise that he writes in the Thriller/Mystery genre, that's what he loves to read. He craves the unexpected and strives to provide that to his readers. He seeks inspiration everywhere, especially while studying and visiting diverse places and cultures. Whether jumping from a cliff in Hawaii or hiking the Plitvica Lakes in Croatia, he's in heaven as long as his wife and four sons are at his side.

Acknowledgements

Thank you to my beta readers. Your insights helped shape this novel. Brooke Maughan, Lupe Merino, Laurie Clark, Luke Barber, Jerry Paskett, Jim Thomas, Paul Gyorke, Laura Martin, Debbie Altom, Tami Weitkunat, Khadijah King, Matthew Sanchez, Heather Brandt, Jewel Roper, Jenny Goetsch, Katie Jablonka, Turning Pages, Heather Kerber, Michelle Blunt, Kathi Ann Starling, Raeann, Amanda Helmann, Cynthia Bryant, Jennifer Harper, Jane Alexander, Hannah Exey, Angie Kellett, Jessica Evans, Erin Sterett, Vanessa Keck, Kelsey Housman, Dawn Resue, Rachel Browning, Wendie White, Jessica Earles, Samantha Becker, Amanda Fuerst, and Michelle Ramsey.

A big thank you to my editor, Jonathan Starke. I also want to thank Amanda Cox, my cover designer. I appreciate your help and kindness.